TAHOE GUNFIGHT

A JOHN POPE WESTERN

G. WAYNE TILMAN

**WOLFPACK
PUBLISHING**
— EST 2013 —

**WOLFPACK
PUBLISHING**
— EST 2013 —

Tahoe Gunfight

TAHOE GUNFIGHT

CHAPTER 1

The man on the black stallion rode slowly down the streets of 1884 San Rafael, California.

He wore a black hat and suit which matched the horse. In a wilder western town, people would have been hiding behind windows wondering who the obvious gunfighter was. Who was he after? Who would die?

The man was tall and handsome, once one looked past his foreboding appearance, and the long barreled stag handled Colt prominent on his right hip.

He rode towards the sheriff's office. The folks who looked up and smiled as he went by saw something else. A golden star on his lapel.

Sheriff John Hunt Pope rode into town with the alertness of his calling.

The sky over San Rafael was as blue as blue can be. Salt air came off the Bay and the June temperature was perfect.

It did not feel like a good morning for a shootout on the tame streets of the county seat. The sheriff never let his guard down. In his line of work, situations can change in an instant.

His beautiful, dark haired wife Sarah had preceded him to town and was coming out of her office as he rode by.

"Hi, darlin'," the sheriff said to his former Pinkerton detective wife. She had more recently been his partner at Wells Fargo. Now, she ran the counties across the Bay for the Harry Morse Detective Agency. It was one of the preeminent agencies in the West.

"I have some follow-up questioning to do for Harry down in Sausalito. I should be back in time for you to treat me to lunch," she said in her usual provocative manner.

"I see your revolver printing through your jacket. Got your short scattergun?" he asked.

"In my satchel. Loaded and I have six more brass shells for it in there, too."

She blew him a kiss, mounted her horse and rode off.

He watched her until she was out of sight. They clicked at their first meeting and the trail to here, had been one full of both romance and adventure. She probably held the record for the most kills of any female law officer. Nobody kept track of such things, but he was sure he was right.

Pope rode to his own office and tied Caesar to the hitching rail in front of the sheriff's office.

He heard shots just after greeting his chief deputy, Bill Isakson. Shots in town were an unusual thing for San Rafael.

Pope quickly stood, loosening his .44 in its holster and moved towards the door. The chief deputy was closer. Pope got there first and carefully peered around the door jamb.

He could not see any threats from his position. He could see scared citizens running for cover.

Pope drew the long-barreled Colt single action Frontier model and stepped onto the board sidewalk.

He scanned up and down the street. The two most likely places to check were a saloon on the left and a bank on the right. This time he was wrong.

The former Wells Fargo detective saw saddlebags and empty rifle scabbards on three horses tied in front of the Wells Fargo office. He walked towards the office, his uncocked revolver held at his side. The dark gun blended with his dark suit and was almost hidden. He had a backup revolver hidden in his left waistband.

The sheriff was beginning to regret not getting a rifle or shotgun.

"Water over the dam," he thought.

Three men rushed out of Wells Fargo, carrying rifles and flour bags. He assumed the latter were stuffed with purloined bills.

He aimed and steadied against a porch column in front of the general store.

"Sheriff! Throw up your hands! Do it now!" he yelled in a voice not to be ignored.

They ignored him. Stupid, stupid men.

He settled the front sight of the 7 ½ inch barrel on the man closest to his horse and pressed the trigger. His targets were seventy-five feet away.

The man stumbled forward, dropping both his rifle and two bags of cash. When one bag hit the dusty street, some of the cash blew away in the wind.

The chief deputy was a man in his sixties. He had worn a badge for thirty-five years. He touched off his ten gauge double barrel shotgun.

"Damn!" he uttered as his man was obviously hit, but not down. He moved across the street and closer towards the robbers as he broke the shotgun open and replaced the three inch long brass shell with a fresh one. Now, he was back to two shots in the long gun.

The chief deputy had been farther down the street from where Pope had started shooting. His position was too far for a tight shotgun pattern. His man had been trying to mount his horse. He had jerked as several of the widely dispersed buckshot hit him. He struggled aboard the horse and slung the money bags over his saddle horn.

The third man was already mounted.

Both men fired their rifles at the two lawmen, though with no success.

Sheriff John Pope unwrapped the reins of his horse from the hitching rail in front of the sheriff's office.

It would now be down to a chase and a second shoot out.

His rifle scabbard on the horse was empty. He saw another option.

"I'm going to take them," he yelled at his chief deputy whose health did not live up to the requirements of the upcoming pursuit.

"Chief, take over the crime scene. Look for victims and get help in case those shots we heard hit anybody!" he said as he mounted and applied spur-less heels to his stallion.

Pope rode hard for the short distance to where the robbers had tied their horses. He leaned down from his saddle without stopping and scooped up the dropped Winchester. Not an amazing trick for a former cowboy

He glanced at the side of the barrel of the 1873, smiled and shoved it into his saddle scabbard.

At a glance, he had read the caliber. 44 WCF. Also known as .44-40. The same caliber as his Colt. So, he had plenty of ammunition if he had to do a lot of shooting.

Pope doubted the chase would be long. The chief

had hit one man with his scattergun. Pope had left one dead in the street.

No matter where he was hit, multiple wounds from the .32 caliber buckshot balls would quickly become debilitating. Left alone, they would cause death from lead poisoning.

Until then, the robber was a threat. The unhurt man was a greater threat.

Pope and his horse were both young and very fit.

"Caesar, we can catch these two before they know what hit them," he said to the horse. He was pretty sure the horse spoke English from past responses when they talked on the trail.

Without more bidding, the black sped up. He could gallop at this pace for hours.

They met some traffic. Wagons and a few horsemen coming southbound.

He could hear the frustrated robbers yell "Get out the way!" as they passed slow wagons or slower horsemen.

As their sheriff of a year galloped past after the two, the northbound traffic knew something was up. Those who lived in Marin County knew their sheriff's reputation as a shootist. He had been known as the "gun for Wells Fargo," until he resigned and became their sheriff. Somebody was going to die today and it was unlikely to be him.

Towards the end of the first hour of his pursuit,

Pope felt he was getting close enough to try his confiscated carbine.

He pulled it from the scabbard and levered the action. It had at least one cartridge from his quick view. He suspected it was fully loaded when the robbery began, unless its owner was an idiot. Which was not a possibility the sheriff dismissed lightly.

Without slowing, he raised the carbine to his shoulder. He got the lead, unwounded rider in his sights. He centered the front bead in the rear buckhorn sight and breathed out. Even though they were at full gallop, the stallion's smooth gait facilitated an accurate shot.

Pope pressed the trigger and the carbine spewed white smoke and flame.

He saw the hat fly off his intended target's head, levered again and shot a second time.

This time the man fell from his horse. The sheriff did not worry whether he was dead as he fell.

Pope saw him hit and flop like a ragdoll. The first hit on the ground was on his head.

The head hit at an awkward angle and Pope could see, though not hear, the man's neck break. When he landed and settled in the road, his head was at an unnatural angle.

"Pard, your friends are both dead. Give it up and stop your horse. I've killed enough men today," he yelled in a loud, matter of fact voice.

The wounded man responded by spurring his horse and speeding ahead.

Pope cursed to himself and wounded the man with a shot just above his right shoulder blade. He fell off the horse hard in the middle of the road.

"Guess this fella was particular about his carbine. Kept the sights true and she looks like she's been freshly oiled," he told the stallion as he sheathed the short rifle.

He checked the last man shot. He was severely wounded. Two cotton bags of the bank's cash were still tied on the saddle.

He collected the fallen guns. Pope took the man's riata off his saddle. He put the wounded man over his saddle and tied his legs beneath the horse's belly. He tied the man's empty gunbelt to the saddle horn with a latigo so he would not roll over.

Pope remounted the stallion and led the man's dun with its cargo back to the first man he shot on this trail.

"You sure are a mess!" he said to the man with his head pointing in an unnatural direction.

He put him over his horse, which was sitting patiently, reins hanging down. Pope tied him face down over the saddle, using more of the first lariat. He was not quite as gentle. This one felt nothing.

Pope removed the two bags of the stolen bills. Treasure is how he thought of it, in his former Wells

Fargo detective vernacular.

He tied the remainder of the lariat to this man's mount, securing it to the reins so he could lead the horse second in line. Pope slung the bags of money over his own saddle horn.

Reins and lariat in tow, he headed back to town leading two horses. One had a dead man. The other, had one who was in bad shape.

Pope knew tying the wounded man this way would be damaging and painful. He knew two other things. He did not have any other option at his disposal. And the sooner the doctor in town saw him, the more chance the man had of living.

As he met traffic, he doffed his hat. He was a naturally polite man. Moreover, they might be voters. Something he was trying to get his head around, since he had been a salaried policeman or detective all of his adult life.

He whistled as he rode. It was going to take Sheriff John Pope two hours to return to town at this slower rate.

He saw the odd, tall body freight wagons along the way in both directions. They were like the prairie schooners his grandfather had led West during the Oregon Trail and the California Gold Rush days. Except, the sides of their wooden beds were twice as high as the Conestoga's. Some were pulled by as many as six or more pairs of horses, mules or oxen.

Pope marveled at these delivery vehicles which plied their routes all year long, through snow and over steep mountain roads.

******

An hour into Pope's return ride, he met a small posse coming to assist him. His chief deputy had put up and coming young deputy Walter Wood in charge of raising and leading the posse of four other men. Unlike many frontier posses in Pope's experience, these men from affluent Northern California were well-heeled. No Civil War muskets or Sears Roebuck & Company two dollar breakopen .32's here.

The young deputy leading the small posse grinned when he saw his boss.

"Guess we weren't necessary," he remarked to Pope.

"It was their choice, Walt. Not mine. One was still alive an hour ago. I did not want to waste time checking him. He needs a doctor not a sheriff. What's the story at the Wells Fargo office?"

"They killed Mr. Branson, the manager. The cashier and the telegraph man are alright. By now, Mr. Branson should be over at the undertakers.

The cashier composed a telegram to the Wells Fargo chief detective about what happened and you killing one and Bill winging another."

"I will write the next one. I think I recovered all

the treasure. Some blew away on the street when the man was hit and dropped the bag though," Pope said.

"The chief deputy managed to gather all of it up before it 'disappeared' into somebody's vest pocket," Wood said.

"Walt, ride ahead and make sure the prosecutor and maybe the judge are around when we get back in. I'm taking it the cashier and telegrapher are eyewitnesses to the murder of Hiram Branson?"

"Yessir."

"Then, the murder is solved and justice has been done. The stolen money had been recovered," Pope said.

"Tell 'em what you found when you encountered me returning. Tell 'em these fools fought the law. And, the law won. End of story." The young lawman nodded and rode off towards the county seat at a gallop.

Pope and the posse returned to a cheering crowd in town. The prosecutor and the judge were both in the crowd, cheering.

"Always a good sign," Pope thought.

Pope went straight to the doctor's office and unloaded the wounded man. He was still alive. He then went to the Wells Fargo office. He drafted a telegram to Wells Fargo's longtime chief detective, James Hume. He had been Pope's and Sarah's boss until management did them wrong after saving the President's life and later breaking up a smuggling ring.

"James Hume Stop All three robbers Wells Fargo office this date are wounded or dead by hand of Marin County Sheriff Stop All treasure recovered Stop JPope Sheriff End." The telegrapher sent it. An immediate response said: "Sheriff Marin County Stop Hume arrives tomorrow. End."

"So, my old friend and boss is coming. I wonder why? The murder and robbery were solved. Figuring who shot the manager will be easy. The only thing left would be to do a full report of the matter and a temporary fill-in for Hiram Branson, the manager who was killed. He was a good man who will be missed in the community. Choosing a manager would not be Hume's job, unless he was assigned to do it," Pope thought.

Hume was, in fact, assigned to put a temporary manager in place. They had an experienced manager virtually next door. Her name was Sarah Watson Pope. And, he had already cut a deal with Harry Morse, who was coming with him.

******

Two of the three most famous detectives in America arrived on the morning ferry the next day and hired a buggy for the trip to San Rafael. Their sometimes adversary, Allan Pinkerton, was near death in Chicago.

Jim Hume and Harry Morse were longtime

friends. Their friendship and work relationship had recently been permanently impaired by a speech given by Wells Fargo's president. Morse had been so incensed he advised San Francisco journalists the true facts about who saved President Arthur from assassination, the Black Bart capture, and the largest roundup of drug smugglers in Bay area history. With the exception of Sarah, the key players were Morse and Pope, not company employees as the executive claimed in his public version of the story.

Morse had spent more time than anyone chasing Black Bart. He had sought him for almost eight years. He, with one of his detectives and Sarah, identified who the robber really was. Morse had arrested him and delivered him to Hume. His part in the speech was relegated to helping two Wells Fargo detectives (Hume and Sarah) apprehend the infamous stage robber.

Pope's name was not even mentioned in saving the President or breaking up the drug operation. Even before the speech, Pope and Sarah had been seething over the company president mandating they be married before going undercover to solve the threats against the President. The speech added fuel to a fire already burning.

The speech was immediately decried by local papers as being one-sided. It had prompted Sarah to resign from Wells Fargo the next morning. She was offered a job by Harry Morse and accepted it instantly.

Pope had applied to the governor to be appointed for the remaining term of Marin's sheriff shortly after. The appointment had been swift and Pope had sent his resignation letter to Hume.

Within a matter of months, bad decisions in a historically well-run company had caused its best two detectives to leave in anger.

Pope had told Sarah when he received Hume's telegram to stand by for whatever was to occur. "It will be an interesting thing to see, at the very least," he told her.

The two friends, with now a discomfort neither wished between them, arrived by ten o'clock. Chief detective Hume went to the Wells Fargo office to question the cashier and the telegrapher.

Morse went next door to meet with his newest detective, Sarah Watson Pope.

"How was your trip across the Bay, Harry?" she asked.

"The water was rough and the atmosphere was cool, Sarah."

"May I be so bold as to assume by atmosphere you are not talking about weather?" she asked.

Morse nodded.

"As angry as you, John, and I were, Sarah, it was not really Jim Hume's doing. I am sure he did not report the cases in the manner they were presented.

Sarah, he could have done more. Instead, he

protected his job and let his integrity fly out the window. This is not the Jim Hume I've known for so many years."

"As you know, Harry, it was a source of great anger for John and me. We were as mad for you as for John's treatment. I only came out better than I should have because I was 'riding for the brand' as our friends last year in Cheyenne would say," Sarah said.

"You deserved every accolade. You found the bloody handkerchief with the Chinese laundry tag. It was the clue leading us to Charles Boles, the rather pleasant gent we called Black Bart for so many years. A man who was afraid of horses and whose unloaded shotgun's hammers were locked in the cocked position by years of rust.

I know why I am here and what Hume will ask you today. I'll let him do it without spilling his beans," Harry Morse said.

"If he is going to ask me to do something, I can imagine it has to do with a Wells Fargo office temporarily without a manager. If I am anywhere near correct, how do you feel about what Mr. Hume is going to say?" she asked.

"It's what I would do if I was him, so I cannot fault his logic. Just see what he says. Mull it a bit and ask my opinion. I promise to give an honest one."

"You always have. You are someone whose word I never doubt. You, John, Israel Pope and, up until recently, Jim Hume.

Now, the wandering eye President, not so much!" she said with a conspiratorial grin which caused her boss to smile.

"After saving him, I am surprised John didn't shoot President Arthur himself," Morse said.

"Don't you believe for a minute he was not considering it!" Sarah said, adding "What's Hume's feeling towards John and me? He was pretty quiet and reserved at the wedding."

"I noticed it, too. And, he did not express anything on the ferry ride over, or in the rental carriage. I really don't know the answer to your question. I suspect it will manifest itself more when he meets with you," Morse said.

The meeting was not scheduled. Hume just walked into the Morse Detective Agency office when he was ready.

"Sarah, how are you?" he asked.

"I'm fine thank you, Jim. And, you?"

"I've been better. On with business though. Has Harry mentioned why I am here?"

"No, he said you wanted to speak with me and he would not preempt your words."

"I have been authorized to offer you the temporary manager's job for the Wells Fargo office here."

"I have a job, Jim. And, I quite like it."

"I know you do. Harry and I have come to an

agreement. If you run the office until we can find a suitable replacement, I will pay you a full manager's salary and you will work half-days. The other half you can perform your Morse investigations."

"For which I will pay you half your salary until you are back on full-time with me."

"So, I will be working for both of you for half a day. Wells Fargo will be one hundred percent of a manager's salary and Harry will pay me fifty percent of my current salary with him?" she asked for clarification.

Both men nodded affirmatively.

I would be crazy to turn down a salary and a half for a month or so, she thought. "As a married woman, I should make sure John concurs. We discuss all matters and decide together. We have since your president mandated our marriage as a condition of employment," she added unnecessarily.

Though he knew she was correct, Hume bit his lip to keep from making a defensive retort. Morse read his now-former friend immediately.

"You deserve a prompt response. Why don't you slip down to the café and get some coffee. I will meet you there shortly," she said.

They nodded and all rose and went to the door, which Sarah locked once all were outside.

She walked to the sheriff's office. She was glad to see Caesar tied to the hitching rail in the front. Her husband was either in or close by. Pope had an office in the corner and she walked in. He and his chief deputy were looking over new wanted posters from the most recent mail.

"May I interrupt you gentlemen for a quick personal matter between John and me?" she asked.

"Surely, Miss Sarah," Bill Isakson responded and he got up and walked out of the office to his own desk and sat down with the sheaf of posters to continue to review them.

"Hume wants me to run the office on full salary until they find a permanent manager. I only have to work half a day. The other half I can do my real job. Harry will pay me half salary until I'm back full-time. Sounds like found money to me," she said to her husband.

He contemplated for a moment, thinking about the deal offered. He wanted to be against it but could not find any downsides.

"My vote is do it. You're right. It's found money."

She leaned over and kissed him on the lips, turned and walked out of the sheriff's department, waving at the chief deputy on the way.

It took her less than three minutes to reach the café via the board sidewalk.

"John and I discussed it. I will accept both of your offers assuming I am assured, Harry, of a full-time job waiting when I return?"

"Of course, Sarah," he said.

"I have already started on some cases here. So, today I will spend time in both offices. The shift times between Wells Fargo and Morse will likely flip periodically according to the needs of each job.

Jim, is there anyone you are looking at as a full-time manager?"

"There's a young man the operations people are going to be talking with. He's assistant manager in a large office. He was a former cashier and knows the ins and outs of how an office should be run. They understand from his manager he cannot arrive here for another month and a half if he accepts."

"I'll try to hold things on an even keel until he or someone else arrives," Sarah promised.

She proffered her hand and shook with both men. Hume left to go to the sheriff's office. Morse stayed to discuss the status of current cases with Sarah.

******

Chief Detective Jim Hume walked into the sheriff's office as Pope was walking out the door. The lean, tough sheriff smiled and extended his hand to his old boss, trying not to show any of the ill-feelings he felt.

"You're looking healthy and fit, John."

"Thanks, Jim. You do, too."

"Do you have a place where you can fill me in on what happened yesterday?" Hume asked.

"Step into my office and we'll talk. Hold on for one important minute."

Pope stepped out to a work area and took two thick mugs from the counter and poured reasonably fresh and very strong coffee into them. He knew Hume drank his black, so he carried both in and set on down on the scarred wooden desk by Hume.

Jim Hume picked up the heavy mug and sniffed the coffee. He took a sip and smiled.

"I believe you make better coffee than my secretary. And, he does a pretty good job."

Pope nodded and began telling him every detail about the robbery, murder, chase and shooting of the three outlaws.

"I am supposed to get the bullet which killed Hiram Branson anytime now. I thought since you were here, you'd like to work with me to test fire the three rifles and three sixguns and determine who killed Hiram," Pope said, knowing his former boss was virtually the world's expert on the emerging science of ballistic forensics.

"An excellent idea, John. Where is the bullet now?"

"A local doctor is the county coroner. He's just down the street. Maybe we should just walk down and pick it up?" Hume nodded and Pope rose to put his coat on.

"I hope he dug it out before he started working on the robber I just dropped off. I shot him pretty badly." Pope said.

"I see you've gone to a longer barrel Colt. And, it looks like a Webley Bulldog tucked in your left side. Any other surprises?" Hume asked.

"I would not be Israel Pope's grandson without a big Bowie in my left boot," Pope grinned as he withdrew a beautiful blade almost a foot long.

"I would have expected no less," Hume said with no intonation. It was just a fact and he stated as so without any fanfare.

They went down to the doctor's. There had been no need for an autopsy. It was pretty clear the cause of death was a bullet through the heart.

"First off, the fellow you dropped off may make it. He has a lot of shoulder damage and has lost some blood. Getting him here reasonably fast made the difference.

I have the offending slug waiting for you and had already measured it," the doctor said.

"The bullet measures .401 inches. So, it's a .38-40 round," he told them. Both knew someone at Winchester had made a naming error in developing the cartridge. The usual protocol was to list the bullet diameter first and the grains of black powder second. This cartridge was forty caliber and the case held forty grains of black powder. It should have been a .40-40 or a .40-38, depending on the particular powder load. Nonetheless, it was an excellent cartridge and somewhat faster and flatter shooting than the more popular .44-40 which also served in Colt Frontiers like Pope's and several lever and pump action carbines.

"The caliber makes our forensic investigation simpler. Only one man carried a .38-40 revolver. He had a matching .38-40 carbine. We only have to test those two to see which killed our manager. Happily, he is our prisoner," Pope said.

They took the bullet and returned to the sheriff's office and picked up the Colt and Winchester 1873 in .38-40. Pope retrieved ammunition from the man's saddlebags and they walked to the livery stable.

"I'm guessing the livery must have a long watering trough," Hume said.

"Exactly. If we used a normal one to capture a bullet, the rifle's faster velocity would punch a hole in the end of the trough."

They explained to the livery stable owner what they needed to do. He was fascinated and chose to watch.

Hume fired the two shots from one end of the trough to another. He angled the muzzles down to achieve the longest travel though water. After the first shot, from the Colt, Pope retrieved the undamaged 180 grain lead bullet and put it in his right vest pocket. He did the same with the same 180 grain fired in the Winchester and deposited it in his left vest pocket.

They thanked the liveryman and returned to the

office.

Pope got his investigative satchel out and removed a magnifying glass. He put a piece of paper on the desk and drew three two-inch diameter circles. He labeled them "murder," "Colt," and "Carbine." Pope then placed the appropriate bullet in its circle.

Hume, using the magnifying glass, compared the striations on the killing bullet with the revolver bullet. They did not match except as to caliber. The striations from the rifling were wrong.

The bullet removed from his manager's body and the Winchester carbine round matched perfectly.

Hiram Branson had conclusively been killed by the robber Bob Lentine using his .38-40 Winchester Model 1873 carbine.

Hume wrote a statement explaining the forensic process and signed it with Pope signing as a witness.

A known stickler for procedure, the chief detective followed court preparation procedures. Now Wells Fargo's files on the robbery were complete except for a murder and robbery trial. Pope made a second signed copy for the prosecutor's files and both men signed it.

The two had lunch and Hume walked over to the Wells Fargo office by himself.

Sarah was already there.

"I heard shots. Did you test to see what gun killed poor Hiram?" she asked.

"Yes, it was Lentine, the last outlaw John shot. The survivor. I'm surprised Ned Buntline has not come calling to write a dime novel about Pope. John's actual kills on the job and off greatly exceed Hardin, Hickok, Earp, Tilghman, and Masterson. Actually, any shootist I can name. Quite frankly so do yours."

"Yes, Jim. It is worrisome. I fear John will draw in gunfighter wannabes. There are only so many face downs God gives you before your number is up," Sarah said.

"It is true. I wish he could keep a lower profile. He's a magnet to violent events, Sarah. There is a lesson to be learned from Abilene's town council firing Hickok in 1871, only thirteen years ago. He just killed too many people. He did what they paid him to do, but in the end, it was simply bad publicity."

"John does not go out looking for it. It's starting to get to him, Jim. He told me he's tired of all the killing."

"Maybe he should hang up his badge and take the permanent Wells Fargo manager job here," Hume thought aloud.

"He'd be certifiably crazy inside of a month. You know him well enough to know it's true. Maybe I should run the office and he should be the detective for Harry. Since most of the jobs are civil in nature, he would not be as exposed to as much violence as being sheriff."

"Your idea has merit, Sarah. You should suggest

it. You know I would hire you as manager here in a heartbeat. As would Harry Morse hire Pope to replace you," Hume agreed.

"I will suggest it. He has already been sheriff here for a year. He may want to wait until closer to election time to decide."

"Well, just remember the offer of Wells Fargo's job for you as manager is short-lived. The offer is off the table as soon as another manager candidate accepts," Hume said.

"I realize your timing limitations. John is not a man to be pushed however."

Hume nodded affirmatively at something he knew to be true.

They spoke for a half hour about how to make the office grow faster and whether the county seat or Sausalito would be the best location for growth.

Hume took out a gold pocket watch.

"I'd better chase up Harry. We only have an hour to get to Sausalito and turn in our buggy before the ferry leaves for San Francisco.

Thank you for taking this temporary job, Sarah. I both appreciate it and have full faith you will handle the office well."

He stood, shook hands and left.

Pope and Sarah spoke about Hume's and Morse's visit during dinner.

"It went better than I expected," Pope said.

"I agree. You know the saddest part? Morse. He has irretrievably lost a longtime best friend. Now they are just business associates at best.

John, you've mentioned several times about all the killing getting to you. What if you took my job with Harry's agency and I became the full-time Wells Fargo manager here?" she asked.

Pope paused, obviously giving thought to the idea.

"It has merit, Sarah. It certainly does. I reckon I am not ready to give up the sheriff's badge yet. It's only been a year. In another twelve months, I will need to decide whether to run for a full four-year term. My leanings now are towards doing it.

I think things will calm down here. There are so many plans I have which are not completed yet. I want to groom Walter Wood. Teach him how to be a detective or at least use investigative skills. Bill will be retiring in five years or sooner depending on his health. I want Walter ready to assume his post."

"What are you going to do about Martha Lane?" Sarah asked about the sister of the young woman who Pope had saved from kidnapers. She was continually inquiring about a law enforcement job.

"Martha's law enforcement career is up to her and her father, not me. I admit, she'd be in less danger with you and me breaking her in than going to work for the San Francisco Police Department and being thrown onto the mean streets right away," he said.

"Me? When did I become a member of the Marin County Sheriff's Office?"

"When you became Martha's mentor and you married the sheriff, silly."

"I guess…. what about Mattie?" she asked.

"Your guess is as good as mine. She has not sent me one of her smoking hot love letters since the marriage ceremony. Almost a year. She must have dozens of them burning in her busy little head by now."

"They damn well better stay there! It's not the head part of her well-developed anatomy I'm worried about!" Sarah said with force.

Pope grinned at her. One day he would learn about dealing with his wife. Maybe. Today was not it. She stamped off, leaving him baffled and no longer smiling. He ended up clearing the table and washing dishes. Even Scout made himself scarce.

******

Marin County had a proportionate number of civil and misdemeanor trials for its population. It seldom had a major felony trial like one for murder.

Robert Lentine wantonly killing the well-liked manager of the local Wells Fargo aroused both anger and interest in the case.

The clerk of the court worked with the prosecutor and set the trial for a week hence. California was still almost thirty years away from its first use of public defenders. Suspect Lentine was at the mercy of the judge and jury as he could not afford counsel and no attorney stepped forward for a *pro bono* defense.

Sheriff John Pope worked with the young prosecutor to round up and question the witnesses. There were two who witnessed the actual shooting. They and the ballistics forensics should be enough for a hanging.

Wells Fargo manager, Hiram Branson, had not resisted. Lentine had shot him to death in cold blood in front of credible witnesses. He had shot at the sheriff and chief deputy, attempted to elude the law, and refused to give up. There was little chance he would avoid the noose.

The trial occurred on schedule.

Sarah and Jim Hume were there to represent Wells Fargo, its deceased manager and its two prime witnesses.

Pope was there as sheriff and witness.

Much of the rest of the town was there, including Pope's grandfather Israel Pope and his wife, Millie.

Pope stood in the front corner of the courtroom as rural sheriffs are wont to do. He planned to go to the witness stand from there.

The clerk called court to order and had everyone stand when the circuit judge came in and sat.

"We are here for the State of California versus

Robert Allan Lentine. The charges are murder in the first degree, felony robbery, and evading law enforcement officers with violence.

Will the defendant, Mr. Lentine, please stand," the clerk said.

Lentine stood stiffly and faced the court. He still had a sling from being shot by Pope and several lesser wounds from the chief deputy's shotgun.

"Mr. Lentine, are you represented by counsel?"

"What?" the defendant asked.

"Do you have a lawyer?"

"Naw. Cain't afford one," Lentine responded.

"Do you understand the charges I have just read against you?"

"Yes."

"How do you plead to the murder charge?"

"Innocent. I didn't mean to shoot him."

"How do you plead to robbing the Wells Fargo office?"

"Innocent. It was his idea!"

The judge got his answer and did not press who "his" was. He left it to the prosecutor.

"Lastly, Mr. Lentine, how do you plead to shooting at the sheriff and chief deputy then riding off, eluding them?"

"Innocent. It was self-defense."

The judge intervened this time.

"Mr. Lentine. I am going to pass on your 'innocent' plea on the murder charge. Let the facts of the case determine whether you shot the man, whether it was accidental manslaughter or cold-blooded murder. As to the robbery, you participated whether it was your idea or someone else's. Do you wish to change your plea?"

"No, judge."

"Alright. With respect to the shooting at the lawmen and riding off to escape, I suspect there will be lots of witnesses who say you did both. Do you want to change your plea?" the judge asked.

"Nope."

"Alright, Mr. Lentine. Prosecutor, please proceed with your opening and witnesses."

The district attorney was the prosecutor. He outlined his case in his opening and called on each of the two surviving Wells Fargo employees.

Both told their stories. He asked both, the same question.

"Did Mr. Branson resist in any way?" Both answered he had not. Both stated Branson was shot in cold blooded murder.

"Did the defendant shoot Mr. Branson?" Both responded in the affirmative in turn.

The prosecutor called on two witnesses who were on the street and saw the robbers exit.

"What did you see when the three men exited the Wells Fargo office?"

"I heard shots. I don't know whether it was one or two. Three fellows came running out with bags. They had rifles in their hands. The sheriff called for them to throw up their hands. They started shooting instead. The sheriff killed one with his Colt. It was a long shot. Maybe seventy-five or a hundred feet. The Chief Deputy fired his scattergun. He hit the defendant and winged him. The defendant and other fella rode off fast. The sheriff jumped on his horse and took off in pursuit. He scooped up one of the rifles from the ground and took it with him."

The second man said virtually the same thing.

"The court calls Sheriff John Pope."

Pope approached the witness stand and was sworn in.

"Sheriff Pope. Please tell the court what you witnessed and what actions you took."

"Chief deputy Bill Isakson and I were in the office when we heard several shots nearby. We ran out to the street to see where they had come from. We saw three men with rifles and bags exiting the Wells Fargo office. I called for them to halt and they began shooting at us. We returned fire, me with my Colt's revolver and the Chief deputy with a ten gauge shotgun. The distance was between seventy-five and a hundred feet. My man fell dead. Bill's was out of range for a shotgun, but he took a couple of pellets and mounted his horse. He was the defendant seated right there,"

Pope said and pointed a steady finger at Lentine.

Mr. Lentine and the other man, who we subsequently identified as Thomas Butler, rode off. I mounted up and commenced pursuit. I only had revolvers with me, so I grabbed the dead man's rifle as I rode by. We later identified him as one Oscar Hammond.

I rode after them for about an hour. They were escaping felons, so when I got close enough, I fired the carbine. I killed Butler or hit him and the fall broke his neck. I am not sure which. Lentine refused to stop. He represented a threat to the people of Marin County, so I shot him. He sustained a shoulder wound. I put him over his horse to bring straight to bring him back to the doctor. A small posse met us on the way back. I sent Deputy Walter Wood ahead to let folks know we were coming in with a wounded prisoner.

At the site of the shooting on the road, I recovered several bags of money. The chief deputy recovered two bags and some loose bills. Wells Fargo audited the recovered money and found every dollar taken during the robbery was recovered.

I formally arrested Mr. Lentine for the charges presented today while he was being worked on by the doctor. The doctor advised me that his wounds may not be life-threatening. It appears by Mr. Lentine's presence here today, the doctor was correct.

The doctor gave me the bullet which killed Mr. Branson. It was a .38-40 bullet. Mr. Lentine was the only one of the robbers who carried the caliber. He had both a .38-40 revolver and carbine.

"Though we knew he was the shooter, we wanted to use forensic science to determine which of his firearms killed Mr. Branson. Wells Fargo Chief Detective James Hume, who is in the court today, and I conducted tests. We determined beyond the shadow of a doubt, it was the rifle Mr. Lentine was carrying when he exited the robbery and he had when I shot him," Pope said.

"Without having to swear Detective Hume in, would you describe how you identified which firearm killed Mr. Branson?" the prosecutor asked.

Pope described the process in detail and in such simple terms people who had never heard the word "ballistics" understood what they did.

"Thank you sheriff. You may step down. Chief Deputy Isakson, will you come to the witness box to be sworn and testify?"

He did and related the same initial gunfight in the street and his actions to ascertain the death of the manager and recover the bag and loose bills.

The prosecutor said, "Your honor, the prosecution has no further witnesses."

"Mr. Lentine, since there is not defense counsel, do you want to say anything in your behalf?" the Judge asked.

"Yeah. I didn't mean to kill the man and the robbery was not my idea."

"Gentlemen of the jury. You have heard the evidence. I charge you with concluding Mr. Lentine's guilt or innocence based purely on the evidence presented here today.

Clerk of the Court, please direct the jurors to the jury room for their deliberation."

As sheriff, Pope, joined by Deputy Wood, escorted them to an adjacent room. The chief deputy stood by Lentine, lest he get any further flight impulses.

The judge said, "Court is adjourned until the jury reaches a verdict. He rapped his gavel.

"All rise," the clerk said. And, the judge went to chambers to wait.

"Looks pretty ironclad to me," Hume commented to Pope.

"I believe so. In view of the testimony, his declarations of not meaning to kill Branson and the robbery not being his idea won't hold any water," Pope opined.

"You gave clear and complete testimony, darling," Sarah said. It was the first thing she had said to him since last night.

He looked at her and nodded. John Pope was still aggravated at his wife for her comments and departure and was not going to let her off quite this easily.

Sarah and Hume went outside to wait. The trial had a large following and Pope promised anyone who went outside the building would receive an announcement when the verdict was in.

He was surprised it took the jury two hours to decide their verdict. One member had argued for manslaughter instead of murder in the first degree for most of the time until he finally understood what he and everyone else had heard from the witnesses.

The foreman of the jury went out and got the clerk. The clerk advised the sheriff, who announced a verdict was in.

The clerk waited for the courtroom to fill and all seats were resumed until advising the judge to come in. He called for order and to stand. The judge came in and sat down.

The jury came back and sat.

"Mr. Foreman. Do you have verdicts on all charges?"

"We do, your honor."

"Please read the verdicts to Mr. Lentine and the court," the judge ordered.

"On count one, murder in the first degree: guilty" Lentine cried out and the judge rapped his gavel and gave him an icily stern look.

"On count two, armed robbery: guilty.

On count three, shooting at sworn law enforcement officers and evading arrest: guilty as charged."

Lentine knew his fate and slumped in his seat.

"Mr. Lentine, please stand," the judge ordered.

"Mr. Lentine, the first guilty charge is a capital offense. The others are serious felonies, especially shooting at sworn officers. I have no choice in this matter. I sentence you to be hung by the neck until dead. The execution will be carried out at San Quentin Prison in this county at the earliest time within the prison's schedule. I remand you over to the custody of Sheriff Pope to await your punishment."

"Damn you! Damn all of you to hell!" he screamed.

Without waiting for the judge, Pope jerked the man from the box and frog-walked him out of the courtroom. Outside the door, Isakson and Wood took him by either side and escorted him to the jail to await his transfer to San Quentin for his punishment.

Pope walked to his office, leaving Sarah and Hume on the wooden sidewalk.

"He must be upset. He never brought suspects in alive before," Hume noted. Sarah did not dignify the comment with an answer. She was worried about her marriage, not how her husband felt about a guilty party being hanged. She knew he would take the hanging with equivocation. She was more worried about the way he took her off the cuff and unnecessary comment. He had never reacted in such a manner in the two years they had been partners and had hardly spoken to her since.

Pope sent a telegram over to San Quentin's warden advising of the judge's decision and asking when he wanted the prisoner delivered for hanging. He received a reply later in the day to bring him any time.

He should be hung a few days later. There was no one to file an appeal, so the process was fast.

Pope and Deputy William Nickels delivered Lentine to the prison. San Quentin was a convenient three and a half mile ride from the county seat.

Lentine was glum and silent on the ride over. They delivered him and were told the hanging would be at nine in the morning one week hence. As sheriff, Pope was expected to be there to advise the judge his sentence had been carried out.

The rest of Pope's day was filled with paperwork. He went home to the cabin at six o'clock. Sarah was already there. Waiting for him.

"Damn," he thought, "here we go again!" He was wrong.

She walked up to him as he dismounted and said "I am so sorry, John. My remark was unnecessary and petty. I love you and trust you. If I cannot compete with an eighteen year old, I should give up and go back to Chicago. But, I am not. My husband, my home and my life are all here in Marin County. And, this is where I will stay as long as you will have me."

She walked over and buried her face in his vest.

"I'll have you forever, if you let me Sarah. There is nobody else I want except you."

She began to sob. He lifted her chin and kissed her wet lips.

After a while, he picked her up in his arms and

took her into the cabin. Caesar was left standing, reins down. Scout was sitting on his haunches beside him. They understood.

Later, Pope came out and led the stallion into his stall for a brushing and feeding without the saddle and bridle. The hound trotted along to supervise.

Sarah was asleep. She had skipped dinner and was sleeping soundly with a smile on her face.

******

Pope got an official telegram from the prison with the date and time for Lentine's execution. Sarah wanted to go as a representative of Wells Fargo, since Lentine had murdered her predecessor.

They rode over on the day of the execution. Pope had to relinquish his Colt and his smaller Webley Bulldog backup. The guard did not ask Sarah if she was armed. He made a seriously wrong assumption, since she had both a .44 and a .38 secreted on her person. Pope did not give up the foot long Bowie in his left boot either.

Sarah sat in an observation gallery. Pope mounted the scaffold. Lentine was brought up, struggling, by jailers.

A photographer took a photo for the prison's file and to release to the newspapers in San Francisco. It showed Lentine with a black hood over his head, a priest, the warden and Sheriff Hunt John Pope standing in a group on the scaffold.

Lentine had been weighed, rope length and counterweights adjusted. The hangman placed the rope around Lentine's neck as he struggled and moaned. The hangman left the scaffold.

It was up to the sheriff to pull the release lever. Lentine was his prisoner, not a prison inmate. Pope performed his job promptly and the prisoner fell through the trap door and came to an abrupt stop out of sight. The sound of his neck snapping was audible to the men on the scaffold. The priest crossed himself and they walked down the steps.

A prison doctor checked Lentine and verified he was dead. The warden had statements prepared and signed by himself and Pope. Pope took one back to his office for court files. Sarah later copied it for her report to Jim Hume. The case was closed once and for all.

"I'm guessing you don't want lunch?" Sarah asked her husband when they got back to San Rafael."

"No, not really. Pulling the lever was a lot different than shooting a man who is trying to kill you. I have never caused the death of a person who was totally harmless at the time. I know he earned his sentence. The world is probably a better place without him.

This just felt different. I need to think about it and deal with it in my head, Sarah."

She squeezed his arm and walked back to the

café near her office. She had not pulled the lever, so she was hungry. She had not had much sleep last night. She was rushed enough in the morning to skip breakfast, save a cup of strong coffee. It was time to make up for it.

Pope walked the certificate of execution over to the judge's chambers. He was in and motioned Pope in the door.

"So, he's met his Maker?" the judge asked as Pope handed him the certificate.

"He met somebody. He will never murder another soul on this earth, Judge."

"Who did it?" the judge asked.

"As the representative of the court, I pulled the lever."

"What was it like? I know you've killed many times. Just not like this."

"I cannot answer. Let me think about it and tell you when I have figured out how I feel about it."

"Fair enough, Sheriff."

Pope nodded at the judge and took his leave.

The sheriff walked back into the office. The chief deputy was having lunch. By coincidence, he was sitting with Sarah Pope at the café.

Pope poured a cup of morning coffee, now darker and stronger yet. He sat down and looked at a pile of papers. Misdemeanor warrants and civil warrants. It did not matter. He received a small stipend on the service of them all.

He sipped the coffee, not recoiling at its heat or strength. Lighting his pipe, he began signing papers and putting them in piles by type.

Pope considered this mindless work. It was relaxing in a way. He did not mind it after years on the trail or walking the mean streets across the Bay.

He stared, unfocused, at the opposing wall in his office. It held a portrait of the governor who had appointed him. In the outer office was a portrait of President Arthur.

Pope did not look so favorably on it each day when he walked in. All in all, he considered Arthur a good President. As long as he stayed away from Sarah Pope.

Maybe this was how Sarah felt about Mattie. A threat. Not as powerful a threat, just one geographically closer.

He shrugged and thought about whether the older sister was going to press becoming a deputy. Pope thought she would, over the protestations of her father. Could he train her how to stay alive against drunks and bullies? Women police officers were virtually non-existent in 1884. There had been a few notable private detective females, including his own wife. As to municipal badge-toting women…. he did not know of a single one. Anywhere.

He had no problem as long as she was tough enough to survive. He knew she, and her sister, were both smart enough. Time would tell whether she pressed the matter at a time where he had an opening.

Pope finished the paperwork as Bill Isakson came in.

"Bill, I have executed a man, done the current pile of paperwork and now I think I'll walk around town and be seen patrolling. Want to join me?"

"I'd be pleased to, John."

The two spent the next hour walking around San Rafael, chatting with people, shaking hands, and stepping into stores.

The following day, Pope would do the same thing in Sausalito. Then Tiburon, Mill Valley, Novato, and Bolinas to finish out the week. He knew his job depended on keeping the peace. It also depended on maintaining visibility and public perception. Sheriff John Pope was going to do both.

He arrived at the cabin to find Sarah had proceeded him and joined forces with Millie for a family dinner at the senior Pope's larger cabin.

"John, we've been talking about harvesting a buck or two for some venison. I think it's about the right time, don't you?" Israel Pope asked.

"I do. What about early Saturday? I have a sneaking suspicion you've already scouted out some likely spots."

"I have. And, they are not too far. Just a bit north and west from here. We'll bring Scout, mainly 'cause he will enjoy it. You and I can sure track deer on our own. Scout's a good boy and deserves a little trail time."

The blue tick hound perked up his large ears, listening. He came over and laid at Israel Pope's feet in response.

"Once you said 'good boy' he knew exactly who you were talking about, Israel," Millie said.

"Darlin', John and I are both proof a good woodsman can talk with his animal partners. I swear old Amos, a mule I rode so many miles and years, knew every word I said. So, did the thoroughbred warhorse I inherited from my Kiowa chief friend. I rode him on the first of my two great retribution trails and for years after."

"It must be contagious, Israel. Kate Warne and I talk all the time on the trail, on the way to work. Everywhere. I don't feel strange about it either!" Sarah added.

"You shouldn't Missy. Your horse is more than transportation in the West. She is sometimes the difference between life and death. When I was gored almost to death by a bear, my mule brought me back on an hour ride. I flat out don't remember a second of it. I'd be dead if he had not delivered me home and to a mid-wife who cauterized my wounds.

And here I am, breathing, over forty-five years later," Israel said.

"Thank God and Manitou for it, Grandpa," Pope said.

"I'm not so sure they aren't one and the same being, Sonny," the old mountain man and bounty hunter said.

"So you think you can schedule going out and fetching some venison in the morning?" Israel asked his grandson.

"I think I can do it, Grandpa."

"Sarah, are you going into Wells Fargo tomorrow morning?" Pope asked.

"Yes, pretty early. I have a few things to wrap up. I should be home by lunchtime," she said.

"Please tell the duty deputy, Walt, I'm out seeking venison for the winter, and I'll swing by after lunch. Grandpa and I should be back here about the time you are," he said.

The two men were up drinking coffee at five the next morning. Like they were every day. No preparation was necessary. Both always had their carbines, Bowie and skinning knives and rope on their horses or their persons. The primary difference was the sheriff did not wear his usual suit and tie.

They rode out, an exuberant Scout leading the way. Israel Pope was a frontiersman. He did not want their hound to run down a buck. They agreed to make a small camp and one would keep Scout occupied with treats and would drink campfire coffee. The other would track deer on foot.

It worked well. Scout enjoyed the one on one time with John Pope. A shot signaled Israel had fired on something.

Israel had seen a large buck by area standards. He had six antler points. In the Wind River Range, Israel would have dismissed him as too small and not worth the powder. In Marin County, he was a keeper.

One carefully placed .44-40 bullet from thirty yards caused the buck to jump. Israel waited ten minutes before tracking him. He did not want the buck to be pressured and run all the way to Sonoma County. This way, the buck would die more quickly. It was important to Israel for the deer not to suffer unduly. It was part of the Indian stewardship he learned and followed.

Israel found the buck less than one hundred yards from where he was shot. Taking the lariat from around his shoulder, he tied the rear feet and threw the lasso over a nearby limb.

He pulled the dead buck up off the ground and bled and gutted him. Israel noted the surroundings for an easy return and walked back to camp.

John Pope handed his grandfather a mug of coffee as Scout greeted him.

Israel scratched behind the hound's ears.

"Yep, boy, I got us one. Don't you worry, Millie fed you some meat the first day I met her in San Francisco. She won't let you go hungry now either!"

Pope went with Israel to fetch the deer and put it over Israel's horse behind the saddle. It was a large enough buck to provide meat for some time. There was no need for Pope to seek another today. Their policy was Indian policy. Take what you need and use all of what you take.

They rode home and butchered the deer. It was the one thing he had learned from his father, a feckless pioneer. They cut stew meat cubes and tenderloin first then steaks from the haunches. In their one departure from Indian culture, they did not save the organ meat despite its iron benefits. Neither liked the taste. Some heart and liver meat was cut up and would be stewed for Scout, who liked it more than they did.

Israel and Millie made a salt brine and covered the meat with it. Some of the bigger pieces would be either sun dried or salted for the coming winter. Much would be removed from the brine and dried on racks in a low heat oven to make jerky. Jerky was always a trail food for both men. Millie used soy sauce on some and molasses on the other for seasoning. Israel said it was much better than what he had made during his trapping days. He told her his tasted like salty old moccasins.

Millie and Sarah had a joint garden with the Three Sisters. It was the triad comprising much of the vegetable portion of the Indian diet. Corn was grown, then squash, then beans to spiral up poles. If Israel did not have bacon to flavor the vegetables in the old days, sometimes jerky was a substitute. San Rafael and Sausalito both had stores with fresh eggs, meat and dried vegetables in good supply much of the year.

CHAPTER 2

Pope received a letter from Martha Lane stating she and her father had come to an accord. She would delay matriculating in college to earn a degree in "something useless for anyone, especially the society housewife she was destined to be."

She said her father would agree to her pursuing her dream to be in law enforcement for a year to see how it worked out. In view of this, she "wondered if the Marin County Sheriff's Office had any deputy openings?"

Pope was aware his wife had a close relationship with Martha, who was the older Lane sister. He put his suit jacket on, the letter in the breast pocket. Pope hastened down the street to find his wife.

Today, Sarah was in the Morse Detective office, conversing with none other than the famous Harry Morse himself.

"Hi, Harry. How are you?" Pope asked.

"Just fine, John. We were wrapping up and thinking about lunch. I have already had four cups of coffee here and need some real food. Otherwise, I will be fidgeting on the ferry all the way across to San Francisco."

"I need to ask Sarah's opinion on something. I'd actually value your input on it too, Harry."

"Join us for lunch and let's talk about it," Morse responded.

After they ordered, Morse his fifth coffee for the day to accompany a roast beef sandwich, Pope handed the letter to him and he read it. He passed it to Sarah to read.

"Well, John, you and I know women can make fine law enforcement officers. And, we are in fine company with people like Hume and Pinkerton."

"We are for a fact. My concern is not so much as a detective. I worry about her on the trails alone, handling sometimes several ruffians with no backup, male or female."

"Do you worry about me, John" his wife asked.

"About your deadly abilities? Not at all. About several ambushing you and overpowering you? Every single day."

"Such a thing could not happen to you?" she asked.

"Sure it could. I just think I have a better chance of fighting my way out of it with my backup Bowie or these big fists."

"No doubt. Could your chief deputy at his age do the same? Or one of your nineteen year old current deputies?"

"I hope so. I cannot really say. In the year here, I have never witnessed any of them take down a couple of thugs who were resisting."

"I trained the women deputies at Pinkertons. Not just how to investigate, also how to shoot, fight, and arrest people. I could teach her those things in the evenings when it would not conflict with either of my two jobs," she offered.

"John," Morse began, "my concern is how your county commission would accept it."

"A good point. They have applauded the suffrage in Wyoming. At one meeting I attended, it was even mentioned Mrs. Morris was a Wyoming Justice of the Peace in 1870," Pope said.

"Well, if the young woman has merit, run it past them. See if their ideas live up to their mouths. She certainly comes from a bright family, her mother excluded. Mrs. Lane would try the patience of Job.

If you hire her, John, and she gets tired of trails and drunks, I might even have a place for her as Sarah's understudy," Morse added.

Pope noted the sign of approval on his wife's face. "She has to watch those tells," he thought to himself. "They can be very dangerous if shown at the wrong time."

"I got approval for a night deputy. I am going to move an experienced deputy in, since the night person would have to handle everything alone. Which leaves me the slot to hire another road deputy," Pope said to the two people across from him.

After lunch, Pope went over to a retail establishment and spoke with the county commission chairman. He pressed how much positive image it might bring on the county, though there would be many naysayers.

The chairman was generally favorable and said they should walk over and speak with two other commission members. Those three were the great influencers. They could be voted down.

"It hasn't happened yet," he noted to Pope.

The two were convinced it was an idea worth trying.

"Martha Lane may be the first female deputy," they said. The other two commissioners agreed. A brief meeting was called for six o'clock, a quorum was present.

The sheriff was authorized to hire a female deputy after a positive interview by him, his chief deputy and the chairman of the commission. The chairman was only participating in this interview because of the political significance of it.

After the turn of the century, two women named Adams and Kopp would be given the deputy sheriff title on opposite coasts. The distinction as to who was first still appears undecided. In 1884, Martha Lane would be the first by a long margin.

Sarah had to return to the San Francisco office for a day with Morse to pick up clues and interview parties on a new case.

Pope asked Sarah to call Martha Lane from the new telephone in Morse's office. He knew the Lane's now had phone service at their residence.

Sarah would outline the interview procedures on Pope's behalf. Sarah would set the time and date for the meeting in San Rafael.

Sarah rode to the ferry with Harry Morse in his rented buggy. Pope picked her up in his grandfather's buckboard the next afternoon.

"How did your meeting go on the new case?" he asked his wife.

"It's a good one. It appears there is an inside criminal in the San Francisco and North Pacific Railroad. He has obtained thousands already by offering continuing business to providers of construction material, employee housing, and others for a percentage of profits. There have apparently been threats of beatings and worse. The victims are too terrified to talk.

It's a variation on the protection racket the hoodlums used against the Chinese in San Francisco a decade or so ago, Harry says. They were originally called 'Noodlums,' with their leader, Muldoon's, name spelled backwards. Somehow the newspapers used 'Hoodlums' instead," Sarah said. "It eventually became 'hoods.'"

"I'm familiar with Muldoon's gangs. They were put out of business by vigilante citizens with axe handles. Where is it occurring?" Pope asked.

"Around Tiburon, where the railroad construction is wrapping up. There are still lots of railroad people there and they will be for a while."

"Did you speak with Martha Lane on the telephone?" he asked.

"I did. John, we could have surely used telephone service during the kidnapping, couldn't we?"

"Absolutely. I think we will have it here in the next year or two. I want the sheriff's office to have one of the first in the county.

"John, she was so excited! I set up a meeting with you, Bill and the county chairman for eleven in the morning day after tomorrow. Friday. Think the chairman can attend?"

"I'll double check. Usually, he can leave his store at any time. His wife runs it for all practical purposes while he politics."

"Want me to sit in?" she asked.

"Not in the meeting. I do want you available immediately after to answer her questions about training, clothes, weapons and the like. Bill and I will cover the law training. I'd appreciate if you would do the hands-on weapons, physical arrest procedures like cuffing, and the fighting. Maybe I'll get her a room at the bed and breakfast where they stayed during our wedding. She had her first deputy-like duty there when she took my Webley Bulldog and guarded Kane's wife."

"I will take her back to the Morse office and talk with her. We should take her to dinner afterwards."

"I agree," he said.

"Oh, and John? I told her she could bring her father if she wished. I emphasized she could not bring anybody else. We don't want Mattie or her crazy mother stealing Martha's big moment."

"Good idea! Thanks for thinking of it," he said.

The next day passed without significant events.

Martha Lane arrived alone on the morning ferry and took a one-horse cab to the sheriff's office in San Rafael. She arrived fifteen minutes early.

Her outfit would suffice for both professionalism and any riding she might have to do to prove herself.

Unknown to anyone else, Sarah had coached her to wear a riding skirt. It was essentially pants cut to look like a skirt and allowed a woman to ride a horse astride instead of side saddle. Sarah was sure she would get the deputy job and would further advise her as to wardrobe and weapons.

She looked like she might be interviewing for a job as school marm. Sarah knew she could be a teacher and so much more. She met Martha outside the office and swept her around the corner for a quick pep talk.

"I've never seen John in an administrative roll such as a job interview. I suspect he will be professional and maybe a little scary. He's taking a big risk, you know. It's not about you not being qualified to be a success. It's about you being maybe the first female peace officer outside of Pinkerton's, Wells Fargo, or Morse. And, we are not really full-time policemen. You would be her! The one!

It will be tough, Martha. There will be narrow-minded men and women who will think it horrible for a woman to be a peace officer. To do what has always been a man's job. I have faced it. So has every woman detective at Pinkerton's. We proved every damn naysayer wrong! You will, too. I have every confidence you will be tough yourself and will succeed beyond everyone's fondest wishes for you.

Now, go in there and impress them down to their boots!" Sarah hugged her and gently guided her to the door.

"You won't be in the interview?" Martha asked.

"No. Assuming you dazzle them, I will be very involved in getting you ready to hit the trail, and maybe hit a miscreant or two with your gloved fist or revolver!"

Martha grinned at the woman she had grown to so admire during her sister's kidnapping. Pope, with help from Sarah and his grandfather had solved the case and returned her sister. He had also almost died as a result, sustaining serious bullet wounds. As Sarah cleaned up the loose ends of the case, Martha and her sister, Mattie, had sat by Pope through several nights at the hospital. Both had developed a crush on the handsome gunfighter. Mattie's had grown into a lot more. Something her sister knew would be a love with no resolution.

She strode in, confidently, and the chief deputy arose to greet her.

"Miss Lane? I am Chief Deputy Bill Isakson. I will be one of the three people interviewing you today. Let me see if the Sheriff and the County Commission Chairman are ready to see you."

He walked into Pope's small office and announced their interviewee was there.

They were ready and the chief led her into the interview.

Both men stood. Pope smiled and extended his hand to her and shook.

"Please be seated, Martha. Gentlemen, this is Martha Lane, who I have known for over a year from a case where her sister was kidnapped in San Francisco.

Please say hello to County Commission Chairman Oscar Harriman. I believe you met Chief Deputy Bill Isakson on the way in," Pope said.

"Mrs. Lane, I don't usually get involved with hiring deputies. Our sheriff and chief deputy are more than able to hire on their own.

Your case requires a bit more care because it will have a significant political impact. Both positive and negative. You will perhaps be the first female deputy sheriff in these United States if hired. Some folks will applaud us here in Marin County for being forward thinking and hiring the best possible person without regard to their gender. Others, will think we are crazy, putting a young woman like yourself in harm's way. Ya just cain't keep everybody happy," Harriman said.

"What do you think about our position?" he asked.

"I am honored to be considered. I got to know the sheriff and Detective Watson—now Pope—when he saved my sister. He almost died doing it. During the time she was held captive, Miss Sarah and I spoke a lot. She, too, is an exception to the general rule. It does not give her any particular pride, nor does it seem to worry her. It's the job she wanted and she went for it. It's the same with me, gentlemen. I always dreamed of being a peace officer. When I met Miss Sarah and saw a woman could live her dream, I knew I could, too," Martha said.

"Miss Lane, what do you think of night rides on lonely trails and having to bring in very bad men alone?" the chief asked.

"I am not afraid of it. Not at all. I know Miss Sarah, the sheriff and you will give me the necessary training. I grew up riding astride, not side saddle. I can shoot pretty darn well and would not hesitate if the need came up."

"I will attest for Miss Lane's shooting. She was taught by the person who taught the female detectives at Pinkerton's how to shoot. I watched. She's a good shot with a variety of revolvers. She'll need some experience with a shotgun and a rifle. I don't see any problem there. We'll teach her," Pope said.

"Miss Lane, how will you deal with the folks who think you have no business wearing a badge?" Harriman asked.

"I will make every effort to prove them wrong. And, if they still don't agree with it, I will give it no further mind. It's their problem, not mine."

"Martha, do you have any questions of us?" Pope asked.

"Just housekeeping details: pay, where I'd be stationed, what equipment would be furnished?" she asked.

Pope told her the starting deputy's pay. It was not impressive to the daughter of a very wealthy man. She did not bat an eye. She quite frankly did not care about the money. Only the job.

"You will be required to furnish a horse. The county will provide boarding and feed and care unless you buy your own ranch along the way," he smiled.

"You will provide your own firearms. We will make suggestions depending on what you seem to shoot the most comfortably after your training. We will provide nippers or handcuffs and ammunition. You'll be required to maintain a high level of weapons proficiency. Trail gear such as ponchos, camping gear in case you get caught out or are trailing someone will be up to you. Don't worry, we will make experienced recommendations. I am slowly making sure each deputy has a Dietz Police Lantern and oil as well as an investigative kit. We will provide those. Virtually nobody else has such a level of equipment. Anywhere in the world, I daresay, outside of Wells Fargo" Pope said.

"Any other questions, Martha?" Pope asked.

"No, sir. I am ready! I want to ride for Marin County, Sheriff!"

Pope turned to Harriman.

"Chairman, would you like for us to meet in private to discuss whether we hire Martha Lane as deputy?"

"I'm ready to cast my vote here and now," he responded.

"Bill?"

"Me, too, John."

"Gentlemen what are your votes?"

"Hire."

"Hire."

Then, I guess it's unanimous. Martha, would you like to be sworn in right now?" Pope asked.

"I would. Could Sarah pin my badge on?" she asked.

"I believe it could be arranged." Pope stood and walked out the door. He found his wife waiting just outside the sheriff's office.

"You are needed to pin a badge on, Detective." She smiled and followed him into his office.

"Martha, please stand and place you hand on the Bible Sarah is now holding. Do you, Martha Lane swear to uphold the Constitution of the United States, the laws of the State of California, and the ordinances of Marin County, so help you God?" he asked.

"I do."

"I now declare you to be a Deputy Sheriff of Marin County, California. Congratulations!" Pope handed Sarah a badge which she pinned on Martha's jacket.

She hugged Sarah, who was brushing away a sisterly tear. Martha then shook hands with the men.

"Well, since I know she can shoot, I guess we better arm her before she walks out the door with a badge showing!" Pope said as he handed her a double action Smith and Wesson breakopen .38 butt first. She immediately impressed the two other men by breaking it open and making sure it was unloaded. Pope handed her a box of fifty .38 S&W caliber cartridges. She loaded it and put the gun in one jacket pocket and the cartridge box in the other.

Pope saw a confused look on Harriman's face. He quickly figured out what it likely was and told him privately the S&W and ammunition had been confiscated from an outlaw. The look changed to a thoughtful and approving smile.

"I will recommend after her training she buy something more potent. Probably a Webley Bulldog," Pope told him.

"They have such a short barrel. Can you actually hit anything with them?" Harriman asked.

"Yes, Oscar. They are amazingly accurate. Which is why I carry one as my backup," Pope said, turning and lifting the left side of his suit jacket up to reveal the butt of the stubby British revolver in an inside the waist holster.

"Maybe I should get one for the shop instead of my Schofield," Harriman mused.

"You could do a lot worse, Oscar. Both are good guns, though." The man nodded and walked back to his shop.

"When does my training commence?" Martha asked Pope and Sarah.

"It's up to Sarah. Honey, if you are busy now, I can ask Bill to start reviewing California laws with her."

"That might be good, John. I still have an investigation plan to prepare for the railroad case. Martha, plan on having dinner with John and me. Probably Israel and your Millie, too," Sarah said.

"Martha, come on back into the office with me. Let's you, Bill and me put our heads together for a few minutes and do some planning," Pope said.

The three sat in Pope's office and he began.

"I have the clearance to hire a night deputy. Which

will give us the patrol deputy slot Martha will fill. We need to figure out how we are going to do this.

Deputy George Dunstan patrols north of town. He has a small ranch I pass on the way in each day from our cabin. The ranch is suffering from his absence. I'm wondering about having him swing into town as part of his patrol for a couple weeks until we can get Martha trained to handle his beat. If he became the night deputy, he would have some daylight to tend his ranch a bit. Bill, what do you think?"

"It sounds like a good solution. I'm pretty sure he'd jump at it. Want me to sell him on the idea?" the chief deputy asked.

"Please do. Let me know if he has any hesitation, alright?"

"I might ride out and find him. Shouldn't be hard. We could ride and talk like a couple old cowboys should."

"How about wait towards the end of his patrol and spend an hour or so reviewing the most important parts of the California Criminal Code with Martha now? Like you did with me a year ago," Pope suggested.

"All righty. Deputy Lane, why don't you get comfortable at my desk and we'll talk some law?"

They did and Pope walked over to the Morse office and advised Sarah what was in the works. He then mounted Caesar and rode to Israel's cabin.

"Hiya, Grandpa! Millie, how would you like to have dinner with new Deputy Martha Lane?"

"I'd be thrilled! Just let me cook right here. I bet she hasn't had a decent meal since I left!"

"You can bet on it. You are the best cook there ever was," Israel responded.

"No question about it. I guess they hired another person to replace you?" Pope asked.

"They did. I actually interviewed her. She is more of a cleaner and less of a cook. I told her to practice the cooking so the mother wouldn't accidentally poison the whole family."

Pope grinned. Millie and the two girls had more of a mother and daughter relationship than a hired help one.

"I have some venison steaks from the buck Israel killed, some fresh squash I can simmer with bacon and a pan of spoon bread almost ready to bake," Millie said referring to the soft corn casserole so popular in her native South.

"I was going to invite everyone out to a restaurant," Pope said.

"Let's get this new deputy started out on a properly filled stomach," Millie said with some finality.

"Yes, Ma'am. Grandpa, do you mind if I saddle your spare cow pony for her until she buys a horse? Your advice in selection of a horse would be real good, too."

"Of course, Sonny. I'll help."

They saddled a small, tough horse named Chico. He was broken to roping and to shots fired from his back. Israel included a canteen with fresh water and a lariat. Ultimately, she would need saddlebags, a rifle scabbard and a tarp or poncho. For now, she was sufficiently equipped.

Pope took the reins and rode Caesar back with Chico behind. He tied both up at the hitching post at the sheriff's office.

"How goes it?" he asked the two reviewing law.

"Real well, John. She's picking it up fast."

"Martha, do you have a valise or carpet bag with you?" Pope asked.

"I do, John or err, Sheriff."

"I've been John as long as you've know me and nursed me in a hospital. Nothing's changed. We don't stand on a lot of formality here. The deputies generally only refer to me as Sheriff and Bill as Chief in the presence of prisoners or other occasions when a little more decorum is called for. By the same token, I'll call you Deputy Lane when required and Martha amongst us," he said.

Pope went into his office for a couple minutes and made a list of things for her to buy, including a small tarp, raingear, a lariat, saddlebags, a rifle scabbard, and a notebook and pencil. He would assemble the remainder of the investigative kit for her, plus handcuffs. For camping, she would need a knife, trowel, hatchet, coffee pot and small grill, small cast iron skillet, mug and utensils.

Walking back out to where Martha and Bill were still going over laws, he interrupted.

"A couple of thinking points, Martha. You will be going up against some career criminals. Men, who are used to bluffs and used to hurting people. They are going to see you as weaker and a potential victim. So, you have to be tougher. You have to develop a stern look to give them. A look of resolve. One saying 'you mess with me and you're gonna die!'"

"I see what you are saying. I also bet you'd say the same thing to a young-looking new male deputy. I will work on it, John!"

"You are dead on, Martha. I have said the same to a similar aged deputy and I am sure Bill has, too.

There's a loaner horse for you tied to the rail out front. His name is Chico. He is a cow pony, brown and white. He has been broken to gunfire. If you need some help choosing a permanent mount, Grandpa or I will help you. Just ask.

Here is a list of things you will need. I suspect Sarah will add to it."

Pope went to the safe and took out several confiscated firearms. He particularly chose the ones upon which he and Hume had done forensic testing in the Wells Fargo office robbery and murder case.

He had hung their owner, so he would not be

needing them.

The .38-40 caliber may be a good choice in a Colt for Martha in case the heavy trigger pull on the Webley was too hard. The .38-40 Colt had a 4 ¾ inch barrel. It was the shortest barrel generally available with an ejection rod beneath. The Winchester carbine matched the caliber and also had a short 16 inch barrel. The caliber had power disproportionate to its milder recoil compared with a .44 or .45.

Pope put the oiled, unloaded handguns and matching ammunition in a flour sack to transport them back to the cabin. He would just stick the short carbine he already loaded into the empty scabbard on Chico's saddle.

Martha and the chief deputy finished the day reviewing the California Criminal Code.

Millie had suggested as Pope was leaving earlier in the day for Martha to stay in his old room at their larger cabin. He was to tell her to bring a weekend bag.

After conferring with his newest deputy, he suggested she ride down to the bed and breakfast and change her reservations to commence on Monday.

He and Sarah met her there and they rode to the Pope cabins together.

The reunion between Millie and Sarah prompted smiles on everyone's faces. Martha took her belongings in and left them in the second bedroom.

Pope and Sarah went to their cabin and dressed

down. Though neither wore a gunbelt at home, both always went armed at all times. Both carried breako-pen .38's hidden in a pocket, either sewn into Sarah's skirts for the purpose or similarly sewn into Pope's trousers. Pope always thought it was dumb men's trousers did not have pockets or a way to use a belt instead of suspenders.

"Martha, your dream of being a policeman, or maybe I should coin a name—police woman—has come true! Are you excited?" Millie asked.

"I am, Millie! And, with the two greatest peace officers I could ever imagine."

"John, I gave Martha and her sister a smattering of tracking on their visit almost a year ago. Would you like me to work with her on more serious mantrack-ing?" Israel offered.

"I would, Grandpa. Maybe let Sarah do some more marksmanship training in the morning with an assortment of guns I brought along. Then, the two of you head out after lunch. Would the afternoon work for you?"

"Yep. Would be fine," the former mountain man, wagon train guide and bounty hunter responded.

An hour after dinner, Israel retired to their bed-room and Pope and Sarah to their cabin. It appeared Millie and her former charge were going to spend most of the night catching up.

******

The next morning, Pope had a series of cans set at varying distance on logs a hundred yards away from the cabins.

After breakfast, Sarah and Martha went out. Sarah reviewed safety and handling and they began trying a variety of revolvers. Martha liked the breakopen .38, the Webley and the short .38-40 Colt.

As Pope feared, the Webley double action trigger was hard for her to pull. Cocked in single action it was fine. Sarah suggested the small .38 would be a good backup. It was not powerful enough to be a stopper with the round lead bullets of the day.

They focused on the Colt single action in .38-40 and the matching carbine for the remainder of the practice. Martha became very proficient with both by the time the session ended. She was taught to clean each gun thoroughly.

Pope intentionally stayed away. The family joined for lunch. After, Martha and Israel rode off for some tracking instruction.

"Before we get to reading sign, or looking for signs somebody or something has been by, we should discuss something basic," Israel said.

"Always be aware of your surroundings. Look behind yourself frequently and to both sides. Not just in front towards where you are going. An attacker, man or beast, can be in a tree or on a cliff above you. Listen carefully and try to identify sounds. Especially sounds which are out of place.

Similarly, retrain your nose to sniff like an Indian, not a so-called civilized city dweller. Practice it. Eventually, you will be able to smell horses. Then, closer, man. You will be able to tell the difference between a campfire for heat and one somebody's cooking on.

Listen to your own self. If you feel hairs rising on the back of your neck, there's trouble. You can bet the ranch on it. It somebody or some situation does not seem right, listen to your heart or mind. It probably is not right.

These things can help you avoid trouble or at least be ready for it.

If you sense trouble, draw your gun. Don't try to outdraw somebody if you don't have to. You are not John Pope. I am not sure anybody can draw as fast and deadly as he can. So, try to be ahead of the card game. Be ready, alright?" Israel said.

"It all makes sense. I will really have to work on the smelling part, though."

"It will be the hardest. The tracking and signs I am going to teach you now are the easy part. They are just common sense and power of observation."

He showed her different animal tracks and then horse and oxen tracks. Israel taught her the spacing showed whether the animal was walking or running. The amount of dirt or leaves blown into the track help to tell age. The freshness of droppings left by animals gave information about how long ago they had passed by.

"Remember too, to listen to your horse. He can hear and smell better than you. If he's getting twitchy, take note. Figure out why. Is it a she bear and cubs? I can tell you from personal experience you don't want to fight a bear. I have twice and the both times almost killed me," Israel told her.

"Look for things which make a track distinct. A notch in a horseshoe. How deep is the impression? If it's a man and the track is deeper than others, he might be heavier. If one of his tracks is deeper than the other, he's likely limping. If they are farther apart and the heel is lighter, he's probably running. Look for blood trails. If it's red, it's real fresh."

Israel's training was so complete Martha wished she could take notes. She consigned as much as possible to memory.

Sarah continued Martha's training all weekend, using the syllabus from her classes at Pinkerton's. Most of the rest, she and Pope knew, would happen on the street and the trail.

On Monday, Pope met with his chief deputy.

"John, I spoke with Deputy George Dunstan. He is real pleased with switching over to full-time night deputy. Like you guessed, it will allow him to pay some attention to his ranch.

He asked if it could start next week. He's a deacon in the Baptist church and he has an important meeting at night on Wednesday," Isakson said.

"That's perfect, Bill. It will give Martha a little more time to season before we turn her loose on the world!

I told Martha to ride over to Schell's horse ranch with Grandpa and take a look at some horseflesh. He raised horses for a long time and has a good eye. She bought sufficient money with her to buy a horse, tackle and whatever else she needs," Pope said.

Further east, Israel and Martha arrived at Schell's. Israel, who had known the owner for years and transacted with him in the past, described the type mount he thought would be good for Martha.

"Israel, I have a smaller cowpony named Maggie. She's older, but with a good five or more years' service left in her. She was used to roping cattle and is not scared of gunfire off her back. She has an even gait and can go on just about forever. She is not race horse fast, I'm betting she would catch up with a race horse after he pulled over to the side of the trail to gasp for breath. You want to take look at her?"

He saddled Maggie and Martha hopped on. The three rode around the ranch. On the way back, Maggie reared up and Martha saw a rattler coiled nearby.

Martha drew the short-barreled Colt and fired instinctively. She hit the snake a few inches below the head, severing it completely.

"Tarnation, young lady! Where'd you learn to shoot?" Schell asked.

"Sarah Pope taught me."

"And, she taught a lot of lady Pinkerton's stuff too," Israel said proudly.

"I didn't even know you were packing, Ma'am!" Schell said.

"I don't have my belt holster yet, Mr. Schell. I hope to get it before I start patrolling," Martha said.

"Patrolling?" he asked.

She flashed the Marin County deputy badge pinned on the underside of her lapel.

"Will wonders never cease? I sure wouldn't want you hauling down on me with your hogleg, Miss."

"I'm sure there's no danger of me doing it, Mr. Schell," she said in the even, matter-of-fact way she had been perfecting.

She agreed to buy the horse, after Israel gave her his secret nod.

"Do you happen to have any tackle, Mr. Schell?" she asked.

"I got all sorts. Let's see what will work for you."

She chose a smaller Western saddle, some saddle-bags, and found a carbine length rifle scabbard.

She rode back on Maggie and her new saddle. Israel led Chico.

"I think you have yourself a fine little mare, Martha. Fits right in with you girls: Martha, Mattie, Millie, and Maggie!" Israel grinned.

"Want to go back by way of town and put your new gear in?" he asked.

"Yessir. I don't have a rifle though."

"Yes, you do," he said, drawing one from his own scabbard and sliding it into her newly acquired weathered, but serviceable one.

"This short trapper length carbine was confiscated with your revolver. Either Bill or John cleaned up both up real shiny for you, Martha.

Sarah said she was going to work at Wells Fargo in the morning and at Morse Detective Agency later on. Let's swing by there. She wanted to chat with you about her new case. I'll take Chico back. Though Millie would have you stay with us forever, and I'd like it too, we both reckon you want to move your stuff into the rooming house and start to establish a presence in San Rafael."

"Though I really hate to leave you all so soon, you are right. I need to get used to being on my own. I also want to look for a more permanent rooming house. Are there any?"

"There's a small hotel in town. They let rooms on a monthly basis. No services as far as I know, but it may work for you. Try the Bay Hotel. It's down the street from where you are now," Israel suggested. "It's also got a small restaurant for times you don't want to cook," he said.

She went by and found they had a room as well as a stable for guests in the rear. She paid a month's rent in advance for her and a small charge for Maggie. The hotel had a porter who would feed and water horses for two bits a day.

Her next trip was to the general merchandise. Israel had suggested some of her purchases at the shop. He also recommended, in addition to a Green River knife for camp, she get a knife as a weapon. Since a Bowie the size he and Pope carried would look like a cavalry sword on her, she found a smaller six inch Sheffield Bowie with an onyx handle and black case. It came with an ankle strap, which she affixed to her left ankle in private. Finally, she found a holster for the Colt and a small gunbelt. They also had an inside the waist holster for the backup .38 S&W. She moved the badge to the front of her lapel now she was gunned up.

Martha went to the Wells Fargo office and saw Sarah was busy. She waved to her and walked down to the sheriff's office.

"John and Bill, I have a horse and tackle and a room at the Bay Hotel on a monthly basis with a stall for Maggie, my horse."

"Looks like you went full deputy on us with the badge and gun showing!" the chief deputy grinned.

"I did. And, look at this!" she lifted the left side

of her jacket and showed them the S&W in its new holster. "I have a small Bowie in an ankle holster. I won't embarrass you by showing it to you," she said.

"A Bowie? Sounds like a certain old mountain man has been influencing you," Pope said.

"Do you think it's too much?" she asked.

"Not really. I carry one everywhere, as does Grandpa. It has saved me before and him countless times. If you were to bump into a Texas Ranger, you'd sure see a Bowie either in front of or just behind his Colt," Pope answered.

"Do I start today?"

"Technically, you are on the payroll as of now. Deputy George Dunstan has ridden the district just north of San Rafael. He's going to switch over to being the night deputy here in the county seat. He has a conflict at night he has to take care of Wednesday of the coming week at church. I'm having him ride you around his beat on the following Thursday. Then Friday, you ride it from then on and he'll start nights here," the chief deputy said.

"Which means you have a week and a half around here or maybe with Sarah, then you start enforcing the law in the county. How are you and Bill coming with the California Code?" Pope asked.

"I think pretty well. Bill, do you agree?" she responded.

"She's catching on fast, John."

"Good. Any time you can spend with Sarah will be time well spent. Check in with her like she said about her new case over in Tiburon."

"I tried to earlier. She was tied up at Wells Fargo. I may walk back over and see if she's free in either office."

"Sounds, good, Martha. Check out with us before calling it a day," Pope said.

She walked to the Wells Fargo office and Sarah was not there. She was next door in her own office. Martha tapped and went in.

"How's your day so far?" Sarah greeted her.

"Busy! Got a horse and gear. Found a room to let. Killed a rattler with the Colt. Got this belt rig, hideaway holster, and small Bowie. I fear I may be a real deputy sheriff now. I have about a week and a half until I start riding my new beat north of San Rafael."

"Excellent. Sit down and let me tell you about my case. Maybe you can go with me to Tiburon during the week and a half and help me solve it. It would be handy having a county officer with me in case an arrest is necessary.

The new San Francisco and Northern Pacific Railway is being constructed. The part starting at the Tiburon ferry landing and beginning its northward trip to Ukiah is partially done. It will stop here, in Novato, Santa Rosa and Healdsburg," Sarah said, pointing to the Northern California wall map.

"The construction has already been good for the economy in Marin County. It has not only brought in lots of jobs, it has also brought new income to a large number of suppliers. These include restaurants for the workers, food in general, clothes, boarding houses, stables and feed, hardware and more. This would normally be all good.

However, there is a problem. Somebody knows what is needed and is going around to merchants of these services and running a protection type racket. 'You want to provide your products or services to the railroad, you have to pay me.' Nobody is talking. The railway company is too new to have seasoned railroad detectives, so they hired Harry Morse to get to the bottom of it and make it go away," Sarah said.

"Wouldn't it be an easy one to solve, Sarah? Just find out who is leaning on the suppliers and question him. If he works for the railway, fire him. Either way, arrest him."

"The problem is twofold, Martha. One, there is a lot of money to be made by these suppliers. It may be to their betterment to give up a percentage, say ten percent, and keep making the money. Two, apparently this person or persons are pretty tough thugs and have beaten some people. I have a list of suppliers from the railway company. There are checks beside the people they know have been roughed up.

I think the approach will be to talk with everybody. See if anybody will say anything. Especially the ones who have been beaten or threatened. It nobody talks, I will have to start conducting surveillance to see who regularly comes by and leaves every business without merchandise. While it won't work for service providers, it may hint about the identity of the strong arm thugs.

The other possibility is rattling the cage may make them come after me. Someone they think will be a soft target. Having you as my backup over the next week or so will be comforting, if you are game to do it?"

"Of course I am! Will we stay there? Will we be undercover, like Kate Warne was at Pinkerton's during the War?" Martha asked.

"The answer to both is yes. You will have to hide your badge and guns. They must be available at short notice though. This is the most dangerous kind of investigating. Our only backup would be each other.

I want to give some more thought about whether we should ride in together or separately and pretend to not know one another. Each has its benefits and negatives," Sarah said. She gave Martha a copy of her investigative plan, complete with key contact people and suspected victims of the strong arm tactics. Martha copied it over the next hour.

"I'm done copying," Martha told Sarah.

"I think I have come to a conclusion about how we should approach this, Martha.

You should pick up some store bought clothes here in town and a used carpet bag to carry them in. Your current wardrobe is expensive and looks it. See if Israel will give you a ride to the San Quentin Point docks in his buggy. From there, catch a stage to Tiburon. Pretend to be looking for a short term job while your brother is on a railway construction crew. Use the suspected victim list to seek jobs at initially. If offered one, take it. Get a room at any of the several rooming houses. All are on the victim list. Watch for signs of tough men or a tough man talking, arguing or threatening with the manager of both.

I will ride into town alone late in the afternoon of the day you go. I'll look for you.

Write the name of your rooming house on a slip of paper. I'll drop my hat near you. You pick it up and hand it to me. If not the hat, we will work out something to pass the location without anyone noticing. Palm the slip of paper and I will read it later. Then I will go to the same rooming house and seek a room. If you are the only woman there, they may even make us share a room, which would be perfect.

Sound like a plan?" Sarah asked.

"It does. I will ride out and ask Sheriff Pope now, to give him some notice."

******

Martha stopped at a shop and purchased a less expensive skirt, blouse, apron and coat. The only weapon she could carry on her person with the coat off was the small Bowie on her ankle. She would carry a purse with the smaller revolver in it and leave the larger Colt with Israel.

She rode out to the Pope cabin and Israel and Millie would both accompany her to Point San Quentin in the morning.

They took the buggy to the ferry dock and she caught a stage for the final ten miles of her trip to Tiburon.

Martha picked the cheapest looking boarding house and secured a room. Upon checking, she found she got the last room and was the only female guest. She thought it boded well for Sarah bunking with her.

She began calling on the targeted stores and companies. The railroad, or railway as they used in their corporate name, had caused demand for products and services to soar in Tiburon. She found a job clerking in the fifth business she visited and started immediately.

The business was towards the top of Sarah's potential victim list. It was a wholesale food company. The manager who hired her said the railroad was its largest current customer. He said he was not sure what they would do to fill the gap when the construction was finished.

Her job was to fill written orders and be a sometimes stand-in at the front counter. She felt it gave her a good opportunity to witness courier pickup of protection of railroad business money and the identity and demeanor of the person who made the pickups.

Sarah arrived by horse and went straight to the construction superintendent's office.

He was expecting her and spoke openly about what he thought was happening. His name was Clyde Beecher.

"Mr. Beecher," Sarah asked after he outlined the problem for her, "have you terminated anyone, perhaps with cause because of misdeeds?"

"Yes, several. I will write down their names for you as well as last known addresses. I know the first man on the list has left town and probably even California. The second two are still here in Tiburon. I have seen both recently."

"Are either tough enough to coerce suppliers to pay for the continued privilege of selling to you?"

"Yes. Both are. Both were crew foremen. Rough and tumble sorts. One is a big bare knuckle boxer sort of a fellow. The other, Hart, is wiry and fast as a snake. Both were fired for punching workers after repeated warnings."

"I see. What do you think of the possibility they might be in collusion threatening suppliers?"

"I guess it's possible, Detective Pope. I do not see them together around town. I am not sure it's confirmation they don't work together on this on the sly," he said.

"Would you give me as close a description on each as possible? I will write them down in my notes as you dictate them," she said.

"Starting with the first, his approximate age, height, weight, build, hair color and style, facial hair, weapon description if you know, and horse?"

After writing the responses, she asked the same for the second man, Mark Lewis.

"Thank you for all your help. I will be in town for a few days. I will pretty much be undercover, so please hold our conversation private. Also, if we meet on the street, don't acknowledge me more than you would any other stranger, please."

She began her familiarization walk around the probable victim companies. When she got to the food supplier, she saw Martha hard at work in an open back room. She spoke with the owner and saw Martha slip out the back door towards a probable privy.

The manager would not speak with her about the threats. He would not even acknowledge them. She saw he was scared. Sarah was not sure whether the fear was loss of business, a broken kneecap, or both. She did not press him. For now, anyway.

She went out the door and walked unseen between buildings. There were two privy's in back. Martha was standing in the doorway of one. She stepped out and said, "All yours, Ma'am!" to Sarah and palmed her a folded piece of paper as they passed.

Sarah stayed in the privy sufficiently long for Martha to get back to work. She walked out and towards her next destination. Reading the unfolded note, she changed direction and walked to the boarding house.

"Do you have any rooms?" she asked.

"All filled up with railroaders, Ma'am" the man said, noticing the wedding band on her left hand.

"I got one young lady what just took a room. You could bunk with her, if you've a mind," he offered.

"Is she a proper young lady? Clean and of good repute?" Sarah asked, playing her part.

"Seems to be. In town with her brother, who is working on the railroad. Won't be here too long, she says."

Recognizing Martha's cover, she took the room. She went up to check it. No lock on the door.

"Two women in a boarding house full of railroad construction men and no damn lock!" she thought.

She saw a carpentry business and walked in. She told the man what she had in mind and walked out later with a wooden wedge for the door.

Sarah put it in her purse and continued trying to interview victims. She did not have any success, other than an acknowledgement by one scared shopkeeper it was occurring and to leave before she got him killed.

The response gave her a particular business she

needed to watch covertly. Luckily, there was a café across the street with some front-facing windows. She went in and ordered coffee. By lunchtime, she added a sandwich to retain her seat by the window. Nothing happened by one o'clock, so she left and walked the block several times, looking in storefront windows for two reasons.

She was pretending to shop and the reflections told her what was happening over her shoulder. She could see threats no matter where she was. From the vicinity of the new target surveillance location, she could see traffic in the food wholesaler's door and out.

Nothing happened and she feared she had been already seen too much in this neighborhood. She moved on and finished her list with no success whatsoever.

It was getting late and she headed back towards the rooming house. Having had experience with fleabag rooming houses while undercover with Pope in New York state, she knew to stop off and buy sheets and pillow cases.

She arrived before Martha and changed the sheets. She spread her work papers on the top of the bed and began scrutinizing them. She heard light steps on the stairway. Martha? They stopped at the door and Sarah reached for her .44 Smith & Wesson. It was sitting on the dresser with a scarf laid over it.

"If you are in there, it's me" came a familiar voice.

"One second!" Sarah said as she bent over and removed her new wooden stopper she had cut earlier today to wedge the door shut.

She opened the door and Martha came in.

"How was your day, Deputy Lane?"

"Fine, Detective Pope. And, yours?" Martha responded, both speaking softly due to the thin walls of the rooming house.

"Martha, did you see anything of interest?"

"I don't think so. Everyone who came in, whether I was watching from the back or at the front counter seemed to be a regular customer. I did fill a number of orders for the railroad's various construction locations," Martha reported.

"I cleared the whole list of target companies. Not a soul would talk to me. Like we discussed, they were afraid of losing railroad business or of getting knee-capped or worse. I'm afraid we have to see one of these men in action, then follow him at a distance. I fear neither of us should make an approach alone. Anyone mean enough to scare this many people is a dangerous proposition," Sarah said.

"Is there a deputy sheriff in town?"

"Only you, Martha. John said he has a deputy patrol this district. He only comes through town once or twice on his patrol."

"What if you wired John and asked him to get him to spend more time here for while we are here?" Martha suggested.

"I wish I had thought of it! I will telegraph him first thing in the morning," Sarah said.

"The two men, Olausson and Lewis, are fairly distinctive. I am surprised we have not seen either in this small town yet," she continued.

"Well, neither has come into the food wholesaler. Like I said, many of the food orders I packed today were for San Francisco and Northern Pacific Railway. A few were for a mining company and one was for a ranch. Not having the Railway business looks like it would put my new temporary employer out of business," Martha said.

As roommates, the two decided it would be alright to be seen eating together. They went to a small, working class diner down the street and had dinner.

Midway through dinner, a man meeting Olausson's description came in with two other men. Neither looked like Lewis. They sat at a table across the restaurant from Sarah and Martha.

Sarah reached over and pressed her toe on Martha's shoe to get her attention. Martha looked up and immediately saw what the detective was cautioning her about.

She looked at Sarah questioningly.

"Let's finish and take a walk around the block on the way back to the room," Sarah said in a soft, comfortable voice.

"Sounds like a good idea. I'm almost finished."

They finished and Sarah slid some money over to Martha to pay. She knew the younger woman in plainer clothes would draw less attention than the detective who had questioned almost every target company today.

Martha Lane was a very pretty young woman and every man in the restaurant looked up when she walked to the counter to pay. Olausson and the men at his table did also. Sarah watched. Their response was wolfish appreciation and not suspicion, she decided.

Keeping her face turned away from the three men, Sarah arose and walked out the door, Martha behind her.

"Let's find a dark spot for you to watch and see what horses they ride. I will rush back to the rooming house and saddle Kate Warne. She can carry the two of us double for as long as I think will be needed. I cannot believe these men rode ten miles into town for a meal. They have to be in a room or house close to this area. I just hope they don't go into a saloon and drink for the rest of the night. See you as soon as I can. Memorize the horses and which way they went. If they split up, note Olausson's direction. Don't follow him alone!"

With those words, Sarah walked off at a fast rate. Martha took the light break-open S&W out of her purse and tucked it in her apron pocket for fast, temporary storage.

She was thrilled at the turn of events. Here she was standing alone, watching for and probably trailing a criminal. She had a badge and a gun. Her dreams had come true. She only wished she could share with her best friend, her sister Mattie.

Ten minutes later, Sarah was still not back. The men exited the restaurant and all three mounted horses tied at the hitching rail.

Olausson was on a handsome black of some size. The other two were on a chocolate brown cowpony and a tall, dark Morgan. Martha was getting to know guns. She came into her job knowing horses well.

The men rode out of town at a walk. Not in any great hurry to get to their destination. Sarah rode up as the suspects rode out of sight. Martha scrambled on behind her and told her what she had observed. She put her hands around Sarah's waist and they rode off at a trot.

A mile into the slow pursuit, Sarah slowed it down even more. She walked Kate Warne, fearful of riding up on the three men unexpectedly.

Several miles later, they saw a ramshackle house or cabin, they were not sure which, on the left side of the road. The three horses were tied up there.

Sarah stopped a hundred yards off and they dismounted. Leaving Kate Warne's reins hanging down, they moved from tree to tree as quietly as they could.

A city girl, Martha was afraid of stepping on a

snake. She thought shoes were going to be a thing of her past and boots would prevail. Now, she was back to ankle high lace up shoes in her current cover outfit. They made it to the edge of the house and listened at an open window.

"Alright, boys" Olausson began.

"This is what I wanted to clue you in on. Anybody who is not interested after I finish should leave before plans are made. No harm, no foul. But, keep your mouth shut or I'll come looking. And, I'll have a ten gauge with me.

A wagon is going to leave San Rafael bank at ten o'clock tomorrow morning. It will have a full month's payroll for all the rail workers, as well as expense money for supplies and all. I heard it could be five thousand dollars!

They decided not to use the train to San Quentin Point, or a Wells Fargo stage. I don't know why.

There should be a driver and a shotgun guard. You all got rifles. It should be easy pickings for an ambush at a curve in the road along the way here.

Anybody want out? Say it now or you are in for the whole deal," Olausson said.

There were no takers for leaving.

"Good! Now, let's put this stickup plan together.

There is a curve in the road about eight miles back towards San Rafael from here. It has a pair of tall pines on either side of the road. There's a lightning-struck tree beside one. Some trees are behind the pine and the burnt out tree. We'll hide in them and wait for the wagon to come by. Moving it this way is really just a dodge because they didn't want the money to go by stage or have a lot of guards. Then, it would look like something. This way, our five thousand dollars just looks like freight.

When it comes around the curve, we will open up with our rifles and kill the driver and the other men.

Be careful about the horses though, we will want to make off with the wagon and leave the bodies hidden in the trees. We will bring the wagon back here and split the money. After we do, we should all head in different directions, one by one. They will have no idea who did it or who to look for. It will be a perfect crime. I want us to be there by one o'clock, in position and ready. The wagon should be along an hour later," Olausson ended.

"So, you got it. The whole thing. Everybody like it? Good. Now, let's celebrate with some Tennessee whiskey." He took out a new bottle, broke the seal and passed it around.

******

"Time for us to go!" Sarah said in low voice. She had taught Martha speaking in a low, soft voice was harder to hear from a distance than a whisper.

The two moved back to where Sarah's horse, Kate Warne, was waiting. They mounted up and Sarah walked the horse down the grass beside the road. When they were far enough away the drinkers in the cabin could not hear hoofs, she urged the horse on.

"Since there is no way to get a telegram to John tonight, I am going to have to ride over from here and tell him what's going on. He is short staffed, so I imagine he will want you here for the arrest of this gang tomorrow. If I take you within a mile of the hotel, can you walk the rest? There is a connector road I take from there back to San Rafael and on to the cabin to get John."

"Of course, I will make short shrift of the mile, Sarah. I can walk the several miles back from here if it's easier for you?" Martha said.

"No. It's too far and your shoes would be painful walking for miles. I'd rather you be in tip-top shape for taking down the gang tomorrow. Go back, get some rest and make sure all your weapons are ready. In the morning, rent a horse from the livery and be ready to meet John and whatever posse he can put together. I'll have him send you a telegram as to when and where. Be at the telegraph office by nine in the morning."

They reached the intersection Sarah had to take. She hugged her young friend and set off at a trot. Martha kept on the road to Tiburon and reached the boarding house forty-five minutes later. She put the wedge between the bottom of the door and the floor. She put the Colt on the bed beside her hand. She stripped and got in. Detective trainee Martha Lane was asleep within minutes.

******

Sarah arrived at the cabin at three in the morning and called out in advance of approaching either her cabin or Israel's.

Both men were at the door, armed, before she could dismount. She told them exactly what she and Martha had heard.

Pope was aware of the cash shipment and how it was being handled. He thought it was cloaked in secrecy. Apparently not.

Sarah went to bed for much-needed rest. Pope and his grandfather agreed to head to the sheriff's office at first light. He wanted two deputies in addition to Martha, who was as yet untried with gunfire popping around her. Maybe two or three experienced, well-armed possemen.

He would have seven or eight men to take on three. He would also have the advantage of surprise.

The tough part was having the wagon driver and guard know they were riding into a rifle ambush. If the outlaws did not commence the robbery, Pope would have no cause to arrest three men waiting in trees. He had several hours to think it through.

He came up with a crazy idea. One which could possibly even work. He dispensed with the idea of possemen. Pope and Israel were in the office early.

He caught the deputy who was transitioning into being the night deputy for the county seat, George Dunstan, as well as Walter Wood. He was beginning to depend a lot on the young Wood. With Israel deputized and Martha, he had five. He would leave the office unattended and include the chief deputy for six.

Six officers against three robbers of unknown proficiency. It should work, he told all except Martha, who was still in Tiburon awaiting her telegram from him.

They concurred it was innovative. Not perfect, probably worth trying. Pope sent the telegram for her to meet Israel in Tiburon by eleven in the morning.

The other part of the plan was to have the railway company delay the actual delivery. They would provide the wagon and team to the sheriff for the planned action.

Israel bought Martha's horse Maggie and her Winchester over with him. Sarah would follow and go into Tiburon and continue her original investigation until Olausson's gang was neutralized. Martha would slip back into town after the lawmen had the robbers under control and continue her undercover work.

Everything was set. By noon, Israel and Martha were set up in woods on the same side as the robbers planned, though further back towards Tiburon. They saw three riders arrive around one fifteen and dismount. They hid in the woods as planned and smoked cigarettes.

"Israel, I can smell the cigarette smoke just like you taught me!" Martha said softly to the senior Pope. He gave her a look of great approval and said nothing as he sat with his Sharps Big Fifty buffalo gun at the ready. Martha had her carbine, though she was not comfortable about her accuracy with it. She had mentioned it to Israel who suggested she not shoot unless she was absolutely sure of her target. He would do the surprise shooting himself. They would be shooting in the general direction of the wagon and an errant shot could kill a lawman. It was a risky proposition.

Around two o'clock, the two waiting in ambush and the three robbers also waiting in ambush heard "Giddyap! C'mon, horses. We ain't got all day!"

Pope recognized the voice as his grandson.

From a distance, he could see the Pope was impersonating the driver of the wagon and had a shotgun messenger. The messenger, his gun propped up between them, was sitting bolt upright on the seat.

The driver stopped the wagon just shy of the curve where the attack was supposed to occur.

"Damn, Bob! The right rear wheel froze up. You

sit here while I check it," Pope said loudly, as if the shotgun messenger was hard of hearing.

Pope hopped down and walked around to the far rear of the wagon, out of sight of the robbers.

"It's froze tight!" he yelled.

"We don't have a jack, or a hammer, or grease to remove the wheel and fix it. We're stuck here until somebody comes along!" Pope said loudly as the driver. The shotgun messenger remained motionless on the seat.

Israel and Martha watched and could feel and almost see the hesitation on the faces of the three robbers. Olausson made a decision he would live to regret. He urged the riders out to the road and the three galloped the short distance towards the stalled wagon, firing and yelling.

The shotgun messenger was knocked over by the barrage of shots.

A much louder "boom" sounded and one of the robbers toppled off his horse as Israel's .50 caliber bullet slammed into him. Martha watched in awe as the scene unfolded in front of her. She raised her carbine. Israel gently pushed it down. "It's my boy's play now, Missy," he said softly.

Olausson and the remaining rider almost reached the wagon when Pope walked around from behind with the chief deputy's long barrel ten gauge shotgun pointed at them.

Deputies Wood and Dunstan popped up from the bed of the wagon where they had lain hidden. Both had rifles at the ready.

"Olausson, this is Sheriff Pope! Drop your guns and throw up your hands!"

The rider beside Olausson raised his rifle. Two rifle bullets and a blast of buckshot at short range toppled him from his saddle, never to rise again.

Olausson dropped his rifle and raised his hands with alacrity.

Pope and the two deputies, now down from the wagon, held him at gunpoint.

Israel and Martha approached him from behind. Martha looked down at the effect of the massive .50 caliber and a close range shotgun blast had on the dead men as she walked past. She shuddered and walked on.

Pope held the ten gauge, its unfired barrel cocked and unwavering with one hand. He held the butt stock tightly gripped between his body and right arm.

He tossed a pair of iron handcuffs past the robber and they landed on the ground five feet beyond him.

"Deputy Lane, handcuff this man from behind, then remove his revolver from the holster. Check him for a knife or other weapons," the sheriff ordered.

She cuffed and disarmed him and gave him a thorough pat down. She removed a dagger from his boot and a derringer pistol from a vest pocket and added them to the pile with his rifle and revolver.

Pope smiled at her and turned to the two other deputies.

"Let's get the bodies disarmed and into the back of the wagon."

Chief Deputy Bill Isakson rode up, leading Caesar and the two deputies' horses. He had witnessed it all.

"John, it looks like the store dummy shotgun messenger wasn't a bad idea after all. I'm afraid we'll have to pay the clothing store for him though. He's sure shot to hell," Isakson said.

He placed the collected guns in a burlap sack and tied them on his saddle. The wagon bed would be occupied by a prisoner and two grisly bodies.

Deputy Dunstan turned the wagon around and drove it back to San Rafael. Pope looked at Martha with a nod of approval and spun Caesar around to join Israel, Bill and his two other deputies.

Martha mounted her horse, hid her revolver and pinned her badge out of sight. She rode back to Tiburon and put Maggie in the livery. Back undercover, she reported the event to Sarah.

"Do you feel comfortable continuing to stay undercover here alone? I need to go back in the jail at San Rafael. It's important to question Olausson about the protection of business scheme, though I am beginning to doubt he's in on it."

"Sure, Sarah. I told the food wholesaler I had to take off for emergency personal business. So, he fired me.

Jerk!" I will walk around and seek new employment and keep my eyes wide open," the young deputy said.

Sarah shook her head in sympathy, touched Martha on the shoulder and mounted Kate Warne for the ride back to San Rafael.

She got back around supper time. Pope was still interrogating Olausson. He came out to greet his wife.

"Anything on the railroad protection racket case come up yet?" she asked.

"No, not a thing. However, I have not broached the subject. I was waiting for you, since I don't know every particular. I'd rather see someone questioned from a position of knowledge. It keeps them wondering how much we know."

"I agree. Your charade using a dummy shotgun messenger must have gone down successfully," she prompted.

"Yes and no. They bought it lock, stock, and barrel. No, because Grandpa had to kill one with his damn Big 50 Sharps and I with Bill's ten gauge up close and personal. We made a mess of both of them.

If you need the names for your investigation, one is Marcus Jones and the other is Red Hammond. I don't have much more on them than those partial names. Olausson did not know them very well, so he was not much help," Pope said.

"May I talk to him now? I telegraphed Harry and he's curious to know if Olausson figures in our case."

"Sure. Let's walk in."

They opened the door and walked in, Pope first.

"Olausson, this is Detective Pope. She is investigating a case for the railroad. The very one which fired you about a week ago. She has some questions for you."

"She's got the same name as you," Olausson said.

"She does. So your continued good health depends on how you cooperate with her. You saw what I did to your fellow outlaw…I have no qualms about tuning your butt up good and proper," in a voice which should have left no room for misinterpretation.

Leaving and closing the door, he took up a position close enough to listen. Or, to rush in and beat the living hell out of Olausson if necessary.

Sarah started off speaking evenly and not in an accusatory or threatening mode. It did not work with Olausson. He was tough and used to pushing people around. He had already figured out the sheriff would be a tough fighter, so his responses had been noncommittal but not argumentative.

Olausson looked at her as if he was undressing her. She ignored his gaze.

"What do you know about the protection racket going one in Tiburon? The one where some thugs are making railway suppliers pay for continued railway business. I have information you are one of those thugs, Mr. Olausson."

He leaned forward and put one hand on her knee.

She could smell his breath as she swung the lead-filled leather sap or blackjack against his wrist. Her second blow was to his jaw. Sarah heard the crack as it fractured and he went down, eyes rolled back in his head.

The door flew open and Pope appeared, both fists balled. He looked down at the unconscious man on the floor.

"Helluva right hook, darling."

She held up the sap. She dangled it from a graceful finger.

"This helped."

He smiled at her.

"Do we need a doc?"

"Afraid so. I think I heard his jaw break when I connected. He was in la-la land before he left his chair.

"Bill? Would you summon the doctor? Mr. Olausson affronted Sarah and she rebuked him rather violently."

The chief deputy walked in and looked at the suspect in the floor drooling on himself.

"I swear I did not hear the shot!" he said grinning.

"No shot, Bill. I hit him. Pretty hard, I guess," Sarah said.

"Bet your hand hurts," he said.

"Not at all," she responded demurely, adding nothing else.

He left for the doctor. Olausson was still unconscious when the doctor arrived. He had managed a groan or two.

Olausson finally regained consciousness. The doctor surmised "He may have a slightly fractured jaw. I don't think it's worth further treatment. The wrist is broken and requires a plaster of Paris cast.

Let's take him over to the office so I can put it on and let it dry and immobilized his wrist. I will give him something to help with the pain and something else to help him sleep. Then, I'd recommend putting him into a bunk in the lockup here in the office where he can be watched more than at the jail," the doctor said.

"We'll do it, doc. Thanks." Bill said and escorted the doctor out of the door.

The chief deputy and Pope walked the still groggy Olausson to the doctor's office. They handcuffed him to a bed in the doctor's to get the cast on and dried.

"Want to tell me exactly what happened, Sarah?" Pope asked when he got back.

"As husband or sheriff?" she responded.

"Sheriff. Your husband does not worry about how you take care of yourself, as long as you do."

"I was beginning to question him. He was giving me lascivious looks. Then, he put his hand on my knee. I considered it to be sexual assault and slapped him twice with my sap. The one my husband gave me, I believe."

"So, you felt threatened and had to react instead of

calling for help?"

"In a nutshell, yes."

"In a nutshell, you knew the sheriff was sitting immediately outside the door?"

"I suspected he was but did not know if for sure. I did not want to risk being rescued mid-rape."

"I will advise the prosecutor Olausson assaulted you during questioning while I was outside the door and your reacted appropriately."

"Thank you."

"You don't have to thank me for the truth, Sarah."

"Alright. I'd still like to finish questioning him," she said.

"Why not let Bill or me finish when he comes out of whatever drug doc gave him to knock him out? I am not sure he will speak to you any more at this point. We'll do it tomorrow."

"Go ahead and give it a try and let me know what you find out."

"Of course," he responded.

Already into a sheriff's second shift, they rode home to a late dinner and early turn-in.

CHAPTER 3

Martha had ridden back to Tiburon after the capture of the lead robbery suspect and the shooting of his two accomplices. She had been struck how violent and messy law enforcement could be. She knew people were wounded and killed. She had just never seen it up close and personal. She determined to not let the blood and gore deter her from pursuing the dream she considered she was now living.

She retried speaking with people Sarah already questioned once she returned. She stopped for the day about dusk. She had made it halfway through the list.

Sarah had told her to not let the food wholesaler know her real identity yet, though the young deputy wanted to go by and flash her star and give him a piece of her mind. Disappointed, she continued to maintain her cover identity in Tiburon.

She ate on the way to the rooming house. It was

dark once she returned. It sounded like every room load of construction workers had gotten a bottle of rot gut and decided to yell, sing and argue the night away.

Martha put the wedge underneath the unlockable door, stripped and put her Colt beneath her pillow, the S&W on the bedside table and, as an after-thought, the sheathed Bowie next to the Colt. She was as ready as she could be, given the raucous noise emanating from virtually each room and the danger with her being the only woman among a crowd of drunken men.

She thought about her lovely younger sister. Mattie might talk a good line about wanting to work with Pope, but she did not have the will and determination to be a deputy. She mainly wanted to steal Pope away from his wife. Martha was concerned it may have a negative effect on both her career and her friendship with Pope and Sarah.

She decided she would talk to her sister about how wrong and impossible it was trying to steal the handsome sheriff. Yes, Pope, at thirty, was only ten years older than her and maybe twelve years older than Mattie. It was not the age. It was how devoted she knew Pope and Sarah were to each other. They would die for one another. They had proven it. Mattie simply did not get the depth it takes to willingly die to save someone you love. She doubted Mattie would ever understand the concept. Martha loved her sister. She was so quick in many ways and so naïve in many others. This was just a big error on Mattie's part though.

She put Sarah's pillow over her head to dampen the noise. She could smell a small whiff of the light perfume her mentor wore in the pillowcase. It gave her comfort and she finally drifted off to sleep as the parties continued.

The next day, Martha continued her attempts to interview railway suppliers. Nobody would talk. It was clear people were as scared now as when she and Sarah started.

She put tic marks on the list and approached the last few businesses.

Martha saw a thin, bald man with glasses enter a store on her list. There was nothing remarkable about either his appearance or him being a customer.

She felt the hairs rise on the back of her neck. Israel Pope, a man who had killed two bears with just a knife, had drilled into her about those hairs during her training.

She went to the store and waited outside the open door and listened.

"I am here for your week's contribution for your ability to stay a railway supplier," the thin man said. "Show me the books. I want to see how much you sold to the railway this week."

The manager, or owner, Martha did not know which, produced a ledger and pointed out a page. The man studied it.

"The tariff this week is twenty dollars. You need to do a better job of selling to the railway or I will make sure you don't sell any damn thing to them!"

The seller started to protest. Martha peeked around the doorsill and saw the smaller man knee him in the groin. As the seller grabbed himself and bent over in agony, the man punched him in the side of the neck. The seller went down and Martha stepped back before being seen.

She knew she had seen an assault committed and threats made. She had a badge. She was armed. She did not have handcuffs, nor did she have any backup. For the big, brawny shopkeep to allow a much smaller man to push him around proved to her he would not help if she intervened and attempted an arrest.

Martha wisely backed away from the door and stepped around a corner. She watched the small, bald man with glasses kick the downed man viciously in the ribs and step out of the shop. He folded bills and placed them in a satchel he carried. He went on to the next business on her list. She positioned herself across the street and watched through the shop's open door. The little man went in, spoke with the manager, looked at a ledger and took some money. He came out the door, unsmiling, and went further down the street.

She continued to tail the man. Once he had finished today's list, he returned to the livery stable and came out in a buggy with a young boy driving. They went south out of town at a reasonable pace. Martha knew if she requested Maggie to be saddled and took off after him, she would be too late.

She decided to break cover and showed her badge to the livery manager from whom she had gotten her horse for yesterday's police action.

"You are kidding! You're no deputy. We don't have no little girl deputy sheriff's in Marin County," he said not believing her.

"Did you hear about the gunfight just up the road, with two outlaws killed?" He nodded affirmatively.

"Where do you think I was? Well, I will tell you. I was there! We killed two men and captured the ringleader. Sheriff Pope is questioning him now."

"C'mon, young lady. Anybody can get a badge. You ain't got no gun. All deputies carry guns."

She produced the hidden .38 so quickly the man jumped back.

She re-holstered it out of sight, her jacket covering it.

"I need to know who the man who just left in the buggy is and where he is going?"

"Alright. I guess you might be who you claim to be. I will be double checking with the sheriff anyway though. The man is Wilson Eckerd. We got a standing deal. Every Tuesday and Thursday, he comes on the morning ferry from San Francisco to visit clients. I send my boy down in a buggy to bring him into town. He does whatever he does and comes back here. My boy takes him back in time for the late afternoon ferry back to Frisco. I don't know any more than what I just told you. He pays cash and tips the boy and me."

"Do you know where he might live in San Francisco?"

"Nope. He's an odd little man. He looks harmless until you look him hard in the eyes. He'd kill anyone in half a second and never look back. I gotta tell you. He scares me. The only reason I send my boy with him is he likes the service we provide with no questions and I don't believe he'd have any reason to hurt the boy or me."

"Thank you. I just saw him assault a shopkeeper. I am undercover and had no way to arrest him. We will do so on Thursday. But, you cannot, I repeat cannot, give him any hint we are on to him. I will be back tomorrow with a detective from the Morse Agency and the sheriff. They will impress upon you how important this case is." She gave him the stare she had been rehearsing and left.

She sent a telegram to Sarah and the sheriff in care of the Wells Fargo office. Martha knew, even if Sarah was at the Morse office next door, she would get it immediately.

Sarah did not receive the telegram the next morning because she was on the way to Tiburon. Pope received it early and mounted Caesar for the ride to Tiburon.

Martha met Sarah outside the boarding house. By mid-morning it was empty as the residents had all gone to work. Only the desk clerk was on duty.

"You got here quickly after my recent telegram!" Martha exclaimed.

"What telegram?"

"I sent you and John one first thing about finding the suspect! He's a small, scary bald man with glasses. I watched him bring a big shopkeep down to the floor with no effort. I then tailed him to the remaining target businesses on our list. I followed him to the livery and watched him leave with a kid driving him to the afternoon ferry to San Francisco.

It took me some doing to convince the liveryman I was a real deputy and he had to answer my questions. He finally did. The man's name supposedly is Wilber Eckerd. He comes on the morning ferry every Tuesday and Thursday and leaves on the late afternoon one."

"You have done well! I will see Harry gives you a bonus for virtually solving our case!" Sarah said.

"I think John will come over once he gets the telegram. The liveryman needs proof I am a real deputy. I did not have my written warrant of deputation with me. Does he know we stay here?"

"He will start looking for us downtown. We should go there to meet him," Sarah said.

Pope arrived on Caesar an hour later.

The two women quickly filled him in on the case developments. They went to the livery to press the owner for more information. In the process, Martha was validated as a Marin County deputy. Pope emphasized the liveryman was to not alert Eckerd. If he did, he faced the risk of becoming an accessory. After speaking with the liveryman, Sarah telegraphed Harry Morse at his San Francisco office. They had a day until Eckerd arrived on Thursday to set up the arrest, which all of them considered to be more than enough time.

The next stop was to the supplier Martha had seen Eckerd rough up the previous day. He had not wished to elaborate with Sarah or Martha. The presence of the county sheriff and his promise Eckerd would be arrested the next day changed his mind about answering questions.

He admitted he had paid over a hundred dollars to Eckerd as had many businesses in Tiburon. He agreed to let Pope and Morse hide in his backroom with Martha pretending to be a customer leaving as Eckerd arrived on Thursday.

Sarah would have preferred arresting Eckerd on Thursday at the first supplier he strong armed.

However, she knew they could repay monies already collected. Sarah would make sure of this by shadowing Eckerd from his arrival in town to his stop at the store where he would be apprehended.

The owner became so enthused at the imminent arrest of Eckerd, he agreed to hold back and argue to make Eckerd threaten him again to solidify the case against him. He also thought once the arrest was made, the others would come forward and testify at Eckerd's trial.

Pope was generally positive about the outcome, though he was realistic enough to know things frequently did not go as planned in arrests. He rode back to San Rafael and returned early Thursday morning well before the Bay ferry arrival.

The ensuing time passed quickly.

Harry Morse and his Detective Lee were both at the Tiburon ferry dock in San Francisco on Thursday. They were separate ticket buyers and their nod of identification of Eckerd was so subtle no one noticed it when Eckerd arrived and bought his ticket. They stayed apart on the ride across San Francisco Bay. Since Eckerd had his usual reservation for the only buggy, Pope arranged for two horses to be waiting for the detectives at the ferry dock. They waited for Eckerd to get in the buggy and leave before mounting and riding into town separately. They rode on to the business where the arrest was to occur. Lee took the horses down the street to a hitching rail and began to appear like he was shopping. Morse went into the business and met with Pope. They were shown to the backroom and sat in office chairs to await Eckerd's arrival.

Eckerd came out of the livery with his satchel and proceeded to make collections in usual order as he progressed through town. Sarah followed him and noted times for each visit along his way.

He moved quickly today and thought he might finish in time for lunch and get an earlier ferry home. He hit the first eight or so quickly.

Eckerd walked into the supplier and was immediately met with resistance. He poked his finger into the owner's vest and threatened bodily harm. Per prior agreement, the man continued to resist and was punched in the solar plexus   and fell to the floor.

Pope and Morse stepped out and Pope said "Sheriff! You are under arrest!"

Eckerd reached into his coat. He stopped at the sight of the large hole in the end of Pope's magically appearing cocked .44 staring at him.

"I wouldn't," Pope said as Harry Morse moved around Eckerd and put both of the prisoner's wrists behind him. Pope reached inside Eckerd's coat and removed a .38 Colt Lightning revolver. He looked at it with some disgust. It was the only undependable Colt ever made. Pope thought of it as a "may-bang."

There was no sheriff's office in Tiburon. They took the suspect to the town office in handcuffs after taking a statement from the supplier about this and prior assaults by the man called Eckerd. Until he questioned the man and with prior advice received from the district attorney, Pope just arrested him for assault and battery. Other charges would be added, after his arrest prompted all of his victims to speak up.

At the town office, Pope, Morse, Sarah and Lee questioned him at length. Martha sat nearby and listened as the seasoned investigators mounted their interrogation. She was impressed with their change from friendly to terrifying and the cleverness with which they framed each question and their responses to the suspect's answers.

They found his name was really Wilbur Raleigh. He was treasurer of the railway company. A senior executive. He only demanded to see ledgers as part of hiding his real identity. He knew what the railroad paid each supplier quite well.

The sheriff and detectives could not find where Raleigh had ever been arrested before. Nor could they determine how such a harmless looking man could so intimidate far stronger, more capable fighters. It seemed the coldness and confidence he exuded was able to scare people who might otherwise be able to destroy him in a fight.

Morse rented the buggy Eckerd used weekly to

carry him back to San Rafael for further questioning and charges. He wired the president of the railway and advised him the case was solved and the identity of the person arrested.

"John, I have investigated many hundreds of cases from being the sheriff of Alameda County to many more years of being a detective. I have never seen one come to an end as befuddling as this one. And, due to the good detective work of two women detectives. Are you sure I cannot hire Martha Lane away from you?"

"I would not stand in your way, Harry. You are a friend Sarah and I cherish and one to whom we owe so much. You ask her and I'll back you up one hundred percent," Pope said.

Later in the day, Martha returned her deputy badge and accepted a Morse Detective Agency one. She became the junior detective reporting to Sarah Pope in the agency's San Rafael office. She was the subject of several favorable newspaper articles, publicity the agency owner loved.

Within several weeks, Pope and his chief deputy found a young cowboy to fill the empty deputy position. He received much the same training as the young woman had.

******

Autumn changed into winter in Marin County. A rare snow fall covered Mt. Tamalpais for a day or two, then melted away.

Pope rode Caesar into town and tied him at the sheriff office's hitching rail.

He went in, greeted Bill, who was always in early, and hung his wool lined canvas duster on the hook in his office. Pouring a cup of coffee, he began reviewing paperwork.

Sarah, who had ridden in with him, went to her office only now. The young man Hume mentioned had taken the manager position at Wells Fargo.

As Pope was taking his first sip of strong black office coffee, the new manager sent his telegrapher hurrying to the sheriff's office with an important telegram.

"Sheriff, you have an urgent telegram from the Governor!" he said as he strode into the outer office. Pope motioned him in, along with the chief deputy.

"Sheriff John Pope Stop Sheriff Placer County murdered Stop Go to Auburn forthwith and take charge Stop Investigate murder Stop. You have dual appointment as sheriff Marin and Placer Stop Advise results Stop Stoneman Governor End."

"I guess I have my work cut out for me," Pope said after reading the telegram aloud. He had not met this governor. The previous one had appointed him Marin County's sheriff upon the resignation of his successor.

"I wonder why me?" Pope asked Bill after the telegrapher had left.

"Probably because you are the only sheriff who has already been a famous detective. And, you are kinda in the news a lot. Politicians note those things."

"I guess I better get packing. You have the reins until I get back. I will send you where to contact me. I'm sure there is a telegraph office in the county seat of Auburn."

He rode the short distance to the Wells Fargo office and showed the telegram to Sarah. His office had a Marin County map on the wall. Hers had a state map, which they immediately consulted.

"Looks like over a hundred fifty or so miles with no train to help. Guess my boy, Caesar, is going to hit the trail again. He'll like it!"

"Do you have to accept the order?" his wife asked.

"Pretty much. I am still an appointed sheriff. The new governor can withdraw the appointment at will. This is a bit of an honor. I'd be politically crazy if I turned it down."

"Well, go home and pack your gear. Say bye to Israel and Millie. Stop by for a kiss on the way north," she said with resignation.

Pope visited his grandfather and Millie when he picked up more supplies and equipment at home.

"You telegraph me if you need some help. Placer is a lot bigger county than Marin. You'll have a lot of area to ride," Israel told him.

On the way back through San Rafael, Sarah gave him a subsequent telegram from the governor. It advised him to meet with the district judge in Auburn to be sworn in and to find out the authorities the governor had granted him.

He could make better time on Caesar than on a stage. He would need his mount anyway. He sent the governor a telegram stating he was leaving by horse today.

He was riding northeast by lunch time. He had a suit rolled up in his waterproof tarp and was riding in trail clothes. Caesar carried Pope's minimal camping gear, some feed for the trip and a bag of vittles for his master.

It was a fourteen hour ride to the Placer County seat in Auburn. Pope camped one night and rode in the following day.

He tied Caesar outside the court building and strode in.

"I'm looking for Judge Warren," he told a clerk working at a desk inside the door.

"Is he expecting you?" the man looked disdainfully at Pope's trail worn outfit.

"He is. I am Sheriff John Pope."

"Oh, I see," the man said, with a quick change in attitude. "Follow me, please, Sheriff."

They went into the judge's chambers where the clerk introduced Pope.

"Ah, Pope. I'm glad to see you. You look like you just rode in," Judge George Warren said.

"I did, Judge, with few stops from San Rafael. The governor said get here fast. So I did."

"While you are standing, raise your right hand and put your left on the Bible on my desk." He swore Pope in as Sheriff of Placer County, perhaps the only man to ever be sheriff of two counties in one state at the same time.

"First, you have all the powers here of a California sheriff. Your job is more to oversee the administration of the sheriff's office than to run it on a day to day basis.

The office is weak for a big county. Since you will not be earning a second salary, I urge you to hire a temporary chief deputy to run things. The county will cover the salary for the chief deputy with part of what we would pay a sheriff.

The governor also told me to authorize whatever subpoenas and search warrants you want.

He also gave you statewide power as his Special Investigator for the duration of this case."

"I am also sworn as a Special Deputy US Marshal. I may not need the statewide authority," Pope said.

"The governor and I did some research. We are both aware of your deputation by the Attorney General and why you have it. Just keep the warrant letter I'm going to give you. It may be politically beneficial up here."

"I will. Thanks to both of you.

Judge, what can you tell me about the murder of Sheriff Littleton?"

"Ashby Littleton was a hard man. He did a good job of maintaining the peace in a large county but was not liked by anyone I can think of. He was brusque, sometimes downright rude. I have heard he beat virtually all prisoners, including those who probably did not deserve it. He will not be missed by anybody, Pope. However, his murderer has to be brought to justice. We have a point to make here. Even if the sheriff of this county is a disgusting bully, you can't go killing him without paying the piper."

"I agree, Judge. Where was Sheriff Littleton found?"

"He was found on the edge of Lake Tahoe near Meeks Bay. It is an area which is not populated as a village. There are a couple brothers who do some haying there."

"What's the name of the doctor who examined the body? And, was an autopsy performed?"

"Doc Smythe here in town examined him prior to the undertaker getting the body. The cause of death was a massive load of buckshot to the chest. There was no need for an autopsy. Since Littleton did not have any known family, he was buried in the local cemetery with a small headstone. We took the money out of his unpaid salary," the judge said.

"Please give me a description of him and of where he lived. I'll have to go through his house and look for evidence of enemies."

"Ash Littleton was six feet or so. Spare build. Graying hair. Average length handle bar mustache. Not a bad looking man, except for his constant angry, sneering look.

The county provided him a small house over on sixth street. It is easy to find. Only one with an iron fence and gate in the front. After you look it over and move any of his personal stuff, it's yours for your duration here. Beats a hotel."

"Thank you, judge. Who's running the sheriff's office right now and do they have any idea about me being appointed temporary sheriff?" Pope asked.

The judge pushed a local paper over to him. The headline was "Governor appoints Marin Sheriff Pope to investigate death of Littleton." The smaller print strapline below amplified with "Pope is famous detective who saved President."

Pope nodded and the judge answered the rest of the question.

"There is no chief deputy. Littleton did not think he needed one. If you want to appoint someone to run the office while you are investigating, we will pay him with the salary you would normally make. Since you are retaining your Marin County pay, you won't be getting a second sheriff's salary here," the judge said.

"Fair enough. I'm thinking the best qualified person and the man I trust most in the world is my grandfather, Israel Pope."

"The famous mountain man and bounty hunter? I forgot he was your grandfather. Isn't he pretty old?"

"Not really. At sixty-five, he can outride, outrun and outshoot anybody else I know."

"The implication is 'except you?'" the judge asked.

"Pretty much."

"Your office. Choose the best man. If he's it, you'll get no push back from me. Bring or send him by for me to meet him."

"I will. In the meantime, my plan for today is to search the sheriff's house and move my meager travel kit in. I will put on a suit then go talk with the doctor, go by the sheriff's office and check in, Who should I expect to find in the sheriff's office?"

"Deputy Otha Deacon. He was a young army officer at Chickamauga. Wounded in his leg and walks with a cane. Was decorated as a hero by Lincoln himself. Runs the office well. He's honest and a good administrator. He was a leader in the army, he has shown no interest in leading here. Which is why he is not chief deputy. Ordinarily he would be. Maybe because of his bum leg. I don't know. I think he could be a lot more.

Are you curious about how they will welcome you?"

"No, sir. Not at all. I am here to do a job. It's not a popularity contest."

"Like you just said," the judge responded, "fair enough."

Pope unpinned his gold Marin County star and put it in his vest pocket. He pinned on the badge saying "Sheriff" across the top of the star's center and "Placer County" on the bottom. It did not leave much doubt about who he was.

He shook with the judge and walked out to Caesar.

"C'mon, boy. Let's go look at the place we'll live for a little while."

The small house was not hard to find. Pope was pleased to see it had a two-horse stall in the rear. There was a tall well-kept dun in one stall. Apparently, someone had put Littleton's horse there after he was shot two days ago. The horse was well groomed and there was plenty of water and feed.

"The man may have been a bully, but he did take care of his horse," Pope thought. He would find out differently upon further examination of the fine animal.

He sat his gear down in a corner and proceeded to search the house thoroughly.

Littleton had .45 Colt cartridges in abundance. Pope set those aside for his grandfather. He found a locked trunk. He left it for now and proceeded searching. He took the man's meager clothes and searched any pockets and put them aside also. There was no chest of drawers. Just shelves on the wall and hooks. There was a privy out back and a small stove for both cooking and heating in one corner of the main room.

He brushed his suit and put it on with the Placer County badge pinned to the left lapel. Mounting Caesar, he rode to the doctor's office and walked in the unlocked door to the surgery.

"Dr. Smythe? I'm Sheriff John Pope," he said to the doctor, who appeared to be in his early thirties.

"Glad you are here. We have been waiting for someone and found it would be you in the morning's paper. I guess you want to talk about the prior sheriff's body?"

"I do. What were your overall conclusions?"

"He was shot up close with a shotgun. Double ought buckshot destroyed his upper body."

"How widely dispersed were the wounds?"

"All nine were in the upper chest, but the pattern was just below the Adam's apple down to the solar plexus and between both shoulders."

"Were there powder burns on the body?"

"Yes, from the wad and generally on the whole chest."

"I'd say if it was close enough for a wide dispersal of burns, yet the shot pattern had opened up, he was killed with a short-barreled shotgun, sawn off sufficiently to do away with any choke constrictions in the barrel," Pope said. "Otherwise at such a close range, the pattern would be no more than several inches in diameter."

"I hadn't thought about it, but logically you are right," the doctor said.

"No defensive wounds on his body? Bruised knuckles? Scratches or bruises?"

"No, Sheriff. None at all."

"Did you go to the body, or was it brought here to you?"

"I went. Why?"

"Did you see the murder weapon?" Pope asked.

"No, there was no shotgun there. The deputy and I looked around."

"Was his revolver still in its holster? And, was it still fully loaded?"

"It was, five rounds and hammer on an empty chamber just like I'd have expected," the doctor said.

"Why was it important to you whether I saw the body there or here, Sheriff?"

"It makes your information more valid since you saw the body at the crime scene. No deputy would have put the gun back in the holster. Nothing unusual about the scene? Ground messed up? Hoof or wagon prints? Did it appear he was killed there? Or, perhaps elsewhere and deposited there? Did the killer extract the fired shell and leave it on the ground? If so, it would be good evidence. Any footprints?"

"Nope. Nothing at all."

"Suggests to me either the sheriff knew his aggressor or did not think him to be a threat."

"I guess I would have to agree."

"Is it your opinion Littleton died instantly?"

"Absolutely. The wounds were horrific. I am sure his heart was shredded. The trauma of the hit probably killed him before he bled out."

"I have not been by the sheriff's office yet. I wanted to speak with you first. What was the name of the deputy who took you?"

"He was a young fellow. Tom Bond, I believe."

"Dr. Smythe, did he mark off the crime scene at all?"

"Yes, I thought what he did was pretty smart. He took his lariat and roped the crime scene off to enable finding the exact spot again, and maybe even keep people off it."

"Excellent! I will commend him. What was the distance to the lake from where the body was found?"

"Not more than twenty feet, I'd say," the doctor replied.

"Anything suggest to you why the sheriff was at the location?"

"There were a few cigarette butts near the body. Maybe he had been smoking while waiting for someone."

"Any idea who?" the sheriff asked.

"No, none at all. Could be he was just stopping for a smoke break."

"You have been a great help, Dr. Smythe. I really appreciate it. I'm going to head over to the crime scene now. I'm going to go to the sheriff's office, but I believe it would be good to see the scene before it's hit by weather or nosey people. Thanks, again."

Pope introduced himself to the deputy sitting behind the first desk. It was Otha Deacon, the Civil War hero and administrative deputy. Pope liked him immediately.

"I'm honored to meet the hero of Chickamauga," Pope said.

"Sheriff, the real heroes died. I'm just the one who lived and was still standing—barely—to pin a medal on."

"I applaud your modesty Otha, but the judge told me the story as I was walking out. I grew up with another different kind of hero. It's nice to have two now."

"Who is your hero?"

"My grandfather. He has killed two bears with just a Bowie knife, fought Indians, has been an Indian, and led pioneers safely to the Promised Land."

"I'm guessing since your last name is Pope and not Boone or Carson, you must mean Israel Pope."

"The very man. Whatever and whoever I am, he made me. For better or worse."

"I'd love to meet him one day," Deacon said.

"I'm hoping he will come here and give us a hand, Otha. My plan is to only be here less than a month, but I am going to be investigating. You will need another strong man to help and to respond to crime and, if need be, chase the miscreants down. Grandpa is the man for the job."

"No offense, but isn't he kind of old?"

Pope grinned at him.

"Give me your opinion on age once you meet him, alright? Also, can you recommend a cleaning woman I can pay to keep the sheriff's cottage clean"

"I can," Otha said and wrote a name and local address down on a slip of paper.

"How far is it out to the spot where Littleton was killed?" Pope asked.

"A good three hour ride."

"I will take tomorrow and ride over there. I would like to look at the location while things are still fresh."

"I'll see you the day after, then."

Pope looked up the cleaning lady and paid her in advance. She said she would do her first cleaning in the morning.

As was his wont, Pope awakened before the sun.

He was still slightly chilled. The house had not warmed much. He would need to check the stove and flue and to see to the wood type and supply. To make sure it was fully operational, Pope unloaded the Colt Frontier model with its seven and a half inch barrel and stag grips. He reloaded with empty shells to protect the firing pin on the hammer. He drew and dry fired at least twenty times. His speed increased with each draw.

He opened the loading gate and ejected the empties for his next practice session, probably the following day. He seldom skipped a day's practice.

Pope inserted a .44-40 cartridge. He skipped the next chamber and inserted four more cartridges. Pulling the hammer all the way to full cock, he eased it down on the sole remaining empty chamber in the cylinder. The gun was carried as a five-shooter, not a six-shooter. With the firing pin over an empty chamber, a drop or blow would not cause it to fire unintentionally. It was the only way a rational person would carry a gun for years to come.

Pope had directions from the doctor. He mounted Caesar and started the three or more hour ride. He wanted to see it and head back before dark.

It was almost one o'clock when he arrived and found the roped off crime scene. He let Caesar stand, reins down and raised the rope to enter.

Pope could see a brownish area on the ground. It was blood and almost certainly where the body had lain.

As the doctor said, it was twenty feet from the edge of Lake Tahoe. Pope took out his sketch book and drew the scene, then measured the boundaries and marked the location where the body was found. He collected three cigarette butts and saved them in an evidence bag. He searched thoroughly for a fired shotgun shell. None was present.

He stood for a while and envisioned what likely happened. Then, he did something he knew would be really painful at Lake Tahoe in the fall of the year.

He stripped to his union suit. He gathered wood and built, but did not light, a campfire.

Boots, clothes and guns secreted, he stepped into the frigid waters of the second deepest lake in North America. He planned to search the bottom in a space fifty feet wide by twenty-five feet out from the shore. With the temperature and depth of the water, he knew it would be difficult. He walked the first ten by fifty foot section, feeling for the shotgun he sought with his feet. Nothing. Damn.

Pope dove into the crystal clear, icy water and began to swim along the bottom. Within minutes, he could feel the cold affecting his abilities. He had never heard the word "hypothermia". He sure knew what it was by feeling how his body felt, however.

He knew he had but minutes left before he would have to get out of the water and light the fire. He was already beginning to shiver.

Pope concentrated on the center of the area he had mentally cordoned off. He felt it would be the more likely place the murderer might have thrown the weapon. If, in fact, the murderer had not just mounted his horse and ridden off with it.

He knew a good detective had to play hunches. This was his.

At the last moment, it paid off. He saw something on the bottom and dove down almost eight feet for a closer look.

It was a sawed-off shotgun! He grasped it in hands so cold he could hardly hold it. He surfaced and dog paddled painfully to shore.

He had to drop the shotgun on the dry land and concentrate on getting his feet to work to move him to the fire site.

Pope had thought ahead and left a box of Lucifer's to light the tender he left in the center of the fire build.

He could not hold the wooden match between two fingers without dropping it as he huddled, shivering, in the wet union suit and tried to light the fire.

Using two shaking hands, he finally got the match to light and dropped it involuntarily onto the tender. The fire flared and the tender caught the kindling, then the larger pieces.

Soon he had a small fire, but a hot one made of resinous fast burning wood.

He walked painfully to his horse and took his blanket rolled in a small tarp from behind the saddle.

He stripped behind a tree and wrapped in the blanket. Pope pulled the tarp around himself and walked, painfully but a little bit better, to the fire. He crouched down and held his hands and feet near the heat.

By the time he was beginning to feel almost human again, it was dark.

He put on his clothes sans the wet union suit. He followed with warm wool socks, boots and jacket. He rolled the shotgun up in his blanket with the tarp on the outside. Pope tied it back behind Caesar's saddle, put the fire safely out and mounted up.

The movement of the horse helped get his blood flowing better.

Pope knew the sheriff's office would be closed now. He rode straight to the house allotted to the dead sheriff. And, now to him. Pope arrived just after dark.

The door was unlocked as most were in the time. He entered and found an oil lamp. Another Lucifer and he had light. He was still shaking a little so he lit the stove. There was enough wood inside to keep it going most of, if not all night.

He went out and walked Caesar back to the double stall. He would have to get the sheriff's horse's name tomorrow. He fed and watered both horses.

Inside, he set the recovered sawed-off shotgun aside. He knew he would find one spent shell and one live one when he broke it open. Tomorrow. Not now.

Chewing a piece of the jerky he always carried in his saddlebags and taking a swig of canteen water, he laid the tarp over the sheets and blanket already on the bed. He laid on top of it and pulled his own wool blanket around him. Pope was asleep within minutes.

******

Once it was light, he really needed coffee. A lot of hot coffee. However, he first searched Littleton's house and moved all of the man's possessions to one corner. The cleaning woman would come in and do the linens, towels and clean the house later today.

Pope had neither the time nor inclination to do more at the house.

He rode into Auburn and went to the sheriff's office. He greeted Otha and set the shotgun on his desk.

"I noticed you brought in a pretty fancy alley cleaner. Is the shotgun part of your armory?" Deacon asked.

"Yes, a short shotgun is. But not the one I just laid on the desk. I believe it to be the murder weapon. I have not opened it, but when opened, I expect we will find the empty shell which killed Sheriff Littleton and probably and unshot one."

"Where'd you get it?"

"About twenty-five feet out and eight feet down in Lake Tahoe from where the sheriff was killed."

"How?"

"I took a swim late yesterday. I think I still have a blue tint to my skin. It was even colder than I expected."

"Good Lord, man the water is like ice! How long were you in?"

"I don't really know. At the time, it felt like days."

"Let's break her open and check the chambers,"

Otha said, getting enthused over the investigation.

Several days in the frigid fresh water of Lake Tahoe had no effect on the gun. A bit of oil and it would be ready to serve another century or two.

Pope picked up the gun and held it with a surprised look on his face. The deputy looked at him.

"What's wrong?"

"It does not break open like a normal double barrel. It appears to have an action which slides back to expose the chambers," Pope said.

He fiddled with it for a minute then slide the top portion of the action back towards him. Sure enough, there was one spent and one live twelve gauge shell in it. Both were traditional brass shells, not the newer brass base with an attached cardboard cylinder to hold powder, wads and shot.

Pope held up the right hand shell.

"I am pretty sure this was the one which killed Littleton."

He examined the gun.

"It appears to be a gun called a Darne. It's made in France. I wonder if we can track it down. I have been around shotguns all my life and expect you have too. This one is new to me."

"I never saw a double where the action slid back instead of breaking open. Long term, it might last longer by not constantly being broken open on a hinge like a normal one," Otha offered.

"Good point. I saw a couple of gun dealers in town. Maybe I'll take a walk and see if any of them can offer any help," Pope said. "I will get some breakfast while I am out. I got back to the sheriff's house late, wet and cold. I have not even had coffee yet."

"There's an already brewed pot on the pot belly stove," Otha said.

"Keep her hot, I'll be needing more by the time I get back. I have to send a telegram, too."

Pope left with the shotgun in a burlap sack. It was too early for the gun sellers to be open so he found a café near the office. He hoped it would be good, since he reckoned he would be taking most of his meals there for the next month or so.

If the coffee, eggs, ham, and biscuits were representative of the rest of the menu, Pope thought he had found a culinary gold mine.

After eating, Pope went to the telegraph office and sent a telegram to Sarah. He asked her to ask his grandfather if he would like to be a salaried Placer County chief deputy for a month or so. A two bedroom house would be shared with him and a good horse would be at his disposal. He could also bring Millie if she wanted.

He then walked to the two gun dealers in town. Neither had heard of or sold a Darne shotgun from France. However, the second dealer had a distributor listing and was able to give him the address of a Darne distributor in New York City.

Back at the sheriff's office, Pope drafted a telegram to the New York distributor and asked what dealers sold Darne shotguns in the Western U.S. He took it to the telegraph office and sent it.

"Otha, the light in the cottage is not good for searching. I want to go search Littleton's belongings thoroughly to see if I can find any clues as to who might want to kill him. I have a feeling there's more to his story than we know."

"He was a gruff, solitary man. He had a mean streak a yard wide. I saw him beat prisoners for no more reason than he just could. I mentioned it a couple times and he came at me. I have not the youth or stability to fistfight a fit man in his prime, Sheriff. I know I should have gone to the judge. I knew if I did, though, Littleton would get even with me.

Nobody's upset he was killed. Nobody at all."

"Do you think any of the prisoners he beat might have killed him?" Pope asked.

"Mebbe. I would not have blamed any of them. Nobody would."

"Think you can come up with a list of names, Otha?"

"I can. It would be pretty short, because most of them got out of town to get away from him once they got out of jail," he said.

"Why don't you write down the names of folks he beat and who are still in the area. We'll talk to them.

I am going to the cottage and do a serious search."

The search turned up only two things of possible value. Both were in the locked trunk Pope jimmied the lock from. One was a photograph of a man, a woman, and a little girl. It had "G. Reasoner, Photographer, San Francisco, California" printed on the rear. The other was a paper strap for cash with ACME Mining on printed on it.

He had left the former sheriff's meager wardrobe with a note for the cleaning lady for her next visit. After she washed the clothes, he would give them to Otha to donate to his church.

Pope went back to the office by midday and showed the photograph to Otha.

"Looks like could be a younger Littleton. Hard to say without the big handlebar mustache he wore here. I don't know who the woman and girl are. He never said anything about having a family. Nobody came here with him."

"Does the telephone connect with the telegraph office?" Pope asked.

"Yep. Just crank her up and tell the operator and who you need. Us, the judge, the telegraph office and a couple rich folks have service."

He called and the operator put him through.

"Oh, Sheriff. You just got a telegram from Sarah Pope. I was going to bring it over," the telegrapher said.

"For now, read it to me. You don't have to say 'stop'

or any of the telegram lingo."

"Alright. She says somebody named Israel is on the way. She says somebody named Millie is not coming yet."

"Thanks. Now, if you would, send a telegram to the photographer I am going to give you here and say I am on the way with a picture for them to identify as part of a murder investigation."

Pope looked at his pocket watch. There was no way he could ride to Sacramento, get on a river steamer and make it to San Francisco in time to see someone at the photography studio. He would do it tomorrow and await his grandfather's arrival the following day.

The Placer County sheriff's office covered a large county. There was a disproportionately small group of people staffing the office. Otha ran the day-to-day operations. There was a jailer and a woman who served as a part time administrative secretary. The lockup held ten prisoners and was generally filled with people the deputies had arrested from around the county and who were awaiting trial. There was a separate jail. People found guilty of misdemeanors served their time at the jail. Felons waited in jail until time to be sent to serve their sentences in the state penitentiary at San Quentin.

Pope would have his grandfather take a look at the districts and their size compared with deputy staffing. He was here to solve a crime and be a place holder. He reckoned it would be his duty to improve the efficiency of the operation.

The cleaning lady had done a good job of cleaning the house, scrubbing the floors, washing towels and bed linens as well as Littleton's clothes.

Pope brought the latter in the next morning and gave them to Otha to give to his church's needy. He then rode Caesar to Sacramento and boarded him for the day at a livery stable near the steamboat dock.

He had read the steamboat trips were a risk due to the constant racing to beat established times. These races were causing boilers to explode.

Such was not the case on this trip. He arrived in San Francisco in the late morning and called on his friend and Sarah's boss, Harry Morse, first. Harry was in the office and Pope told him about the case. His only clues, he said were the rare shotgun and the photograph.

Morse suggested maybe Littleton was a false identity. More than one outlaw had changed his name and crossed over to the lawman side of the street. Pope considered the idea and promised to not only explore it, but to keep Harry apprised. If anyone alive loved a tough mystery, it was his friend Harry Morse.

He went to the photographer's studio. The owner was a small, gregarious man. He examined the photograph.

"Sheriff, this photograph had to be one I took,

though I cannot call the name of the family off the top of my head," photographer Edward Lee said.

"It is an early gelatin silver print. They were made on photographic paper coated with gelatin which has light sensitive silver salts in it. I would say from the coloring of the paper over time, it would probably be from when I first opened. Luckily, I had a wonderful mentor in this business. I bought it from George Reasoner. It was established so I kept the name.

George taught me people, including ancestors, would return and ask for copies. So, I learned to put a tiny serial number on each photograph and record it in my book." He pointed to the tiny series of numbers on back of the print.

Lee went to his backroom and returned with a book which had 1870-1880 on the cover. Taking a magnifying glass he wrote the number from the back of the photograph on a slip of paper. Lee looked up the serial number.

"Aha! This is the Charles O'Brien family and was taken in 1872! Does this information assist you?" he asked.

"I believe it will be crucial to solving the murder I am investigating," Pope said as he noted the information in his leather notebook. "Thank you, Mr. Lee. I appreciate your cooperation. If this works as I hope, you may read about the conclusion in the San Francisco papers."

Pope returned to Harry Morse's office and found the owner reviewing case files.

"I have a name and year for the photograph," he told the detective.

"And, I may have the source to get more details. I have found US Census data to be invaluable. Let's go to my record room and take a look for 1870's for the City and County of San Francisco. They became a consolidated city-county in 1856."

Within minutes, the famous detective pointed his finger at a listing for Charles O'Brien, wife Marie and daughter Sophie. O'Brien's occupation was policeman, his wife was a housewife. The ages listed were thirty, twenty-nine, and ten years old. Pope noted all, including the address. He knew from his police days it was a modest neighborhood where a cop would be likely to live.

"Thanks, Harry. I'll let you know what I find."

Pope went to the San Francisco police headquarters first and looked up a detective lieutenant.

"Well, it's my old protégé!" Howell exclaimed as Pope walked in and grabbed his proffered hand.

"Howdy, Lieutenant. How are you?" Pope greeted his boss when he was a San Francisco detective.

"Busier than I ought to be at this stage in my life. Got some more Chinese smugglers in Marin?" he asked, referring to a big case they had worked together a little over a year ago.

"Not any I know of. I am also temporarily sheriff over in Placer to investigate the murder of their sheriff. Which is the real reason I am here, other than to also buy you lunch."

"Lunch is always good. A new lunch joint opened up between here and the harbor. We can go there. What's up with the murder investigation?" Howell asked.

"SFPD had a policeman named Charles O'Brien back in the seventies. I don't know when he quit. But he's listed in the first census of the decade. He is a person of interest in the murder. I'd like to find out as much about him as I can."

"Let's walk down to the Personnel office," Howell said and headed out the door to the hallway, Pope following.

"Jack, you remember John Pope. He was a detective here. I taught him all he knows and he went off and became a famous detective and now sheriff," Howell said to the personnel head. "He needs to find out about one Charles O'Brien. Probably a patrolman. Back in the seventies."

Jack led them back to a file room. He opened a file drawer and pulled through some folders before removing one.

The three sat at a scarred wooden table as Jack went through the folder.

"Appears we had to let O'Brien go. He was accused of taking bribes. Big ones. He was only here for a few years. We didn't have enough evidence to prosecute him. We did have enough to fire him."

"Jack, do you remember what he was like?" Pope asked.

"It's a while back, but I remember he was surly and meaner than a snake. Nobody liked him."

"Is this him?" Pope asked, handing him the family photograph.

"Yep. It's him alright. What did he do after here?"

"I am not sure until three years ago at which time he was appointed sheriff of Placer County by the then-governor to serve out a deceased sheriff's term," Pope said.

"Maybe he changed."

"Does not sound like it. He showed up on his own. Any idea what happened to the wife and daughter?'

"I always suspected he beat them. Maybe worse. He got his kicks hurting people. As I remember, she was foreign. Maybe French. Could be she went back to wherever she came from and took the daughter with her. I just can't really say, Sheriff."

"Thanks, both of you. This is a big help. Good or bad, I need to find out who killed O'Brien/Littleton. Your information gets me closer to doing it," Pope said.

Howell took Pope up on lunch. He always did.

"John, what will you do now in the investigation?" he asked.

"I am going to go to the old neighborhood and see if anyone remembers him or what happened to his wife and daughter. The girl would be about twenty-two now. Maybe she or the wife are still in town. I will run through the later 1870's census to see if they are listed. Then I'll head back up the across the bay and up the river to Sacramento, pick up my horse and ride back to Auburn. I have Grandpa coming up to help me out a bit."

He shook with Howell and headed back to Harry Morse's office.

"Harry, can we take another quick look at the next census and see if the family still lived at the address? And if not, whether there was a single listing for mother and daughter as Marie and Sophie O'Brien."

Their review of the next census did not show a listing for either. not.

He thanked Harry and took a long walk to the neighborhood where the O'Brien's lived in the early 1870's.

Pope's first stop was to the house where they had lived. The woman of the house said they had just bought it three years ago from a man named Brown. She had never heard of the O'Brien's. He asked her if any other neighbors had lived there back in the early 70's. She responded the older lady next door had. She hinted the woman was a "busybody."

Pope knew nosy neighbors often fill in important

missing details.

Mrs. Schultz was around eighty and had lived there since before the Civil War. She poured him a cup of coffee and they sat in overstuffed chintz furniture in her parlor.

Pope chatted politely with her instead of using his normal police interrogation techniques.

Mrs. Schultz hinted O'Brien was a "mean *polizist*," which he took correctly to mean a mean policeman in her native German.

"Did he beat his wife or daughter?" he asked carefully. She nodded. "Perhaps worse?" he asked. She nodded again.

"When did they leave?" The response was around 1873. It would have been about the time of his termination from the police department.

"Mrs. Schultz, do you know where they went?"

"I don't know. He left first and Marie told me she and the girl would try to get back to either Montreal or France, her homeland. Then, two or three weeks later, they were gone."

"Did you ever see either of them again?" She had not. He thanked her and tried several other neighbors without further success.

Pope made it back to the docks in time to catch the late afternoon steamer back to Sacramento. He reclaimed his stallion and rode to Auburn. The office was closed by the time he arrived in the county seat, so he went to the house.

His grandfather was due sometime tomorrow. Since he told him there was a good horse there, he reckoned the older Pope would travel by stage since trains did not run from Marin County to Auburn.

He stopped in town to eat something light and rode home and called it an early night.

******

Pope beat Otha to the office the next morning. He already had coffee made by the time Otha arrived. He filled him in on his findings.

"There won't be any way to find out where the former sheriff's wife and daughter went in 1873. The old lady said Marie O'Brien wanted to go to French-speaking Montreal or home to France,"

"There would not be any ship or stage or train records to help us. People paid their cash and boarded. Names might have been given on steamers, but those come and go so fast there's no way of tracking them on manifests," Otha said.

"Otha, do you have a chart showing the deputies and their districts, or is the map of Placer County the only one?" Pope asked.

"It's the only one. I marked the districts and the deputies in pencil so they could be updated without starting over."

"That will work. I want to give my Grandfather a good idea of how spread out the county is and what deputies we have patrolling it. Is there any telephone service between here and the several deputy substations?"

"One day maybe, but not currently," Otha said. "The substations are in big enough towns to have telegraph offices, so we communicate with wires. The substations are barely a ten by ten room," Otha added.

Pope walked over to the map.

"I don't see a substation near the lake," he said.

"We don't have enough calls for service yet to warrant one."

"I bet it changes dramatically before too many years," Pope thought aloud.

He walked over to the telegraph office and sent a telegram to his Marin County chief deputy asking if things were going alright. He got a response within five minutes noting things were going well and giving a late afternoon arrival for Israel Pope.

He reached in his vest pocket and pulled out the currency strap with "ACME Mining" on it.

It reminded him another trip to the telegraph office was necessary.

He drafted a telegram to the Sheriff, Washoe County, Nevada to find out if there had been a robbery at ACME Mining Company near Reno in the 1870's or early 1880's. Around mid-morning he received a response saying there had been a significant robbery with the company president murdered in 1879. Pope wired back he may have some information on it related to a case he was working and would be there within several days.

Pope spent the time before Israel's arrival signing or stamping documents regarding tax matters, and foreclosures. The next pile of paperwork included acknowledging subpoenas and civil warrants to be served. These sheriff duties were not exciting, but Pope looked at them unequivocally as just part of the job.

He heard the stage arrive, always an event at an 1880's town. Smiling, he put on his coat and walked out the door to greet one of his two favorite people in the world.

He watched his grandfather step down from the red Concord. He was tall and fit at sixty-five, with longish white hair and a well-groomed handlebar mustache. Israel was wearing a dark suit and a dove gray Stetson hat. He could have been a US Senator.

In reality, he was one of the greatest of the living mountain men and wagon train masters. He had led hundreds of families to both Oregon and California. Once he began to raise his grandson, he stayed closer to home. He was a feared and highly successful bounty hunter. His skills as a mantracker may have exceeded his exceptional ones tracking four-legged creatures. He was unschooled but well-read and could converse in any company.

Sheriff John Pope was convinced he was looking at the wisest man alive and still one of the most dangerous.

The two approached each other and clasped in a firm hug.

"Thanks for coming, Grandpa. I need someone to take charge while I'm gone investigating. This murder is a tough one. No witnesses, a probable identity change and few clues. And the governor wants it solved yesterday," he said in a voice unheard by anyone else.

Israel, carrying his 1873 Winchester carbine in a leather case, walked to the boot of the stage and recovered a large carpet bag which his grandson grabbed to carry into the office.

"Otha Deacon, senior deputy, meet Israel Pope!"

"Are you the Deacon from Chickamauga?" Israel asked as he proffered his hand for a strong clasp between two men who had seen the devil and come back alive.

"I am. It's an honor to meet you, Mr. Pope. I look forward to working with you."

"It's Israel and the honor's all mine. What do you go by?"

"Otha."

"Otha, we'll get along well and I'll help you keep

this place called Placer County as safe for its inhabitants as we can," Israel said.

His grandfather was that way. His charm immediately drew people to him. Unless he was going to kill them.

"Let me unlimber my carbine, in case something untoward was to happen. Where do you want me to set my bag, Sonny? Er, I mean Sheriff."

"Put it in my office. You can use it. I will be traveling around investigating most of the time you are here. Instead of me swearing you in, let's see if Judge George Warren is available," Pope said.

Israel slipped his long-barreled Colt out of his waistband and into a belt rig which he strapped on. Pope knew Israel's inimitable Bowie was also hidden somewhere on his person. Just as his was.

They walked into the court and the judge's assistant checked, then announced them.

After greetings, Judge Warren said, "My folks came to California first by wagon train. I finished law school and came later. You led them. It was the one when Indians attacked and you took a group of ex-army men out after them. My father was one of them. He speaks highly of you to this day, Mr. Pope."

"Thank you, Judge. It was so long ago, I don't remember the names, but they were all good men. They fought hard and saved the rest. They were rough times, Judge. Very rough."

"They were. And, they required men tough enough to succeed. I told your grandson to bring you by. I have wanted to meet you. I will write my father and tell him we met. He's over in San Francisco now."

"Judge, we'd be honored if you would swear my grandfather in as Chief Deputy instead of me doing it?"

"I will. You pin the badge on him."

The swearing was done on the same Bible as Pope had held his hand on. The badge was pinned on and if anyone ever looked the part of a Western lawman, Israel Pope in his black suit, white hair and mustache and long Colt surely did. They thanked the judge and walked back to the office, looking more like father and son than men another generation apart.

"You know, Sonny. If it had not been for the war party, your own father might be walking beside you right now."

"I reckon he would Grandpa. But, I am pretty pleased and confident to have his father here."

Otha spotted the badge and congratulated the new chief deputy.

"Otha, why don't you take the chief over to the map and show him how the county breaks down for our patrols. And would you give him some insight on the men who ride for us?"

"By the time you are through that, I will saddle and bring Littleton's horse back here for him to ride home after we have dinner. I'm sure neither of us wants to cook tonight.

Otha, what's the horse's name?"

"Jeb. Named for the enemy. Jeb Stuart."

Pope shrugged. He was not sure who was the enemy in the war. Both were right and both were wrong and maybe three quarters of a million men died to prove it was their side which was right.

Pope walked back to the house, leaving Caesar tied out front of the sheriff's office.

He pulled the tackle down and saddled Jeb. As he was saddling him, he saw spur scars. The no good sonofabitch! The scars made Pope infuriated at the man whose murder he was investigating. Pope had never left a mark on any animal he had ever ridden, including on several pursuits and running gun battles. There was no excuse to wear sharp spurs and hurt the animal upon whom your life might depend.

The horse was glad for the attention and the chance to stretch his legs. Pope rode in a few miles out of town talking to the horse in a friendly conversational tone. The horse was a good one. He had a good gait and Pope surmised he could run long enough to chase down most miscreants. He turned the horse back towards town and trotted in until he got to the main street and slowed him to a walk. He tied him to the hitching rail. Israel came out to look him over. Pope pointed to the scars and watched his grandfather's anger grow. He had never known his grandfather to hate a single soul. Including the warriors who had killed his second wife and the ones who later killed his son, daughter in law and little granddaughter. Pope's family.

He not only knew the anger his grandfather felt, he shared it.

Israel shook his head sadly and spoke softly to Jeb as they followed Pope on Caesar down the street to a fancier restaurant then the usual café at which Pope dined.

They ate, returned to the house and put the horses away.

Pope had picked up new sheets and blankets for the second bedroom and Israel moved in.

"What are your plans tomorrow?" Israel asked.

"I am going to ride over to Lake Tahoe and meet with a contact from my Wells Fargo days, to try to get more information on Littleton. Or, O'Brien as the case may be. Then on to Reno to the sheriff's office. I have a growing suspicion O'Brien was in a robbery of a mining company there in 1879. I want to see what I can learn about the robbery. Especially the suspects. How about you, Grandpa?"

"I'm learning a lot from Otha. Why isn't he the chief deputy?"

"I asked him the same thing. He's highly respected in the community. He says he just does not want the responsibility and does not feel he is up to the riding and physical exertion which comes with the job."

"My guess is he could do it. If he does not want to, well, I guess it's best he not take the post. It's Placer County's loss though," Israel said.

CHAPTER 4

Pope left for the telegraph office in the end of the Wells Fargo office. He had an idea and acted on it.

Allan Pinkerton, was on his last legs when he accompanied Sarah to essentially say goodbye to him a little over a year ago. He had died several months ago and Sarah went to Chicago to his funeral. He was buried in the Pinkerton plot next to the first female detective, Kate Warne. Warne had succumbed at thirty-five of pneumonia. Her location would have been the usual location for Pinkerton's wife, which caused some dissention in the family.

Pope knew there had to be a story there. He did not press Sarah for it, knowing her affection for the secretive Scot.

Pinkerton had started a card file of criminals. The idea was picked up by another odd little man in the Nation's capital in the 1920's and is in use to this day.

Pope wondered if the Pinkerton file had anything which would help him regarding the robbery of the ACME mining company in 1879.

He sent a telegram to Sarah to see if her relationship with Pinkerton's sons would weather a request from outside the agency. He would be gone for several days, so even if she got a rapid response, he would be unaware of its contents until he got back.

Pope woke up to the rich smell of good coffee. Nobody made coffee better than his grandpa.

They sat around the table drinking coffee and chatting like in their old days.

"I am going to the southern rim of the lake to check with an old contact and then ride up to Reno and meet with the sheriff about the ACME robbery. My gut tells me O'Brien and Littleton were the same man and he was in on the robbery. I know the cash wrapper is not concrete proof, but it's a good clue. It could be the reason he let someone come up to him. Like an old gang member, perhaps."

"You are the detective, Sonny Boy. I reckon what your instincts tell you are at least half the solution of a thorny case. Clues and the right questions are the other half. It's not so different from tracking a man you're after on a bounty. 'Where would a wanted man go?' is instinct and carries more weight to a good manhunter than the same question about regular non-criminal man just traveling through" Israel said. Pope nodded.

He had heard his grandfather say something similar before, but it bore repetition.

"You gonna get some ham and eggs in town before heading out? Not much in the way of vittles in the little South Tahoe village."

"Sure isn't."

"Say hello to Bertie for me if she's still there," Israel said.

"You know her?" Pope asked, surprised his grandfather knew the pretty prostitute in the village at the southern end of the lake.

"Not biblically. She helped me with information on a fella I was hunting up for a bounty a few years ago. She had just moved there. Nice lady. Would make somebody a real fine wife if she was away from where she lives."

"I thought so too, Grandpa. She helped me find a man I was trailing for Wells Fargo. She's too good a person to be a soiled dove."

"A woman has to eat. Not like she can take any old job a man can. She's gotta be a cook, a cleaner, darn clothes or be a wife. Sometimes those jobs are taken and prostitute is all what's left. It's not right. But, it's the way of things."

"I'll say hello to her for you."

Israel took out a twenty dollar gold piece.

"Give her this. Tell her I gave her two bits and caught the guy on her information three days later.

She deserved more than two bits."

"I will."

They rode into town and checked in at the sheriff's office. Nothing was happening. They ate at the café and brought Otha back a ham biscuit though he had said he ate earlier.

"I might want to keep Jeb, Otha. How might I go about getting him? Now the sheriff is dead with no kin, does the horse belong to the county?"

Otha shrugged unknowingly.

"I'd say ask the judge. He'd know if anybody did. It was not a sheriff's office horse. It was his, wasn't it, Otha?" Pope asked.

"Yep. He rode in on Jeb. Jeb's a good horse who deserves a kinder owner. I'm betting the judge will say 'just take him.'"

"Alright. I will see you fine gents in a couple days. I should be getting a telegram from Pinkerton's by way of Sarah. Read it and see how it plays into the investigation."

"Adios!" Pope doffed his Stetson and headed out the door. He slipped his Winchester into its saddle scabbard, mounted Caesar and rode off.

Four hours later, he rode into the village at the south end of Lake Tahoe. He stopped and spoke with the owner of the small general merchandise, rode through town and looked at Bertie's door. No bandanna was tied on the door handle to signify a customer was being entertained. He dismounted and tapped on it.

She came to the door smiling and fresh as a daisy.

"Miss Bertie, I came by here and spoke with you a couple of years ago on a case," Pope began.

"I remember you. The Wells Fargo man. Your badge says something different now and it's not hidden."

"Yes Ma'am. I'm your sheriff temporarily and I'm looking for some more help."

"Coffee?" she asked.

"Always," he said.

They sat on the porch and sipped.

"First off, some years ago, a tall man who looked just like me except with white hair and white handlebar came through bounty hunting. He gave you two bits for some information. It later panned out for him. When I told him I was coming here, he said to give you this. He said he underpaid, so here's the money with interest."

He gave her the twenty dollar gold piece.

"Pope? I remember him! An older you! Your father?"

"May as well be. He raised me from ten years old on. But, he's actually my grandfather. Before he was a bounty hunter, he was a mountain man. One of the last. The man who killed two bears with a knife."

"Not at the same time, I hope."

"No, Ma'am. Different times and different bears."

"I certainly see the resemblance. You are going to be one handsome old man, Sheriff."

"I'd settle for just making it to 'old.' Doesn't always happen in my business."

"Thank him. He's a charming man. The apple sure hasn't rolled far from the tree. So you left Wells Fargo?"

"I did. My wife was a detective too. We got a raw deal from one man. It's a great company overall, but we were tired of traipsing around the country anyway. So, I took a sheriff job in Marin County and she does detective work for Harry Morse in San Francisco."

"The man who caught Black Bart?" she asked.

"She actually found the clue leading to his identification. She was there for the arrest."

"Women may get ahead yet, but it's a long road I fear."

"I fear too. But with people like her leading the way, it's going to happen. Wyoming has had women voting for years and even has a female justice of the peace. I swore in a young woman deputy in Marin, but she's now a Morse detective."

"You keep saying Marin, yet you said you were my sheriff. I don't understand."

"I'm both. The governor asked me to investigate the murder of Sheriff Littleton and serve as sheriff in both counties until I did."

"Littleton is dead? I hadn't heard."

"He was shot at the edge of this lake several days ago. Shotgunned. Probably by someone who he knew or at least didn't fear."

"It wasn't me. Though I had every right to kill the bastard," Bertie said.

"Why, Miss Bertie?"

"He came by here every few weeks. Beat the hell out of me during his visits. I could always count on bruises and a black eye or two. Great for subsequent business," she said bitterly.

"He never paid me a cent for services rendered or beatings taken. He was a piece of garbage."

"So, I am beginning to find out. Did he ever identify himself by another name?" Pope asked.

"No. The only name he cried out once in the middle of things was 'Marie,' but I never found out who Marie is. Or, was."

"You have just given me a very valuable clue, Miss Bertie. I have to get going and meet with the sheriff over in Reno. Please take this for your time," he said handing her ten dollars.

"You don't have to give me anything."

"Well, I want to, so please take it. Be careful and be safe. Do you have a gun?" he asked.

"No, I don't. Probably should."

He took a .38 revolver he brought from the office's confiscated guns and handed it to her.

"It's loaded with fresh cartridges. All you have to

do is pull the trigger. No cocking necessary. Point and press the trigger until you don't have to anymore."

She shed a solitary tear and mumbled something in appreciation. Pope smiled at her and touched her on the arm. He got up and mounted Caesar and rode off. What a nice human being going to waste, he thought once again.

******

It was dusk by the time Pope got to Reno. He found a hotel and checked in after leaving Caesar with a stable to be brushed, fed, watered.

The next morning, he met with the county sheriff.

"What can you tell me about the ACME Mining Company robbery here in 1879?" he asked.

"First off, sheriff, why?" his contemporary asked.

"I am investigating the murder of the sheriff of Placer County, California at the request of the governor. I found a bill wrapper possibly taken from the robbery. It seems to be related to the murder case, but I am just gathering clues right now."

"A lot more detective work than most sheriff's do," Sheriff Blake observed.

"I was a Wells Fargo detective for some years. It's in my blood, I guess. I have a strong chief deputy running things in my absence and have been given pretty free rein by the governor and local judge to track this thing down wherever it takes me."

"Alright. I was sheriff then and investigated the robbery. Four men entered the mining company office. All were masked. The apparent leader was a tall man the one living witness said. He was lean, about six feet one, and maybe late forties. He was the shooter. Killed the mining company manager and wounded the accountant who was our witness.

They ransacked the safe and got away with five thousand eight hundred all in wrapped twenty dollar bills stacks. No coins. No gold. What they got was the payroll for the next day.

I always figured it was an inside job. They knew when and where to get the most money."

"Is the accountant still around?" Pope asked.

"No, he got terrified and skedaddled back east somewhere. I don't know where. He was not a very good witness."

"Can you tell me about the guns they used and the horses and direction of escape?"

"They had good horses. Which told me they were probably cowboys. The leader supposedly had a big horse. One of the men on the street when they came running out saw them and said he liked the tall man's horse."

Pope described Jeb to him.

"Yes, sounds about right. No conclusive by any stretch, but certainly close to the description I got.

You asked about the guns. I called them by designations one through four. One was the leader. He had a Colt's revolver. Standard single action. Two had a sawed-off shotgun. Three and Four carried rifles and had revolvers holstered. The rifles were described as 'Winchesters,' but could have been Marlins or whatever. I don't put much store by the blathering of witnesses." Pope nodded. He was interested, though in the description of the leader's horse."

"Sheriff, do you know if they had bedrolls, canteens and lariats on their saddles?"

"I don't know, Sheriff Pope. Not a clue."

"Did anyone call another by a name in the commission of the robbery?" Pope asked.

"Not as I know. And, the only witness is now who knows where."

"Did a posse assemble and chase them?"

"Kinda. By the time I got enough men together with guns having a possibility of actually going 'bang', the robbers were way ahead. We rode hard but we did not see hide nor hair of them."

"How about the bullet which killed the owner. Whatever happened to it?" Pope asked, thinking about comparing it with Littleton's gun.

"I don't know. It may have been taken out by the doc, been a pass through from such close range, or been buried with him."

"Is the doctor around so I can find out about it?"

Pope asked.

"He's buried not far from where the mine owner is. Died last year. He won't be a good source," the sheriff said with a slight smile.

What happened with the company?" Pope asked.

"The company went bankrupt due to the robbery and miners walking off the job. It was bought by a speculator and is making a pretty penny now."

"Could the speculator have engineered the robbery just to take over the company on the cheap?" Pope asked.

Blake grinned at him.

"If he did and I find out, I will personally shoot him."

"Why would you shoot him?"

"Because the idiot is my brother-in-law!"

It was Pope's turn to grin.

"If he bought right and is making a lot of money, he doesn't sound too much of an idiot."

"Even a blind squirrel finds an acorn sometimes, Sheriff. And, my brother-in-law is one blind ass squirrel."

"I see. Well, let's mark him off the suspect list. Did you have any gut feelings who may have been behind this robbery. Former employees of the company, for example."

"I always reckoned they were cowboys in town for a drink and heard something about getting paid tomorrow. Some drunk miner probably said something."

"Makes perfect sense. Especially with good horseflesh. Not generally indicative of miners, I'd think," Pope said, and the other sheriff signaled his agreement.

"Sheriff Blake, were there any other armed robberies by a gang in the general period of the ACME one?" Pope asked.

"Not here. I seem to remember a bank robbery over in Pershing County. There was a new little bank in the county seat. Lovelock. The robbery put it out of business. Was just before the one at ACME."

"Who's the sheriff over there?" Pope asked.

"Bill Dawson. Been the sheriff there for years. He did not have the staff or makings for a decent posse to chase down the robbers. I think the US Marshal put out a wanted poster, but nothing came of it. I don't remember any details," the sheriff said as Pope took copious notes before slipping a photograph out of his notebook.

It was the photograph of the O'Brien family.

"Do any of these people look familiar, Sheriff?" he asked.

Blake studied the photo. He took longer than one would if he was dismissive.

"Maybe. I cannot name the woman and the girl to save my life. The man is not familiar, though he fits the general physical description of the lead ACME robber.

"Can we talk one hundred percent off the record?" Pope asked.

"Yes. Of course. I'd like to see a solution to this robbery. Finally!"

"It is beginning to look like to me your head robber was a man named O'Brien. You are looking at him and his family maybe seven years before the robbery. He was a crooked San Francisco policeman. He was fired. SFPD does not know where he went, or whether his French wife and their daughter went with him, back to France or where."

"French, you say?" Blake asked. "French rings a bell. Hey, King. Get in here!"

The deputy who had showed Pope in came in the door on a run.

"What's up, Sheriff?"

"Look at this picture from—when Pope?"

"Fourteen years ago."

"Do you recognize this woman? Think French accent," Blake said.

Deputy King, a man in his fifties, thought hard. His face was almost comically screwed up as he deliberated.

"Got it! She was the cleaning lady at the mining company which was robbed five years ago. ACME!"

"Did she leave just after the robbery?" Pope asked.

"Not immediately. Maybe six months. She and her daughter up and went to…let me think. Oakland!

They moved to Oakland because she got a job there."

"Did she have a husband," Pope asked.

"Not while she was here in Reno. She might have had one earlier. I mean she had the daughter and all. Though I guess having a child does not mean she ever had a husband. I remember her as a hard-working woman. Cleaned the mining company spic and span. They lived in a little shacky house over in the outskirts of town."

"Deputy King, do you remember her name?" Pope asked.

"Not her real name. Everybody just called her Frenchy."

Pope and Blake looked at each other.

"So, you think the lead robber was this man, O'Brien. He got the inside information from his French wife who worked at the mining company?"

"Yes. Now, the wife was supposedly beaten regularly, so she may not have been part of the scheme. In fact, they may have already been separated since Deputy King does not remember a man about the house. Would you mind if he went to the neighborhood with me and we talked to some long term residents—if any—and tried to get some more information?"

"All three of us will go. King get our horses ready. We'll be right out."

The deputy left.

"I think you are holding back something important, Sheriff," Blake said.

Pope nodded.

"I cannot prove it yet, but I believe O'Brien, the abusive husband of Frenchy, is the man who became Sheriff Littleton of Placer County and who was murdered close up by a sawed-off shotgun this week."

"Damn!" was all Blake could say. Pope felt the same.

They rode over to the neighborhood where the woman called Frenchy and her daughter had lived.

"Old Mrs. Perrin has lived here since before the cows came home. Everybody else has wandered in in the past few years. I patrolled this area before I took on the office deputy job," King offered.

They went to the Perrin residence and found a woman well into her eighties.

"Howdy, Mr. King. Who's these gentlemen you got with you?"

"Mrs. Perrin, this is Sheriff Blake, my boss, and Sheriff Pope from over to Placer County in California. We need to pick your brain about the lady called Frenchy who lived here a while back with her young daughter."

"I remember her well, gents though I haven't got a clue what I had for dinner last night. It's how it gets when you get some years on.

Frenchy was a nice looking and decent woman. Worked hard and raised her little girl right. Had a mean looking man who'd come by every few months and spend the night. I'd hear yelling and fighting. He would leave the next morning. She'd be trying to hide bruises and all. Pretty clear he worked her over every visit. She should have shot him."

"Mrs. Perrin, is this Frenchy, the girl and the man who visited?" Pope asked, handing her the O'Brien photograph.

She fumbled around in her purse and extracted a pair of ancient reading glasses and put them on. Examining the photograph, she finally said "yes."

"Do you remember Frenchy's given name and her last name?"

"Nossir. I sure don't. I just know some years ago they up and moved to somewhere near San Francisco."

"Mrs. Perrin, was it Oakland?" King prompted.

"I believe it might have been," she said.

"Did any other men show up at the house with the man who beat her?"

"I remember he had three fellas meet him one morning as he was leaving. It was towards the end of the time Frenchy and the girl was there. They rode off together. Them horses had gear on them, like they was going on a long ride," she said.

Pope put his notebook away and the men thanked the elderly lady.

"You have helped us a lot and we really appreciate it, Ma'am," Pope said as they got up to leave.

"This story is filling out nicely. I will ride over

to Lovelock and dig around. Then, I will check the census for near 1879 for Oakland and see if I can find Frenchy and her daughter," Pope said.

"Thank you both for your help. Sheriff, I will let you know what I find out, particularly if I learn any more about the ACME robbery," Pope said as they shook hands and he rode northeast heading to Lovelock between the Trinity and North Humboldt Ranges.

As he rode further north toward the mountains, it got windier and colder. He turned his collar up.

"Caesar, this is like what we used to do. Nice getting on the trail again and sleeping out, huh boy?" The horse whinnied and shook his head.

The road was a clear one, but there was virtually nothing along it. Pope searched for and found a decent place off the road to camp in a group of trees.

He unsaddled Caesar and led him to a stream to drink. He then took a bag of feed out and gave it to him to supplement the grass underfoot.

Pope boiled some of the stream water in his coffee pot with a handful of coffee beans in the bottom. He took out some biscuits and some ham he picked up in Reno and had a trail dinner. With Caesar free, but knowing he would not wander off, Pope stoked the Montana fire pit and pulled his blanket up and rolled up in his tarp. Soon, he was asleep, lulled by the wind in the trees and the smell of the dwindling fire.

Pope rode into Lovelock by midday. He went

straight for the sheriff's office and found the Pershing County sheriff leaned back with his boots on his desk. He was an older man, with a sweeping mustache. He wore a Slim Jim holster with what looked like a S&W Schofield from the exposed black rubber butt.

"Sheriff Dawson? Sheriff Blake over at Reno said you might be able to help me."

"Oh? How might I help?"

"I am Sheriff John Pope from Placer County, California. I'm investigating a murder. The clues have led me to a robbery you had at your bank here about five years ago."

"Yep. Never caught those four. I talked to Blake. We both wonder if they were the ones who robbed his mining company. By causing our new bank to go under, they did a lot of harm to this community, Pope."

"What can you tell me about the robbery, the men, their mounts and weapons? And, the take?" Pope asked.

"The lead man was mean. He shot the cashier for the pure hell of it. There was no need, the man was gathering cash as fast as he could."

"What did he look like?"

"He wore a mask. I talked to several people inside and outside the bank separately. All told me he was tall and lean. They guessed he was around late forties in age. He had a rifle on his horse, a handsome chestnut or a dun. I disremember which. Two other robbers carried rifles. Not short carbines, full length rifles. The last man carried a scattergun with the barrel and butt stock cut off real short. He swung it around and terrified everybody."

"Did the leader look anything like this man? I know you didn't see his face."

"I didn't see him period. But he looks like the descriptions I was given after the fact."

"The man he shot," Pope began, "where did he get hit?"

"He caught a .45 in the right shoulder."

"Where is the bullet?" Pope asked.

"The doc dug it out and gave it to him. He was the cashier, Joe Ford."

"Do you know where Mr. Ford is today?"

"He's right down the street cashiering the new bank."

Pope smiled. If he could get the bullet and compare it to Littleton's revolver, he would have tied him to one robbery.

"Sheriff, as a Wells Fargo detective, I learned how to take a bullet and associate it with a particular gun. We always won in court, it's so positive. I need the bullet badly."

"Walk on down and ask Ford for it. I'm sure he kept it."

"Before I go, I understand the Marshal printed some wanted posters for the four robbers. Do you still have one?"

"Hell, I got about twenty-five. Give me a second and I'll give you some."

A few minutes later, he had drawings of all four robbers. There was four hundred dollar reward for information leading to the capture, death or solution of one or more of the robbers. It did not have an expiration date. Pope had another idea and kept it to himself as he folded several copies and put them in his jacket pocket.

"Sheriff, these men were equipped like cowboys. Do you think they came from a ranch in the area?"

"I was and still am pretty certain they came from the Bar D, about five miles north of town. The owner, Jacob Douglas, refused to talk to me. Which made me all the more convinced. He's a hard man. I have a strong feeling he used a running iron on many of his cattle," the sheriff said, indicating Douglas was a rustler.

"I'll give it my best," Pope said, leaving with the posters folded in his notebook.

He rode to the Bar D from the sheriff's directions.

There was nobody at the house, so he rode around until he saw five men branding some cattle. He rode over.

"Howdy, I'm looking to talk with Jacob Douglas. One of you folks Mr. Douglas?"

A large and mean looking man in his mid-fifties

rode over.

"I'm Douglas. Who in hell are you?"

"I'm John Pope, Sheriff of Placer County, California. I am investigating a murder and think you can help."

"First thing is I don't help no lawdogs. Second is you ain't got no jurisdiction. This is Nevada, boy."

"First thing is it may save your ass for helping me. I am watching you change brands with a running iron. I could arrest you right now. Second thing is I am a Deputy US Marshal, so I have all the jurisdiction I need to put nippers on you."

"And, you are going to try to put nippers on me when you are outnumbered five to one?"

"I am. I'll probably have to kill you first and a couple of your men if anybody tries anything," Pope said as he slipped off and away from Caesar.

From the corner of his eye he saw movement. In the split second it took him to spin around, his Colt was already out and cocked. He saw two cowboys, more likely rustlers, pulling leather.

Pope killed them both and turned to Douglas, who was groping for a gun he carried hidden below his vest.

"Die now or die of old age. Makes no never mind to me" Pope said as he levelled the gun on Douglas' chest and watched the other two men trying to figure out what to do over Douglas's shoulder.

Douglas dropped his gun and so did the two behind him.

"This was your stupid call, Douglas. It didn't have to go this way," Pope told him in a low growl.

"Now, turn around!" Pope snapped the handcuffs on Douglas behind his back.

"You two put your dead compadres over their saddles and tie them on tight enough for a five-mile ride back to Lovelock. Do it now!" he ordered.

Pope rode behind the men, holding them at rifle point into the county seat. Riding down the middle of the road attracted enough attention to draw the sheriff out to see what was going on.

"Sheriff, I went out to talk with Mr. Douglas here. I caught these five using a running iron to change the brands on some cattle. The two idiots over their horses tried to draw on me, so they were clean shoots. The two others were thinking about it, but a wave of smart swept over them. Douglas refused to talk, but I bet he will talk with me in the cell."

A deputy joined them and walked the two into a cell. The sheriff sent for an undertaker to the two bodies.

"All of their guns are at the ranch where they dropped them by the fire used to heat the running iron."

"Deputy, go out there and pick up the guns and record the evidence of brand changing by running iron," Sheriff Dawson ordered. The deputy was on his horse and heading out of town immediately.

"Sheriff Pope, let's have a chat with these fine citizens. I have an idea and want to talk with the prosecutor before I get involved." The sheriff walked off towards the courthouse and Pope escorted the three men into the sheriff's office. He put two in one cell and Douglas in one the farthest away from his two employees. If he was going to give directions on what to say, Pope wanted him to yell so he could hear it.

Sheriff Dawson returned shortly and motioned Pope into his office and shut the door.

"I worked out a deal with the prosecutor. If Douglas talks and gives us enough to figure out who robbed the bank and everything else, he and his two cronies can walk away from the branding charges. They will have to return all cattle to the rightful owners following a newspaper article and be escorted by a deputy and me. I am only two months away from my reelection vote. This should help it, both solving the bank robbery and showing Douglas for the rustler he is. Voters like to get their stolen cattle returned, son. You need to keep such things at the front door to your brain."

"You cut a good deal. I will accept and follow your advice. I got too big a dose of federal politics a year ago being assigned with my wife to identify a group intending to assassinate the President."

"Was it you? I read the Justice Department borrowed two Wells Fargo detectives. I figured it was because the federals did not know who to trust on their own team."

"Pretty much," Pope said.

"Did the assassins get tried?" Dawson asked.

"No, but justice was served."

"By your long-barreled Colt?" Pope nodded.

"Justice is mine, sayeth Colonel Colt," Dawson intentionally misquoted then crossed himself just in case the Lord took exception to it.

"Let's go talk to the formerly untalkative Mr. Douglas," Dawson said. "Speak up as you see fit."

They unlocked the end cell and walked Douglas to the sheriff's personal office and closed the door.

"Did the bank robbers work at your ranch?" Dawson asked.

"Go to hell," Douglas responded. Pope stood up and elbowed him across the face, dumping him off the chair and onto the floor.

"You show the Sheriff the courtesy he's due or this will be the worst half hour of your pathetic life," Pope said.

"Did the bank robbers work at your ranch?" the sheriff repeated.

Douglas glared at him and Pope stood up again balling up a fist he hated to use.

"Yeah. They did. I didn't have anything to do with the robbery. But they was my boys."

"Who is this man?" Pope asked sliding the O'Brien family photograph across the table.

"O'Brien and his family."

"Was he the leader of the gang?" Pope asked.

"Yes. When I heard what they were planning I fired the lot of them. I kept it to myself to stay out of trouble."

"Give us the names of the other three," Dawson said.

"Tom Holt, Ron Lock, and Wesley Rait."

"Do you know if they did the ACME robbery in Reno?"

"Not for sure. But I think so. I think they had several robberies planned. The descriptions in the paper sounded like the four of them."

"Where did they all go?"

"No idea. I never saw any of them again after they left the ranch."

"Including O'Brien?" Pope asked to make sure.

"Including O'Brien."

"One last question, Mr. Douglas. Did any other cowboys leave soon after O'Brien?"

"Not from my ranch. He had a couple others he drank with in town. They moved on about the same time as him," Douglas said.

"Any names?" Pope asked. Douglas shrugged and shook his head.

Pope and the sheriff looked at each other. They got up and took Douglas back to his cell.

The sheriff went over to the prosecutor and spoke.

His deputy had come back and confirmed the brand changing operation. The prosecutor and sheriff went to the judge's chambers while Pope interviewed each of the other two separately.

He was sure they robbed the bank. Pope just needed more compelling proof than Douglas' speculation. He was also relatively sure from separate surprised looks, neither had anything to do with the ACME robbery. Pope reckoned O'Brien picked up some new people for it.

Dawson came back and he, a deputy and Pope took the three surviving members back to the courthouse. They appeared before the judge in a hastily planned session.

The prosecutor presented evidence. The defendants were not offered counsel. They were about to get a deal they could not turn down.

The judge stared at them a long time. Long enough to make even these hardened cowboy squirm.

"Alright gentlemen. You have heard the evidence against you. It is compelling. I'm going to give you a choice because your boss, Mr. Douglas, has cooperated on a very important case unrelated to your spurious escapades with a running iron.

Here it is: we can charge all three of you with rustling and go forward with a court trial. Or, you can accept a deal. The deal is, no charges will be brought against any of you. However, you will have to physically return every head of cattle, even with the modified brands, to the original owner. The sheriff and some number of deputies will accompany you to each ranch and assure this compact is fulfilled.

If the three of you wish to meet in the corner to discuss your two options, go ahead and take a few minutes," the judge ended.

The three men met and spoke in low voices. Douglas said doing this would keep them out of prison. It would also brand them as rustlers throughout this part of Nevada. He would have to sell his ranch and all of them would be well-advised to relocate immediately upon finishing the return of the livestock. Lock noted they stood every chance of being lynched by stockmen from whom they had stolen cattle. Douglas agreed but said he thought the possibility of maybe being lynched was not as bad as definitely being sentenced to a long stint in prison.

They concurred and accepted the deal.

******

"Thanks to you, Sheriff Pope, my bank robbery has been solved after five years. We know from your subsequent questioning O'Brien took a larger share and disappeared. We know our surviving two and the two you killed have long since spent their money."

"My big disappointment is they did not admit to the ACME robbery. I don't believe they did it. I also suspect a gang member, probably from the ACME gang, killed O'Brien in his new life as sheriff. It was probably done in an effort to get the larger share of the money. I am concerned one of these men was identified with a sawed-off shotgun with both barrel and butt stock shortened. Not a usual weapon for a bank robber in the Western United States. Neither man admitted to using one when I questioned them.

I am going to go to the bank cashier now and try to get ahold of the bullet we think O'Brien fired into him. I can prove O'Brien shot him by comparing the rifling marks on the lead with a bullet fired into several feet of water with O'Brien's gun and recovered.

The bullet will solve the murder at ACME. The murderer is dead, but at least we know who it was. And, it will prove O'Brien and Littleton were one and the same person. Thanks for your help. I will let you know how this all ends," Pope said as he left.

Pope walked across the street to the new bank with the former bank's cashier, Joe Ford.

He entered and saw the cashier behind the brass bars protecting the bank from the rest of the world on the door side of the bars.

"Mr. Ford? I am Sheriff John Pope from Placer County, California. I know who shot you five years ago, but I need your help proving it."

Thirty minutes and a longer explanation later, Pope walked out of the bank with a two hundred fifty-five grain .45 Colt bullet in his vest pocket. He promised to return the man's cherished souvenir of the robbery.

He camped again on the way back to Auburn and arrived there late the next day.

Pope brought Israel and Otha up on the case. They set the forensic tests for the next morning.

As in the past, Pope used a long watering trough to catch the bullet. The last time and this time, his grandfather had the honor of firing.

They announced a forensic test to the folks in town and Israel fired Littleton's .45 Colt at one end of the livery water trough. He aimed so the bullet would go virtually the full length of the trough under water. Pope rolled up his sleeves and retrieved the fired bullet from the bottom of the trough on the other end.

They took it to the wooden sidewalk in front of the sheriff's office. A crowd gathered around to see something new in the way of police procedure. Pope went in and reappeared with a powerful magnifying glass from his investigative kit and a sheet of white letter paper. Taking his pencil from a vest pocket, he drew two several inch diameter circles five inches apart. He labelled one "Littleton's gun, just shot." The other was "bullet used in Lovelock robbery." He put the bullet from the watering trough in the first one and the one removed from the bank cashier in the other, explaining its origin to the crowd, which included the judge and the prosecutor. Normally, it would have been a silent process, but he was playing to a crowd.

He carefully examined the striations on each bullet then put them side by side and turned them over in unison as Israel held the glass.

He looked up and made his announcement.

"The bullets were definitely fired by the same gun. The bank robber five years ago in Lovelock, Nevada has been positively identified as a man named O'Brien. O'Brien was also identified from this photograph," which he handed to the judge to look at as others looked over his shoulder. "The description of the man whose real name was O'Brien is the same as the description of Sheriff Littleton whose gun we just shot the bullet from. It is logical to conclude O'Brien the robber and Littleton the sheriff were the same man."

A murmur ran through the crowd. The judge asked "Did Littleton do the ACME robbery where the mine owner was killed?"

"Yes, Judge. He did. I have evidence but am continuing to get more to prove it conclusively, while I search for his murderer," Pope said.

"Does it matter, now he's dead?" someone in the crowd yelled.

The judge answered.

"Only if it contributes to identifying his own murderer, likely a member of his ACME robbery gang," the judge said.

"Would the bullets stand up in court Judge?" The judge looked to Pope.

"When I was a detective for Wells Fargo, we used this method to convict a number of people and, yes, it stood up in court every single time."

"What would it take to conclusively prove Littleton killed the mine owner?" the judge asked Pope.

"I guess digging the body up and taking the bullet out. It was never recovered and put into case evidence. It could have been a pass-through too. Exhumation might prove it, but what are we going to do with the proof? Do we want to try him and convict him posthumously?"

The judge thought for a minute and said, "No, it would be a waste of the court's time. Good work here, Pope."

After the audience had dissipated, he added "And, I approve of your selection for chief deputy. Israel Pope should stay on in Placer County. I believe I could get the Governor to appoint him sheriff."

"Thank you, Judge," Israel said. "But I have a nice place in the woods in Marin County and a pretty, younger wife now. We can smell the ocean air most days. And, my neighbor is my boy, here. I finally have a life on my own two feet instead of a horse's back all day long. I'd make Otha the sheriff and find some energetic young sprout to do the riding and shooting. He runs the office as it is."

Otha turned a bit red, and the judge had a thoughtful look on his face as he turned back towards the courthouse and the three lawmen went back into the office.

True to his word, Pope sent Ford a telegram saying he was shot by a Bar D cowboy named O'Brien and his bullet proved it conclusively. Pope told him his bullet was being returned by post.

"You know, Sonny, the bullet does not conclusively prove O'Brien shot the banker. It proves the gun he was carrying when he was sheriff was used to shoot the man. O'Brien could have bought, won, or stolen the gun afterwards," Israel said.

"True, Grandpa. We are dealing generalities and probabilities here. It really does not matter since O'Brien, also known as Littleton, is dead. But, it fits in nicely without hurting anybody. And, it gives some closure to the banker who would have wondered the rest of his life who shot him," Pope said.

"All true. Littleton being dead makes it a moot point," Israel replied.

"Chief, do you really think I'd make a good sheriff?" Otha asked.

"Absolutely. You proved your metal at Chickamauga. You have run this office for years. Hire a young rabbit with his tail on fire to be the riding and shooting chief deputy and you would have it made," Israel said with Pope nodding agreement.

"What's next, Sonny Boy?"

"I sent a telegram to Sarah to ask her to see if Pinkerton's had any record on the ACME robbery or on O'Brien. I have not heard yet. Now I know his wife and daughter may have moved to Oakland after Lovelock, I need to check with Harry Morse's census file for a later date and see if I can locate them. I might see if Sarah wants to meet me at Harry's office in San Francisco and help. She got real good at looking up files at the Congressional Library last year."

"You just miss her, admit it. And, missing her is a good thing."

"I do, Grandpa. This is the longest we've been apart almost since we met."

He sent a telegram to Sarah with his idea. She responded back she needed to meet with Harry Morse anyway and could meet him at Harry's office tomorrow afternoon and spend the night in San Francisco with him.

Pope automatically cleaned the corrosive black powder residue from Littleton's Colt and looked at it closely. It was a gunfighter's gun. It had the shorter four and three quarter inch barrel. The front sight had been removed for a faster draw. It was clear its owner was not interested in shooting distance beyond which he could smell the breath of his targets. The grips were black hard rubber and two notches were carved in the right grip. The gun was kept in good shape. The only thing wrong with its appearance was a large amount of expected holster wear on the blued cylinder and barrel and on the case hardened frame. On a whim, he took it to the local photographer and had a picture made of it. He picked up the photograph before lunch.

Having farther to go, Pope rode to Sacramento and boarded Caesar. He bought a ticket on the late after-noon Sacramento River to Bay steamer. He arrived in San Francisco and found a hotel for two nights.

Once he settled into the hotel room for the night, he turned the gaslights up and took out his notebook and the wanted posters and photographs in it. He studied them closely and decided to send a telegram to the US Marshal for Nevada and ask if he was aware of any robberies in his district other than the Love-lock bank during the 1879 to 1873 period. He drafted it and would send it in the morning.

He turned in early, glad to sleep in a real bed after several nights camping on the trail.

The next morning, he requested a bath and after, got a shave and haircut. He sent the telegram to the Marshal in Carson City. He specified the hotel name in San Francisco if the response were to be made today, his office in Auburn if later.

He went to the Harry Morse Detective Agency office at the approximate time his wife was supposed to arrive. She came in shortly after. Morse was on an investigative trip out of town.

He and Sarah went to the file room and searched the Oakland census records for each year after 1879. They looked for both Marie O'Brien and Sophie O'Brien. Sophie, they opined, should have been old enough by the last census to rate her own listing if her mother had left the area and she had not.

After an hour, they found an address for the two in what appeared to be an apartment in Oakland. They immediately set off for it.

No one was there when they arrived late in the afternoon. It was a time when most people were at work, so they asked neighbors whether they had seen the man in the O'Brien family picture visiting the two women. None had.

From across the street, Pope and Sarah saw the two women arrive at their building at six o'clock. Sarah and Pope immediately went in and climbed the stairs to apartment 208 and knocked.

A very pretty young woman in a gray work dress answered. The Popes identified themselves and were invited in.

"Why on earth would an out-of-town sheriff and a detective want to see us?" Marie O'Brien asked, her French accent faded somewhat with the years of speaking English. They could tell she had been as lovely as her daughter, but hard work, probable abuse, and time had aged her prematurely.

"Do you know a man named Ashby Littleton? He was my predecessor as Sheriff of Placer County, California," Pope asked.

Neither woman blinked as Marie said "No," and her daughter shook her head.

"Mrs. O'Brien, when was the last time you saw your husband, Charles O'Brien," he said as he handed her the family photograph.

She gasped and said "Where did you get this?"

"Please answer and we will explain after," Sarah said.

"I guess it must have been four years ago. Sophie and I left him five years ago. I never divorced him. Too much expense. He found us here after we left Nevada.

Now, you tell me where you got our picture."

"It was in the possessions we found belonging to Sheriff Ashby Littleton," Pope said.

"Why would he have it?" Sophie asked, speaking for the first time.

"Would you describe your husband's and father's horse to us?" Pope asked.

"Why?"

"Please respond, it will help us explain a lot to you."

"He was big and brown."

"What was his name?"

"He was named after some rebel general."

"Jeb Stuart, perhaps?" Pope responded.

"Yes! Papa called him 'Jeb!' We never knew why a man who was born in County Kerry would care about Confederates, but he was almost obsessed with them," Sophie said.

Pope thought, "hence the new first name, Ashby, after Confederate Brigadier General Turner Ashby."

"The sheriff called his big, brown horse Jeb," Pope said.

"Do you remember anything about the revolver he carried?" Pope asked.

"Of course not!" Marie exclaimed. Pope looked at Sophie.

"I helped him change it," she said.

"How, Sophie?" Sarah asked softly.

"I held it when he sawed the sight off with a hacksaw."

Pope handed her the photo of Littleton's Colt.

"Yes! I believe this pistol is his."

"Ladies, I am afraid we have come to a conclusion here. And, it's bad news for you," Pope said. The two women looked at him expectantly.

"We believe Charles O'Brien was a bank and mining company robber who changed his name to Ashby Littleton and became Sheriff of Placer County. He was murdered a week ago on the California shore of Lake Tahoe."

Marie O'Brien let out a long breath. It sounded to Sarah and Pope more like relief than sorrow.

"Are there any suspects?" Sophie asked.

"We believe a gang member from one of the robberies probably killed him. A very particular and odd sawed-off shotgun was used."

"How do you know? Did the murderer drop it?" Marie asked, still not showing sorrow.

"No. I recovered it from Lake Tahoe," Pope said.

"Mrs. O'Brien, you are not reacting like most women who just found out their husband, even former husband, has been murdered," Sarah said.

"Charles O'Brien was a cruel, hateful man. He deserved whatever he got for the abuse my Sophie and I suffered at his hand. I thought we had escaped him, but he showed up here a year later. He spent the night, had his way with me and, as usual, beat both of us. He left afterwards with a friend and we have not seen him since. He is a piece of garbage and the world is better off with him dead," the former wife said with emotion. Then, she asked "Did he leave any money behind?"

"Only some old clothes, the gun and Jeb the horse. If you want, I will give you twenty-five dollars for Jeb right now for a bill of sale." The woman nodded. They consummated the deal with the exchange of cash and a bill of sale before the Popes left.

"Towards the end, when you left him, did he

have any friends come around? Names would be most helpful to us."

"He had a pard. His name was Willie Smith. He was the one who came by the next morning and Charlie left with," Marie said.

"What was he like?" Sarah asked.

"Tall and real skinny. Red hair and mustache. Nervous acting," Marie said.

"He wore his gun on the left and real low, like a gunfighter," Sophie added.

"Do you know what happened to him?" Sarah asked the two women.

"He liked the area around Lake Tahoe. I think he had a cabin on the Nevada side," Marie said. Sophie nodded.

"Have you ever heard Willie Smith use any other name?" Pope asked.

"Not really."

"He was creepy. I was always nervous the way he leered at me and stayed too close. Even when I was a little girl," Sophie added. "I hope he's dead too."

"I will look for him. Right now, he'd be the number one suspect in the murder of your husband and father," Pope said.

"Why worry about him? Charlie or Willie? Neither one is worth the effort," Marie said.

"Good or bad—and I suspect bad—O'Brien, with his new name, was Sheriff of Placer County. We cannot let his murderer get off free just because nobody liked him. Justice should serve everybody, not just nice people. It's the way our system is supposed to work. I have no qualms in quick justice. Two of O'Brien's bank robbery gang tried to pull leather on me and both died right then and there. Willie Smith will, too, if he gets stupid."

"John, unless you have anything else, we should get out of their hair and let these ladies fix their dinner."

"No, I'm done for now. Give me one of your Morse cards please." He took her card and wrote his name and contact information for both counties on the back and gave it to Marie O'Brien.

They left and walked to a busier location and hailed a hansom cab to take them back to the hotel. Both were quiet, lost in their thoughts. Both felt they had learned a fair amount of information from interviewing the late outlaw's family. Meeting the mother and daughter gave a more personal look at the case and at the former sheriff. It also gave Pope another area to search for the murderer.

"You didn't ask Marie whether she gave her husband inside information about the mining company," Sarah asked.

"I know. If we pursue the potential accessory angle, the poor woman will probably go to prison. Don't you think she has suffered enough?" Pope asked.

"I love you," she said.

They had dinner at a little fancier restaurant than they would usually select. After all, they had been apart for a while. They returned to the hotel and bed.

Pope stared at the ceiling of the hotel room contentedly. He could smell the faint but sweet aroma of the long, black hair splayed across his chest as Sarah slept, head on his shoulder. He had missed this. A lot. Neither was perfect. But they were near perfect together. No male partner could have his back more proficiently than the woman lying beside him. They had only slept for a few hours before rising at six in the morning.

A quick breakfast, then a hansom cab to the docks, Sarah for the ferry across to Marin County, and Pope for the steamer across to the Sacramento River and up to the state capitol. Caesar awaited him there for the ride to Auburn.

The case of the murder of the former sheriff was coming together. The case of the bank robbery was solved. An unexpected bonus. It he could find Willie Smith and either through ardent interrogation or tying the Darne shotgun to him, perhaps solve both the sheriff's murder and the ACME murder.

Pope would see what telegram awaited him from the US Marshal, then head back to the rim of Lake Tahoe and begin talking to people.

He arrived in Sacramento on the steamer and reclaimed his horse. It was mid-afternoon by the time he tied Caesar to the hitching rail at the sheriff's office.

Pope walked in and greeted Otha. He heard "Ah! The prodigal grandson returns!" from his office as the distinguished chief deputy emerged.

"A productive trip?" Israel asked.

"I believe so. Let's all get some coffee and gather around. I'll tell you what I found out and what I think about it. Then, you give me your read on it," Pope said.

After a concise and detailed rendition of what he had learned and what he made of it all, the two other lawmen sat quietly and sipped their coffee thinking.

"Before we opine, you have a telegram you need to look at from the US Marshal over in Nevada," Otha said.

He handed it to Pope who slowly read it aloud, as if savoring every word.

Pope set it on the desk they were sitting around in his office.

"So," he began. "There were two unsolved robberies. One was a hundred miles north of Reno, the other the same distance east. Both were in 1880. Which is why nobody thought to share them with me. Too far away in their thinking. A grand total of two thousand dollars, mixed between paper, coin and gold dust was taken and never recovered. One mining company delivery. One mining company headquarters. Nobody shot. Vague descriptions. No surprise there. But, the driver of the delivery wagon said the leader was a tall, wiry man on a handsome, big brown horse.

And the treasurer in the mining company on the second one said one man had red hair. Willie Smith has red hair. The other intriguing comment is the gang did not ride off together. Two went one way and two went another.

Perhaps O'Brien and Smith made off with the treasure and the other two either met them at an agreed upon location later or got swindled out of their take?" Pope thought aloud.

"The Marshal's and the Reno sheriff's thinking about distances was pretty small-minded it seems to me," Israel offered. "Jesse, Frank and the Younger brothers rode from Missouri all the way to Northfield, Minnesota eight years ago to rob a bank. They were shot to pieces by townspeople. They may have seriously underestimated what hard working gun owning people would do to protect their town and their money, but they rode a lot more than a hundred miles to learn it. More like four or five hundred miles," Israel said.

"Probably why I was not told. Well, the descriptions are just more pieces to the puzzle. A description somewhat fitting O'Brien and one fitting Smith. Not conclusive, but the clues are building up," Pope said.

"It's sure looking like, being the snake he was, Littleton or O'Brien more properly, held back on some of the cache of money from four robberies and one of the robbers, likely Smith, killed him for it," Otha said.

"My thoughts exactly, Otha. Now to prove them. I'll have to find Smith and have a little chat with him."

"What is your schedule, John?" Otha asked.

"Well, if Willie Smith has been living somewhere on the rim of Lake Tahoe for four years, he's probably unlikely to move away in the next day or two. Today, I will meet with the judge and fill in what I've learned so far. He may have some guidance which will help me decide my next actions," Pope said.

He went to the office phone and cranked the lever. The operator came on and he asked for the courthouse.

The call came in o the clerk's office and Pope was told to hold for a minute. The man came back on and said the judge had a half hour beginning at eleven this morning. Pope said to tell the judge he would be there at eleven and hung up.

"I sure wish we could do this between here and San Rafael. And, Reno too."

"Probably will sooner than you think, Sonny Boy," the man who led pioneers West in covered wagons observed.

Pope was at the courthouse at eleven and ushered into the judge's chambers.

"Glad you came by, Pope. I know you've been on the trail and I've been wondering if you had any success."

"I think quite a bit. I will give you a full briefing and then prepare one for the governor," Pope said.

"No need to worry about the governor. We are friends and communicate one way or another almost daily. He and I went to West Point together and served together in the war twenty years ago. His roommate was Stonewall Jackson. Mine was a young fellow who got hit with a Confederate artillery ball in his first battle. Needless to say, it was also his last one."

"Sorry about your friend, Judge."

"Me, too. Now, what have you learned since we spoke almost a week ago?"

Pope gave him a detailed recounting of his travels and what he had learned. He ended with his conclusions about who Littleton had to have been and the forensic evidence strongly suggested he had participated in a mining company robbery in Nevada and had shot the treasurer with the gun known to be Littleton's and further identified by O'Brien's daughter as her father's.

"It would take some well-crafted testimony in a court case. But, we don't have a court case about Littleton's life before he changed his name and became the sheriff here. You have apprised the sheriff in Reno and the US Marshal in Nevada of your findings?"

"I have apprised them evidence points to Charles O'Brien being the leader of possibly two gangs which robbed one bank and three mining companies in 1879 and 1880. The sheriff over in Reno knows I suspect O'Brien and Littleton were the same person but does not have the additional evidence from his wife and daughter or the horse description confirming it. I have no reason to share the new information with him," Pope said.

"No, you don't. What's next?"

"I am going to do a bit of sheriff work here in Placer County, then ride over to Lake Tahoe for a few days. I think it's my best chance at finding Willie Smith, the red-headed outlaw who I think killed the sheriff."

"Think about whether the county would have any real benefit of tying the murder back to Littleton being O'Brien. Littleton could have run into a red-headed outlaw who killed him because he was sheriff. Who is served by the world knowing the dual identity?"

"Nobody, I guess, Judge."

"Good, I will apprise the governor where we stand on this and that you are doing an exceptional job investigating it. One, it's true. Two, it will help your reelection over in Marin County if the governor likes you and throws some campaign money your way."

Pope nodded, liking the idea.

"Now, a new topic for our last ten minutes before I have to meet with the clerk and the prosecutor. I have been thinking about your grandfather's wise suggestion about appointing Otha sheriff once you finish your work here and return to San Rafael.

The idea has merit. He's a proven war hero, liked and respected by everyone. He just cannot jump on a horse or do a walk down street shootout. Then, how many of those do we have in Auburn? The idea of getting a solid chief deputy and having him do the heavy lifting while Otha runs the operation is a good one.

I have spoken to the governor about this. He, of course has to appoint someone to serve out Littleton's term.

We would like you to come up with a new chief deputy and train him to be an alternate sheriff. If he does a good job, he would be the likely candidate when Otha decides to retire after a term or two.…. a lot less time than many have to wait.

It may add a little time on your stay here. Or, it may not. Before you say anything to Otha, I'd like to review this with him in front of you and your current chief deputy this afternoon at three. What do you think?"

"Judge, I think it would be a solid approach to take for policing Placer County. I will tell the other two we have a meeting at your request at three and we will be there," Pope said. He stood and they shook hands. Pope walked out of the door thinking having senior military officers as judges and governors beat all hell out of just lawyers with stars in their eyes and existing politicians.

"The judge has some ideas about the sheriff's office and I think they are real good ones. We have a command performance with him at three to talk about them."

"You seem to have had a preview, John," Otha prompted.

"I did, but he asked me to let him introduce them in his own way, Otha. So, my lips are sealed except to reiterate my agreement with his thinking."

Otha pretty much knew what he was going to hear. It would be about him being appointed to serve out Littleton's term. He had kept as low a profile as a man called hero could keep for the last twenty-one years. He knew he had let his disability get the best of him, though plowing ahead and doing his duty in this job.

Maybe it was time to officially do what he had been doing for years. Running the sheriff's office as the sheriff.

Otha had come to have a great deal of respect for the temporary young sheriff. Many in the West already had respect for his grandfather.

He would keep an open mind and see what the judge had to say.

They sat in the judge's chambers at three o'clock. Judge George Warren outlined his proposal as clearly and logically as he would prepping a jury for a murder trial.

Otha had already decided on his answer.

"Otha, what do you think of all of this? Would you accept the appointment?"

"Judge, you laid out a convincing scenario. This captain listened hard to the colonel. I will accept and give it my very best, once John finishes his responsibilities and is ready to go back to San Rafael."

"Excellent! While I know the badge will stand in the shadow of the Medal of Honor President Lincoln pinned on you, I will still be highly honored to give you the sheriff's oath and see your wife pin the sheriff's badge on your chest. You have truly earned both, Otha!" the judge said.

"Does the governor have to approve this?"

"He already has, upon Pope going back to Marin County.

Otha, do you have some ideas for an existing deputy to be your chief?"

"I do, Judge. Deputy Tom Bond who patrols the eastern section of the county. I think three things would more than prepare him. First is some instruction on tracking by Israel. Second is evidence, investigative, and shooting by Sheriff Pope. Last is some on the responsibilities of the office by me."

"Judge, while I have not had the chance to meet Bond face to face, I was impressed he had the ingenuity to rope off the murder scene. It made it easier for me to find and to work it," Pope said.

"Let's get this Deputy Bond in, clue him as to the

plan. See if he would transfer to work out of Auburn. Make sure he is amenable to a fair amount of preparation before he is promoted," the judge concluded, signaling the end of the meeting.

The three lawmen walked back to the sheriff's office

"Otha, I knew you were a hero, but I did not realize you won the Congressional Medal of Honor pinned on by Honest Abe," Israel commented on the walk back.

"I just did my duty, Israel. I was able to rally my men to Horseshoe Ridge and help hold the line against the Confederates. It cost a lot of men and cost me full use of my left leg. We were able to retire back to Chattanooga in the darkness. By that time, I was being evacuated in a wagon and worrying about going home with one leg. Thank God, they did not arbitrarily whack it off as they were so wont to do in those days.

President Lincoln said, despite it being the worst Union defeat in the Western Theater, holding the line allowed our army to regroup in Chattanooga and saved many Union lives."

"Can you ride, Otha?" Pope asked.

"It's chancy, John. If I use my hands to put my left leg in the stirrup and real quickly throw my right leg over, I can often mount up. But, just as often, my left leg gives away and I end up on my butt underneath the confused and scared horse. If I get mounted, I can stay on, but it isn't pretty for a man who grew up riding."

"How about a buggy?" Israel asked.

"You haven't seen it, because I live down the street and limp to work with my cane. But, I have a buggy with a modified entry on the right I can mount just fine. I could move it here and use it if sheriff's duties required me to go somewhere important. Haha, I could also politick from it!"

"How's your shooting, Otha?" Pope asked. "I know you were an army officer, so I reckon pretty good."

"It's probably fair enough for most sheriff incidents. Not in your class, John, but who is? In the war, I carried a big old Colt .44 Army. I also carried a .22 spur trigger Smith & Wesson. Kinda weak, but it was as accurate as hell. I learned to put my bullets in the eye. Always worked for me. I moved up to the .32 model you've seen me wear every day. While it is not a .44 or .45, it was what Wild Bill carried to the card game in Deadwood when he was murdered eight years ago. It sure was not the power of his gun which got him killed, it was sitting with his back to the crowd."

Pope took out his left hand gun, the Webley Bulldog and broke it open before handing it to Otha.

"Drop the cartridges on the desk and dry fire this one some. See if you like it," he said. "It's fairly powerful and far more accurate than you'd think. Take it outside of town and fire it some. I bet you end up liking it a lot."

Pope opened his desk drawer and handed Otha a box of Webley cartridges. He also took out one of his original shorter barrel Colt .44's and placed it in the left hand, inside the waistband holster where the Webley usually rode. The grip printed some through his coat. It was square instead of rounded like the "bird's head" grip on the Webley. But, he was the sheriff, why should he care?

"Otha, how do we contact Tom Bond? Is there a location out there where he checks for telegrams?" Pope asked.

"Not really. He rides in here weekly to do his reports, pick up wanted posters. And, comes in when he has an arrest to put in the lockup."

"When is he due in, if he does not have an arrest first?" Pope asked.

"Day after tomorrow."

"What's the chance of me catching up with him if I ride out that way?" Pope asked Otha.

"It's about slim to none, John. He covers a lot of territory and makes a point to keep it unpredictable to keep lawbreakers uncertain."

"How old is he and what's his background?"

"He's thirty-five. Was an unsuccessful miner, then a successful cowboy. He got married and needed a steadier income. Rents a place near where Littleton was killed. Maybe five miles away."

"Think he'd like moving back here?"

"I believe he would really like it. Both of him and his wife are from this area."

"Sounds good, Otha. I guess we are stuck for a few days in view of the distance to the edge of the lake. I hope this works out for everybody. Maybe I'll ride back to his district with him and start some detective training. Then, look around the lake for signs of Tom Bond. Grandpa, will you ride out with him next week to do some tracking skills?"

"Sure thing. You know how I like teaching needed skills. Have done it all my life. Learned a helluva lot from my old mountain man mentor who died some months into our trapping expedition towards the Wind River Range. Was the trip where I met your step-grandma. She was the most beautiful woman I ever beheld. Now, don't tell my Millie I said so!"

"I'd never tell on you. You loved her then and she died. You avenged her and mourned for nigh onto a quarter of a century. You are more than entitled to memories. I'm just getting around to making mine now."

"All true. You did some avenging yourself, boy. I was and am as proud of you as a man can be. Otha, did I tell you the story? No? Well, get some coffee and sit down for a rip-roaring true tale of horror and the vengeance delivered."

Pope walked out the door to do some patrolling. He knew the story. He had lived it as a ten-year old.

It was good as a story, but it reminded him he no longer remembered what his father, or mother, or toddler sister looked like. His main remembrance of her was seeing her long blonde hair blowing as a scalp. It was on the teepee of the chief of the war party who had killed everyone he loved. A man he allowed to live one second longer and was the only man he ever murdered in cold blood.

He shivered on his warm autumn afternoon and walked on, doffing his Stetson at townspeople and stopping to chat with some. He wanted to wrap this investigation up. Which meant finding Willie Smith and bringing him to justice. One way or another. He did not care which way. He had become inured to killing. It worried him periodically. Until the next man drew a bead on him. Or, was too slow. Most were. One out there was one who was faster. Now, with Sarah and one day his grandfather to look after, he could not be as nonchalant as in the past over losing a gunfight. He had responsibilities to his family. And, he had responsibilities to the citizens he served.

Pope found folks in all the towns and villages he had visited during his police, Wells Fargo detective, and sheriff careers had been decent hardworking people. The bad ones were in the minority. It was his duty to bring them in, on the horse or over it as they chose.

He planned to offer the choice to Willie Smith.

If he was still in the area. If he was still alive. Pope's gut told him Smith was both. And, Israel Pope said "listen to your gut, it has powers of logic your brain doesn't have."

It would be nice to pass such wisdom to a son or daughter one day. But it was not in the cards for him and Sarah.

He stopped himself from walking along so pensively. He needed to keep more alert for danger. Even in this rather peaceful California town so far from the frontier.

Pope circled back around and went into the office.

"Grandpa, you ready to ride back?" He was and they bid adieu to Otha Deacon, a good man. Hopefully, the next sheriff of his county.

******

The Pope's still had not filled a larder for regular cooking at the cottage. Dinner was sandwiches and coffee.

"I think this whole thing with Otha is a logical solution. Tom Bond sounds good, though we haven't met him. I am hoping he will work out well and fill in the duties Otha simply can't perform," Pope said.

"Me, too. This has been a good trip, but it's time to head home soon, Sonny Boy."

"I know Millie's tough. With Sarah having to travel on cases, often at no notice, I hate to have

Millie in a remote cabin alone. Maybe we should switch things around, Grandpa. You train him with tracking and awareness first. We can make him chief deputy and release you to go back to Millie. Let him transition to Auburn as soon as possible and I will go to the lake alone. It's the way I operate best any-way—riding with you or alone."

"Sounds like a good plan to me. Let's see how it materializes," Israel said.

They sat outside and smoked their pipes for a while, then the older man turned in. Pope sat longer, enjoying the wind and solitude. He still was mentally trying to connect every aspect of the multiple cases and see how they tied together. The murder of the sheriff less than two weeks ago. The murder of the mining company president. The bank robbery. And, the two heretofore unrelated robberies in Nevada.

He thought about the two O'Brien women. What a raw deal they had drawn in life. He feared the pretty daughter would look as beaten down at forty as her mother. At least she would not be beaten down with fists like both had been. Unless she drifted into a re-lationship with an abuser like her father. He had seen it happen all too frequently as a San Francisco police-man and later as a detective. He did not understand the cycle of violence. He guessed folks eventually came to believe it was normal. They feared a change from their normal more than the hateful reality of being beaten. Either way, it was a sad situation and neighbors and the police turned a blind eye to it.

Pope listened to the dwindling noises of people as they drew their day to a close. Doors shutting. Horses neighing. The odd dog barking. The last vestiges of cooking fires fading. It was interesting to him. He preferred the solitude of wind in the trees. Of Sarah sleeping by his side. The thought reminded him of how long he had been up and busy today. After spending time with Tom Bond over the next day or two, he would be back on the trail. He needed to buy some trail food and pack some feed for Caesar. There was still plenty of browse where he was headed. But, his equine partner deserved a treat. Pope got up and stretched. He went in and unlike most, threw the latch, locking the front door. He could hear his grandfather snoring in the next room. Israel Pope's presence was always a comfort.

Pope hung his clothes on wall pegs and slipped below the blankets. It was not cold enough yet to keep a fire stoked all night. He was asleep quickly.

In what seemed like no time, he heard his grandfather yell "Up and at 'em! The sun will be up soon. We can't sleep our lives away." Words he had heard in the morning for years.

He splashed water on his face and dressed. He would get a shave at the barber shop near the office.

"Breakfast is my treat, Grandpa. The cheese sandwiches we made had last night did not fill the void. Steak and eggs would, with lots of coffee. And maybe a glass of orange juice here in civilization."

"I'm sold. Let's saddle up and get to it."

Both men walked out in dark suits with prominent badges and matching stag gripped long barrel Colts prominent. They were riding within minutes.

Fortuitously, Tom Bond rode in a day early. He had a prisoner in tow, nippers in the front so he could ride. The man had gotten in a fight at a small bar near the lake and cut his opponent. Bond had a written statement and a bloody knife.

It looked like it would be a solid case.

Once the prisoner was booked into the holding cell, Bond was invited into the Pope's office to speak with him, Israel, and Otha. He was average height and weight with a mustache and thinning brown hair. He had a ready smile, but there was something about him showing he could become very tough immediately if necessary.

"Tom, you've done well out there in the lake district. How would you like a promotion and to come back to Auburn?" Otha asked.

"Promotion, Otha?"

"Promotion to chief deputy with a ten percent salary increase. Otha would be appointed sheriff by the governor. You and your wife could stay in the county house Littleton used for as long as you need, rent free.

Y'all might want a bigger house or more land, but it's your call," Pope answered.

"I'd like it. I know my wife sure would. She gets lonely out there and I worry about her by herself at night while I'm here in Auburn. There's nobody around our cabin five or six miles from the lake," Bond said.

"What we have in mind is three branches of training. You are an experienced deputy. You don't need deputy training. What we can offer is Israel Pope, current chief deputy. He is a former mountain man. Nobody can teach you to track better. I can help with how to structure investigations and search for clues. I have had a lot of experience gunfighting. Maybe I could share some of it. Otha can teach you how to run a sheriff's actual office. The administrative stuff."

"It sounds good to me, Sheriff. I'll get started any time."

"We thought about the tracking first. But there's a flaw in the plan. Your wife will be out there alone wondering what happened when you don't come back tomorrow," Pope said. "Otha, do you have another, closer, deputy coming in today?"

"Yep. Mack MacKenzie."

"See if he can stay here for a couple of days and back you up. Grandpa and I will ride out with Tom. He can get a dose of tracking on the way back and the next day. I will go on to the lake and start snooping around for Willie Smith."

They agreed on the plan and went to the general merchandise for supplies and the café for biscuits and cornbread already made.

"By the way, Grandpa, I have something for you," Pope said as he handed the bill of sale for the horse Jeb to his grandfather.

"Mrs. O'Brien is the next of kin. She needed money more than a horse, so I bought Jeb for you. I know you liked him a lot. So, you are riding out towards the lake on your own horse."

"Thank you, Sonny. Let me pay you for him."

"No. My gift. I could not pay you back in a whole lifetime for putting up with a snot nose kid and teaching him almost everything you know. My gift to you."

Israel patted the horse and said, "Well big boy. I guess you are stuck with me now. I promise I will never scar you with a spur like the previous sonofabitch did. You got my word on it. We'll talk about it and much more as we chat on the trail."

They left town quickly and rode until dark. Pope and Israel briefed him on the case but held off on Littleton's real identity.

It looked like rain, so the Pope's lashed their two tarps together for a shelter for all three. Their usual fire pit provided some warmth and coffee with little smoke. It was lesson number one for Bond.

"Tom, do you know the name Willie Smith?"

Pope asked as they ate cornbread with honey and drank coffee.

"I don't know the name. What does he look like?"

"Tall, skinny with red hair and a red mustache. Apparently, no beard. At least when my source saw him last. He was a pard of a murderer and robber named Charles O'Brien. We are not making a big deal of it, but O'Brien changed his name to Littleton."

"The sheriff? Damn! I knew he was more than just mean. I remember seeing a man around the lake who matched the description. I think he has a cabin somewhere and comes and goes a lot. I never gave him much thought. Figured he must be a teamster or something. Robber never crossed my mind. Not much of anybody who lives by the lake makes their money there. Lots of cabins are left vacant for months as men leave to go on trail drives, drive freight wagons, cowboy, work mines seasonally. You name it. It's one reason I always hated leaving my wife there alone. The area is pretty deserted and the ones who come and go are kinda questionable to me," he said.

"I know you said you did not know exactly where he lived. Any idea about what approximate part of the lake?" Israel asked.

"Maybe the middle of the California side. The general area where Littleton was gunned down. There are three cabins together near there. I can vaguely identify the owners on each end. No good bums.

The middle one, I just can't visualize who lives there. Maybe the red haired fella?"

"I talked with the doctor you took out there. By the way, you did well roping off the crime scene. One less thing in your crime scene investigation training. Anyway, the doctor said the buckshot was in a wide pattern on his chest. When I asked if there were powder burns he said yes. Well, a shotgun does not scatter as much as people think at close range. For him to have had powder burns and a wider pattern both meant the choke was wide open. Which strongly suggests a real short barrel where the choked part was sawn off.

Does a sawed off with the butt stock sawed just after the pistol grip ring a bell?"

"I saw the body and the wounds. You couldn't miss them and they were fresh. I never connected the wide pattern but still having closeup powder burns.

My mistake. I have never noticed a shotgun like you described in my patrols. But I have a question. I can see how you determined the barrel was short, but how on earth did you figure the butt had been sawed?"

Israel grinned as Pope removed the Darne from his bedroll.

"One like this one, huh?" Bond asked.

"No. This one specifically."

"It wasn't at the scene. I searched real hard and did not see it."

"It was. Just somewhere you did not look. And, I would not have expected you to look where I found it. I do now, however.

I searched a grid fifty feet wide from the shore and about as far out as the average person could throw it," Pope said.

"You dove in the ice cold water?" Bond asked incredulously.

"I did. And, it was colder than I expected. I shivered for a long time, even wrapped up in a blanket and one of these tarps. By a fire. When I found this French shotgun, it had one spent brass shell and one loaded one. I am pretty sure it's the murder weapon. I can tie a bullet removed from a body back to a particular gun, but I can't do it with a shotgun. Smooth bore means no rifling marks on a bullet. But the circumstantial evidence is really strong this is the one. It had not been in the water long either. Not a spot of rust anywhere on it."

"I don't see a pin where it breaks open," Bond said.

"The barrels are fixed and the top part of the frame slides backwards. Like this," Pope opened the action for Bond.

"I never saw one of those, Sheriff."

"Me either. It's made in France. One of the men in O'Brien's gang had a sawed-off. I cannot say for sure it's this one, but it gives us something to work with. I've tried this one and like it a lot. Think I'll keep it. No usefulness as evidence. No problem about ownership since the owner threw it away."

Bond took the short shotgun and examined it before handing it back.

"I don't blame you. It seems to me less likely for the action to weaken over time, not swiveling on a pin every time you open or close it."

"When it's daylight, I will show you the crime scene drawing I made of the site you roped off. Protecting it like you did is paramount. As a policeman in San Francisco, I took a lot of notes. Still do. But, it was Wells Fargo which taught me to document crime scenes, how to search, ballistic forensics and how to testify. I helped recruit my now-wife Sarah aboard. Since she was an experienced detective for Pinkerton's, the late Allan Pinkerton had her do the training for incoming female detectives. She and I combined our experience for remedial training for Wells Fargo detectives.

I hired a female deputy at Marin County. She spent her first week learning on a case with Sarah for Harry Morse Detective Agency. The young lady resigned quickly to be picked up by Harry as Sarah's protégé," Pope said.

"I cannot believe there are women wearing badges. It's a new concept for me."

"Pinkerton started it with Kate Warne before the war. She may have been the greatest of all, though I think Sarah is. Sarah has a larger kill record than any Pinkerton agent, man or woman. More than the true record of most gunfighters."

"You are kidding!"

"She's up to six kills. All seen by me or otherwise verified."

"Sheriff, you said you would give me some gun-fighting pointers. I guess you have a pretty good kill record yourself." Bond said.

"My boy does, Tom. He killed his first six or seven at ten years old. I will tell you the story later on," Israel added.

"And, as a lawman, Sheriff?"

"I don't keep a real good count. Around fifteen, I reckon."

"These are people drawing on you or actively shooting at you?" Bond asked.

"Yes. Now I think of it, closer to twenty. There were three in the Presidential assassination case alone last year," Pope corrected himself.

"I think I better listen real careful to you."

"Maybe, maybe not. I have been real lucky. None of the times I have been shot were fatal. Obviously!"

"Yeah, but the two during the kidnapping of Mattie Lane almost did the trick on you," Israel added. Pope just nodded. His shoulder and leg both still hurt in damp weather.

"Changing the subject, maybe after you check in

with your wife and share the news, you can point us up to the cabin where the red-headed man may live. You two can go off and do tracking training and I'll poke about," Pope said.

"Glad to, Sheriff."

They arrived at the small house the Bonds rented. As expected, his wife, Ann, was pleased with the promotion and move. She invited the Popes to have dinner with them in a few hours. Israel accepted. Pope needed to begin his investigation into the whereabouts of Willie Smith.

"How about the chief deputy and I ride to within a mile or two. I'll put you on a path to the lake. There will be road circling the lake. You were on it five miles south when you took your swim. When you hit it, turn left or north and ride about a mile and a half. You will come to three cabins on the road. They are maybe half to three quarters of a mile apart. The red-haired man's could be the center one. The second one you will come to. Who knows if he's there. I don't know a thing about this man except he's a transient. Gone as much as he is based at the cabin. It all clicks into place if he's a robber with a wide territory of targets. Just be careful, Sheriff. You are one man. He may have three or four there," Bond cautioned.

"I will, Tom. Grandpa, I'll probably see you back in town in a couple of days." They nodded to each other and Pope lightly heeled Caesar down the path.

CHAPTER 5

In what was some of the prettiest country he and Caesar had ever ridden, Pope felt he was in hostile territory. He slipped his rifle out of the saddle scabbard. It was not his pistol caliber carbine, but the larger .45-70 caliber Model of 1876. It threw a five hundred grain bullet. Twice the weight of his Colt's bullets. It had over a ton of energy, over three times what the .44-40 had in a Winchester carbine. Even more compared to a shorter barrel handgun.

Like his mountain man grandfather, Pope rode ever on the lookout. He had his big rifle across the saddle for quick use. He scanned ever direction, including up and behind and blew air out of his nose frequently so he could smell man or beast closer.

He could smell the freshwater lake well before he saw it and turned off the path into the woods to his left. He rode about half a mile and dismounted.

"Caesar, you stay here. But come running if I whistle!" he said to the black stallion who he reckoned understood everything he said.

He walked through the woods, close to the perimeter road. He saw the first cabin and knew he was within perhaps a half mile of the target cabin.

It did not appear anyone was in the first one. There was no smoke coming out of the chimney. It was surely getting cold enough to heat one's abode for the night.

Pope looked up at a very gray sky and the first word he thought was "snow." This was going to be a colder night yet.

Passing behind the cabin, he noted no horses in the small corral or open stalls.

He went on to the cabin where he hoped to find Willie Smith, the red-headed outlaw.

He found this cabin was not occupied either. No smoke, no horses. Nothing. He smelled a faint aroma of hardwood smoke further down the trail. Cabin number three. He heard a few hogs rooting around in the back and raising a ruckus.

Pope whistled and heard a whinny in response. Soon, he saw the black horse trotting towards him. He mounted and rode to the cabin. Pope put the big Winchester in the scabbard and slipped his smaller four and three quarter inch barrel Colt into his right jacket pocket. He moved the sheriff's badge to the outside lapel of his heavy coat and mounted.

"Hello the cabin!" he cried out in a stentorian voice.

In a minute, a slight man with a shotgun opened the door and stepped out.

Pope thought stepping out was foolish, but did not have time to worry about it.

"Howdy. I am Sheriff John Pope. What's your name, sir?"

"How do I know you are the sheriff? I thought Littleton was."

"Mainly because of the badge on my lapel. Littleton was shotgunned to death some days ago not five miles from here. You want to identify yourself now?"

"Nope. None of your business. Now get the hell off my land!"

Pope was not one to argue with a ten gauge. He turned Caesar and walked the horse out of sight. Leaving him in the woods, reins down, he walked to the rear of the cabin. He could hear the man moving around inside. Pope figured the big bore shotgun was leaning in a corner. There was a rear door on the cabin. It opened inward, just as Pope wanted.

Pope drew the long-barreled Colt from beneath his coat and kicked the door in. He stepped inside almost on top of the terrified big mouth. He swung the seven and a half inch barrel and it laid against the side of the man's head just above his left ear. He went down hard.

He checked the unconscious man and took a pocket knife off him. He looked around the dirty cabin and saw only the shotgun. It was propped in the corner just as he supposed it would be.

Pope broke it open and extracted two three inch shells. He rolled them under the dirty unmade bed and put the gun back.

He drew up a chair and sat watching the man. He began groaning and moving some. Finally he opened his eyes. The first thing he saw was the gaping hole in the end of Pope's .44 a foot from his face.

Pope took his left hand and slapped him across the cheek to help him gain some attention capability.

"When the sheriff asks you a damn question, you answer! And, if you ever point a shotgun at me again, I will take it away from you and stuff the barrel down your throat. All the way 'til it sees daylight. Do you understand me?"

The man, not secured, glowered at Pope and spat at him. The blow came before he could recognize a fist was flying towards his face. A left uppercut connected with his jaw and he went down more deeply unconscious this time.

Pope put the man on his bed. Taking a pillowcase off a pillow, he removed the Bowie knife from his boot and cut wide strips. He tied the man's wrists to the metal headboard, spread as far apart as the man's arms would reach.

Pope had seen a bucket outside. He thought

it might be used as a slop jar to avoid trips to the privy on a cold dark night. Apparently, the man had flushed it out with pump water, though it was still none too clean.

Pope brought it in and dumped the water on the man's face. He woke up sputtering and spitting out water no man wanted to swallow.

Pope sat back down in the cabin's one chair and stared at the man.

"That warn't right!"

"Neither was pointing a shotgun at your county sheriff. Or, spitting at him. I strongly considered shooting you. It would have been a clear case of self-defense. Charging you wouldn't have really mattered though. I would just drag your sorry ass around back and toss you in the hog pen. You'd have disappeared by morning. I may still do it," Pope said.

"Now, last time. What is your name?"

"Cletus Paulson."

"Cletus, who lives next door to your right?"

"Red haired fellow."

"Hmm. Odd name. Can you do better?" Cletus shook his head.

"Where is he?"

"Don't know."

"What kind of schedule does he keep?"

"What do you mean?"

"How often does he leave? Where does he go? Does

anyone come to visit?"

Cletus hesitated. Pope stood and picked up the bucket. He sloshed some of the vile water around to prove it was not empty.

"Still thirsty?" he asked.

"He leaves every few weeks. He comes back a couple days later. Sometimes, a few men come with him. But, they don't stay."

"Think he's due back soon?" Pope asked.

"Likely so."

"Do you know Sheriff Littleton by sight?"

He nodded.

You ever see him over there?"

"Once."

"Look like they were friends?"

"Yep."

"How long ago was it you saw Littleton there?

"Week or so ago."

"Really? About when he died."

"If you say so."

"I don't have time to wait for the red-headed man. I believe his name is William Smith. I will come back from Auburn to talk with him," Pope lied.

"You gonna leave me like this?" Paulson asked.

"What would you do if you were me?"

The answer was beyond Cletus Paulson's level of comprehension.

Pope went over to the table and picked up a rusted

kitchen knife. He stabbed it into the wooden tabletop next to the bed.

"You stretch real hard and get the knife. Cut yourself loose. If I see you coming at me with the scattergun, you are a dead man walking. I will put a .45-70 ball through your noggin and watch as your head explodes. It would be a sight to behold. If you think I'm kidding, think again. I'd as soon kill you as look at you."

"I'll come back by looking for Red. I'll check on you. If you have not figured a way to cut your bonds, I will cut you loose and drag your dead body out to the hogs."

Pope walked out the door, glad to get some cold clean air in his nose after the filth hole he just left. He went behind the Smith cabin and fed Caesar. It was snowing pretty hard now. Smith had some nice, seasoned stove wood dry below a makeshift roof. Pope borrowed some and walked Caesar back with the load of wood.

He decided to set up camp far enough away to not attract attention but close enough to see goings-on at the cabin.

Using his trowel, Pope dug two pits. The ground was too hard to dig a tunnel between the larger fire hole and smaller draft hole to suck in and supercharge air to the fire. He gouged out a trench with the trowel and covered it with sticks. He covered them with dirt and ended up with a substitute tunnel. It was a trick he and his grandfather swore by on the trail.

He made a low shelter with the small tarp and put his blanket and the saddle blanket underneath it. He collected some evergreen boughs to make a mattress to keep him off the cold, hard ground.

Pope heated water in the coffee pot and washed his hands with part of the hot water. He made a cup of coffee with the rest. He drank coffee, had some of the left over cornbread having given the biscuits to his grandfather. He chewed some bison jerky and decided to call it a day. This part of California was still almost frontier. It still attracted trashy folk like Cletus Paulson. Maybe not for long, he hoped before dozing off.

He awoke cold in the middle of the night. The tarp was drooping from the weight of snow.

He checked on Caesar, who seemed well. The big horse had grown his winter coat. No matter he might feel cold to the touch, the slight unmelted snow on his back told Pope the horse's coat was insulating well. It was holding his body heat in instead of going through the coat and melting the snow.

He wished he had hay instead of feed. The hay would generate more heat as he digested it. Pope put the coffee pot back on the restoked fire and melted snow to make sure Caesar had sufficient water to combat dehydration. He filled a folding canvas bucket he carried as part of his trail gear and placed it near the horse.

Pope went back to bed after stoking the fire with more wood. He learned the hard way tonight it was time for two small tarps. One for a shelter and the other to cover up in after he rolled up in his blanket. He would go to the little village on the south end of the lake tomorrow. He could accomplish two things. He could see Bertie and ask if she knew of Willie Smith or at least a red-headed slim man in his forties in the area. Second, he would see if the small general store in the village had a second tarpaulin for him. It would buy him another day or two to watch for Smith's return.

Pope awoke at dawn. It was really cold. The first thing he did was to walk over and talk to his equine partner as he checked him to make sure the cold, snowy night had not had a negative effect on him. Caesar appeared healthy and alert. Pope melted him some more snow for his water bucket and cleared a place to put out some feed.

He then saw to himself and made coffee. He finished the remaining cornbread and ate several strips of jerky. He wondered whether his grandfather had stayed with the Bonds last night instead of camping out. Old or not, Israel Pope had slept outside, blizzards included, more than he had slept in a real house. Inside or out, Pope was confident his grandfather had slept well and warmly.

He saddled Caesar and covered the fire with dirt first and snow second. Pope left the site looking like it had never been touched by humans. He rode south around the shore to get to Bertie's.

She did not have the "busy" bandana on her door latch. He called out and she came to the door wrapped in a blanket because of the cold.

"Come in, Sheriff. There's coffee on."

He sat in the warm cottage and she poured a cup of really good coffee.

"What can I help you with?" she asked.

"Miss Bertie, are you aware of a tall, skinny red haired man in the area? He is in his forties. Lives in a cabin on the California shore about five miles north."

"He's never come here as a client. But, I have seen a man who matches the description over at the store every now and then. He seems to come in for a while then leaves for a while. Is he an outlaw?"

"He is. I think he is the man who shot Sheriff Littleton."

"So, you are looking for him to give him an award?" she smiled.

"Not quite. I think Littleton, when he used his real name, Charles O'Brien, was a gang leader and the man I described, Willie Smith, was his number two. I'd like to put the nippers on Smith and take him in.

Have you seen him lately?"

"A couple of weeks ago, maybe less. Actually, now you remind me, it was around the time Littleton was murdered."

"Good information. I appreciate it. May I ask you something?" Pope said.

"Honey, men have asked me about anything you could imagine. Fire away."

"If you had the money, would you ever consider moving away, changing your name and either getting a job or running a small business?"

"What an odd question! I never figured I'd have the money to do such a thing. But if I did, I would leave the area where I am known as Bertie the whore and use my real name and do anything different than this. Why do you ask?"

"My policeman's nosiness I guess. You have too much class to be doing this."

"Thank you. I am not sure you are correct, but I appreciate the thought.

I would not go to a large place like San Francisco. I hate big cities. Maybe somewhere like Sausalito or San Rafael would be the right size," she said.

"They would not be too close to here to preserve your privacy with a new life?"

"I don't think so. Most of my clients are local or are men who make runs between Nevada and here. I should be alright heading west to towards the Pacific."

"Thanks for being candid. Again, I should not have

been so forward, but you are a good person and I'd like to see you doing something which would give you more happiness than this probably does.

I guess I better get over to the store and question him about Smith. Thank you for the coffee and the information. I hope it leads to Smith's arrest. I like him for three serious robberies. One includes a murder, though I believe he did not pull the trigger."

As he rose, Bertie got up and gave him a surprise hug.

"You are a nice man who cares about people. I know, I've read about you being a gunfighter. But deep down you care. Thank you."

He smiled at her and walked Caesar over to the store. The proprietor told him the man with red hair lived up on the shore five or so miles north, validating he was the one about whom Pope was curious. He said he had seen the man around the time the sheriff was killed and not since. He did not know what he did for a living or what his name was. Perhaps he drove a stage or freight wagon. He always gravitated towards Reno, not the California side. He said the man would be at his cabin a week or so then gone for a couple weeks or more.

"Have you ever seen anyone visit him?" Pope asked. The man had not.

"Have you seen him with a shotgun with both the barrel and the butt stock sawed off?"

"No, I never saw him with one of those. He wears a revolver. Looks like the butt of a Schofield sticking out of his holster. And, carries a carbine. I have not seen any sort of shotgun though."

"My last question is unrelated. Do you happen to have a small tarp in stock. Maybe five by six feet or so?" Pope asked.

"I think I do. Let me check in the back." He did and Pope bought it on the hope he would be warmer tonight. It was larger than he originally wanted, but not too large to include in his regular saddle carry items.

"There is no livery in the village. Is there any other place I could get some hay? Maybe two night's worth for one horse."

"I got some of it in the back. Let me put some in a bushel sack for you. Anything else?"

"Some vittles would be good. I am on the trail longer than I expected."

"How about a pound of dry pinto beans and side of bacon. Will you be in one place long enough to simmer beans?"

"Probably two days, so yes," Pope said.

Pope paid the man and rode back out towards Smith's cabin.

His prior night's camping spot was a good one. It was far enough away from the cabin only an Indian or Israel Pope could detect the smell of wood smoke, beans and bacon or coffee. Yet, he was close enough to sneak over and watch the cabin, then come back to camp around dark. He doubted Smith would return from his travels after dark. It was just a chance he would have to take.

He dug out his fire pits. It was more difficult than he expected because the ground had hardened due to the inclement weather. Pope took his tomahawk deeper into the woods and found two fallen saplings and cut them for a front frame for his shelter. He laboriously dug two deep, narrow holes and planted the saplings. Using latigos he always carried, he tied the third one across the top. A bit more hatchet work yielded stakes to hold the back of the new, slightly larger tarp to the earth. Long pieces of heavy cord tied to stakes in the ground held each of the front supports down. He stepped back and looked at his shelter. It would keep most rain and snow off his bed. He gathered kindling and firewood and set them inside the edge of the shelter to keep them dry. More evergreen boughs built up his makeshift mattress. He gathered some large rocks from the very cold stream nearby and used two to hold his small iron grill and the remainder to build a small deflector to send heat from the larger pit into the shelter.

He filled a small pot with beans and put them on to simmer all day. Slicing off five strips of the bacon, he cooked it halfway on the grill before adding it to the beans with a little of the bacon grease. Tonight's dinner was going to be better than last night's was.

There were still several hours surveillance time left today, so he rolled his original tarp and picked up the .45-70 lever action rifle and a canteen and walked through the woods to watch the rear of Smith's cabin. The outlaw's horse would be there if he was. Unfortunately, there was no horse in the small corral or open front stable.

Pope leaned the big Winchester in a crotch in a tree and made a seat out of the folded tarp adjacent. He sat and waited, listening carefully, smelling for sign and chewing bison jerky. After three hours and two sips from the canteen because of the five salty strips of jerky, he packed up and went back to camp.

He stirred the beans with a large spoon and sampled a spoonful. They could use a bit more simmering but were perfectly suitable for the night's dinner.

Pope made coffee and ate the beans. More cornbread would have been nice, but a hot meal was good and filling nonetheless. He melted more snow for the bucket he used to water Caesar and gave the horse a third of the hay he got from the village general store.

He would watch the cabin for another full day and leave for Auburn the day after tomorrow. Two more rations of hay would cover Caesar's needs.

A lot of the snow had melted during the day, but the sky was foreboding. He was pretty sure more snow would fall tonight. The sky was not of epic blizzard proportions, but he knew he was right about snowfall starting again during the night. He would be a bit better prepared tonight for a comfortable evening sleeping below the California stars, invisible though they may be.

It started snowing several hours after dark. The wind went through the air hole on the fire set and superheated the fire in the fire pit. He added a couple larger pieces and retreated under the tarp and blanket. He asked Caesar if he was alright and got a whinny he took to be a positive.

Pope loved the wind noise as it went through the trees. It was almost as sleep inducing as a burbling stream. He fell asleep quickly thinking about Sarah and whether his grandfather was camping in this weather on the way between the lake and Auburn.

He wished Scout was with him. He missed the hound. He knew it was more important he protected Millie. The dog had fallen for her after she gave him meat scraps and let him sit in her lap for ear scratches during the Lane kidnaping incident.

He finished the beans and bacon the next morning with more coffee. He cleaned out and packed the pot and grill. Pope went to watch the suspect's cabin as before.

He gave up by midafternoon and took his camp down. He cached the poles, rocks and the new tarp out of sight in the woods, covered with his bed's spruce boughs.

The fire holes were filled and leaves were put on top to hide their existence.

He saddled Caesar and started back. He would have to camp one night before arriving at Auburn but anticipated the weather would be better as he approached Auburn's almost five thousand foot lower elevation.

Pope camped the same way, except for not having a shelter. No snow was falling so he settled in on one tarp, covered with the blanket and pulled the other half of the tarp over himself. He was insulated and almost waterproof. He slept well and rose before dawn and rode in, arriving late afternoon. Israel Pope was there. He was dressed in his dark suit and looked none the worse for wear.

"Good to be on the trail with the stars shining above again, Grandpa?" he asked.

"Sure was. I like my life but have to admit I still like sleeping out instead of with a roof overhead."

"You will always be a Kiowa blood brother, won't you?"

"To the day you shovel dirt on my coffin."

"By then, I will be too old to lift a shovel. We'll have to hire a younger man to do it. I plan on you beating the century mark before you join grandma and White Feather."

"Yep. If there is a happy hunting ground, at least those two were best friends. So, there won't be much screeching. Not so sure when Millie joins us later. She's a quiet woman, but I still would not want to make her mad."

"Gentlemen, I interviewed a replacement deputy for Bond. I'd sure like your opinion on him since you are the current sheriff and chief deputy," Otha said.

"Glad to opine, Otha. But, it should be your choice. you will be the sheriff sooner than later," Pope said as his chief nodded agreement.

"He's local, so he is available for y'all to interview."

"Why don't we do it, for appearance sake if nothing else. Once he's aboard, I think he should get the same orientation Grandpa and I gave Bond. I have not done the shooting part yet, so they can both get it at the same time. Then, he should ride the district with Bond. Nobody is more familiar with it."

"Want me to arrange the interviews for later to-day?" Otha asked. Pope nodded assent.

"I will try to get him in about three then," Otha said. "His name is Wilbur Hastings. He's like Bond in many ways except younger. About twenty-five. Former miner, then cowboy. Good looking kid."

"Look forward to meeting him, Otha." Israel said.

Hastings came in. All three lawmen interviewed him. They excused him for three minutes as they agreed unanimously to hire him. Pope called him back and swore him in. They were down to one last badge left in the office. Otha pinned it on Hastings vest.

Pope noticed he was unarmed, as were most men on the street in town.

"What revolver do you have?" he asked Hastings.

Hastings turned a bit red and admitted his only revolver had taken a trip down a mining sluice into a fast running stream and he had lost it. As a cowboy he had relied on his .44-40 Marlin carbine.

"Otha, do we have any decent .44 WCF revolvers in the confiscation drawer?" Pope asked, using the original name for .44-40.

"I'm not sure, Sheriff," Otha said.

"I'll go in the drawer and poke around," Pope said, getting up and walking no farther than the corner of his office.

He pulled through the holstered handguns and checked the calibers. There was a Frontier Model with the short Shopkeeper barrel without an ejection rod. It seemed fairly new and was well oiled. It showed holster wear from the holster which accompanied it. Pope took it out and handed it to the future deputy.

He passed his first test by immediately putting it on half cock, opening the cylinder gate and checking to make sure it was unloaded.

"You might want to carry a quarter inch wooden dowel with you to poke out empties since you don't have a rod under the barrel," Israel suggested as he picked up a fresh box of loads for it from the supply shelf and handed it to the deputy.

"Do you go by Wilbur, Will or what?" Pope asked.

"Will, Sheriff."

"Will, how's your horse? Up to long trails and fast runs?"

"He sure is! He was my cow pony. He loves to run."

"Do you talk to him?" Israel asked.

Hastings hesitated, not sure how to answer without looking silly.

"Spit it out, boy," Israel said.

"Yessir, Chief. I talk to him all the time. He likes it and kinda answers."

Israel turned to his sheriff grandson and said "I knew I liked this young man. He's going to be alright."

The next day both Popes rode out to the lake with Hastings. They had to camp overnight en route as always. They found Bond and his wife packing and planning to move in several days. They would use their buckboard and camp in it on the way back to Auburn. By a letter with family members they found a small ranch to buy on the outskirts of town. They would not need the small house the county provided its sheriff. Hastings, a bachelor, liked the cabin they were renting on the lake and met with the owner to take over the lease. Things seemed to be falling into place.

Except Willie Smith still had not shown up again. Pope did his investigative and shooting training for the two deputies. He was glad to see both were good shots. The key, he knew, was being a good shot when someone was trying to kill you by sending lead in your direction.

Wyatt Earp, made famous at the gunfight in Tombstone several years ago, had said something Pope thought was valid. "Fast is fine. But accuracy is final. You must learn to be slow in a hurry."

The new future chief deputy and his district replacement rode the district the next day with Israel teaching tracking and awareness. Bond told Pope he would move his wife back to Auburn in two days. He planned on Hasting's orientation to be done by then.

Pope went back to his snowy campsite. Smith was still not at his cabin. Pope reset the camp and took up his watch position again for several days.

With no activity at the cabin, he rode back to Bond's. Everyone was there and ready to move. As he did not have all of his gear with him, Hastings joined the group on the trip back to Auburn.

Both Popes were pleased with Otha's choices for his chief and the replacement deputy after their training was completed. The only fly in Pope's ointment was Willie Smith's absence. He needed to close the case and could not without Smith. He was sure he could get a warrant and issue a wanted poster. However, not completing a task would grate on him.

It was not a matter of ego. It was duty and professionalism. He had been tasked by the governor to solve the murder. Though he had solved several crimes, this one was his primary task. And, he was going to finish it.

They stopped halfway for the night and rode into Auburn midday.

He had a telegram from Marin County chief deputy Bill Isakson waiting for him. It had just arrived this morning.

In it, Bill said he had come down with some sort of grippe and the doctor was caring for him. He was quarantined in the doctor's office. Could Pope return for a few days until he was up and back at the office?

Pope stopped at both the café he frequented and a general merchandise to get travel supplies. He told Otha to send a return telegram saying he was on the way.

He left the Placer County Sheriff's Office in the best hands ever as he headed Caesar west toward the Pacific.

******

When he got back to the office, Bill was still sick and maybe worse according to the doctor. Pope pulled deputy Walter Wood in for the duration of Bill's absence.

He went through the several day's unread mail.

Nothing of great importance was there.

Pope walked over to the Wells Fargo office and saw a balding young man sitting at the desk Sarah used during her split duties. He guessed the company had put a permanent manager in place.

He walked next door. Detective Martha Lane was at the desk.

"Hi, John!" she said. The words prompted another young woman to run out of the back room and throw her arms around him. She planted an unsolicited wet kiss on his lips and held it until he extricated himself from Mattie Lane.

"Oh, I've missed you so much!" she exclaimed.

"Hello, Mattie. And, Martha. Where's my wife?"

"She had to go to Tiburon again on another case," Martha said. "She should be back in an hour or so. We weren't expecting you back for a while."

"Indeed. I am not supposed to be here. But, the chief deputy has a bad case of the grippe and I got called back from my investigation in Placer County."

"Have you determined who killed the sheriff?" Mattie asked. It was apparent she had been clued in by her sister or by listening to Sarah.

"Yes. Now I just need the proof and to interrogate him."

"Are you going to soften him up?" Mattie asked.

"Not unless absolutely necessary, Mattie. I have to get back to the office now. Tell Sarah I am in town," he said as he unceremoniously retreated from the young woman he still tasted from two minutes ago.

He walked briskly down the wooden sidewalk, patted Caesar on the way to the door and went into his office and closed the door.

An hour later, a beautiful raven-haired woman walked in and opened his door without knocking. She had an amused look on her face.

"Raiding parties, gunfighters, rattlesnakes and mountain lions don't phase you, but I hear a nineteen year old little rich girl caused you to run out like your pants were on fire," his wife said stifling a laugh.

"Unlike the others you mentioned, I cannot shoot her," he responded seriously.

"Not to worry. I will probably do it myself anyway. She's smart as the dickens. It's a shame she is so in love with my husband. Otherwise, I'd hire her along with Martha."

"Don't even joke about it, Sarah. How long is her visit? Short, I hope."

"Not necessarily. She is finished with school and did not matriculate in a college this fall. Conceptually, she could stay as long as she wants," Sarah said.

"Have you checked on Bill?" she asked. "He was doing better yesterday."

"Not today, I am afraid. The doc won't let me see him. He's quarantined in the room in the doctor's office. I'm told the next step would be to transport him to San Quentin and put him in the prison in-firmary for twenty-four hour care. The doc says the ferries are real strict about not taking anybody with a contagious ailment, so a San Francisco hospital is out of the question right now. I had to talk with Doc from across the room. I yelled through the door at Bill and told him to get well. He answered, but weakly."

"I didn't know he took a change for the worse. Are you bringing someone else in to cover in the mean-time?" she asked.

"Walt Wood is coming in tomorrow for the du-ration."

"Did Israel come back with you?" she asked.

"No, he's needed up there. He's a great lawman, Sarah."

"I think Millie is getting lonesome. I don't blame her. Like you, he's comforting to have around."

He grinned at her.

"How about dinner? A fancy place if you want."

"No, we should get back to Millie. She has not been alone for years and seems sad."

"Of course, honey. Have you been staying with her?" he asked.

"I have. She should stay in our spare bedroom tonight, or we in hers. She has not lived alone since she was a young wife during the civil war. Even then it was not in a cabin in a remote area."

"We'll do anything we need to make her feel and

be safe.

On another subject, how is Martha coming along in her detective training?" he asked.

"Very well. I hate to say this for several reasons, but in listening to the two and having both help me at the office, I am afraid Mattie is the brighter one. She grasps concepts like what is required to charge someone with a serious crime better than her older sister."

"It's a shame. I had hoped Martha would work out for you and Harry. She certainly seems to have everything required to ride a beat as a deputy."

"I suspect she would. And, she might be a good detective yet. However, I doubt she will ever be a great one," she said.

She locked the office and walked her horse, Kate Warne, back to the sheriff's office. He locked it and they mounted and rode home.

"How's my Israel?" was the first thing out of Millie's mouth when she ran out to greet them.

"He's great. Grandpa is a fine lawman. I will send him back to you real soon. I am closing in on the end of the case which drew me to Placer County. I just need one more thing to happen. However, we have made some changes which might even allow me to release him sooner. I can also take you back with me in a day or so. You could stay with us. We have a two bedroom house up there."

"Releasing him sooner sounds good to me. Let me think about going back with you. I will let you know before you leave. How long are you here for, John?"

"I don't know. I can't afford to stay long at this point in my investigation. I have brought a good deputy in to take Bill's position until he gets back. He has been instructed how to reassign deputies to cover his district while he's in San Rafael.

I admit, Millie, I am very worried about Bill Isakson. He's not in the greatest of health to begin with and this grippe really has him down. He is too contagious to send to San Francisco on a ferry. I think the next few days will be crucial for him."

"I will pray for him, John. You should too. I know your and Israel's religion is more Indian than anything else but pray however you do it. Just do it please. Bill is a fine man and deserves all we can do for him," Millie said.

"I agree, Millie and I will. I'll send a telegram to Grandpa tomorrow with your request, too."

Pope and Sarah went to their cabin for him to unpack and gun down a bit and for her to change from business attire. Millie, used to preparing large dinners, invited them to eat with her. Her cooking was very difficult to turn down, as was her company. Though just in her fifties, she had quickly become an important motherly influence on both of them.

Dinner was a hearty stew with store bought beef

and vegetables canned from her own garden. Her yeasty rolls with fresh butter were excellent.

It was clear she craved company and they gave up the privacy they both wanted to stay with her in Pope's old room for the night.

The next morning, she rode into San Rafael with them. Sarah drove the buggy and Pope led her horse on a long lead. Scout merrily trotted along with them. Millie accompanied Sarah to the office. She was eager to see the two girls she had virtually raised. Mattie's arrival had been a surprise to everyone and Millie had not had a chance to visit with her. Scout elected to stay with the women.

Pope checked with the doctor on the condition of his chief deputy. Isakson had a rough night, the doctor reported but his overall condition had not worsened.

Pope went to the office. Acting chief Walt Wood was already in and going through telegrams and accumulated mail. None of them were particularly important.

His next plan was to walk over to the Isakson home and check on the welfare of Bill's wife.

"Miriam, I just came from the doc's office. Bill had a rough night, but this morning does not seem any worse for wear. The doc is holding off taking him over to the infirmary at San Quentin. He's optimistic he can bring him back to good health himself.

Is there anything you need? Shopping or money-wise? Just let me know now, or if I am back to Placer County, go by the Harry Morse office and tell Sarah."

"Thank you, John. I am fine. If I need anything I will let one of you know. As to food, I have a larder packed full of vegetables I have canned. Things like meat, butter, beans, milk and the like are just a short walk away.

How are you getting by without Bill in the office?" she asked.

"It's not as easy as it is with him there. He's done the job so long he knows it better than anyone. Deputy Walt Wood is standing in for him until he gets back."

"Walt is a good boy. I remember when Bill hired him. If I can talk Bill into retiring, I think Walt would make a good replacement."

"He would. But let Bill recover. He has a lot of good years left. Whether it's wearing a badge or fishing and napping, I'll support his decision all the way."

He walked back to the office.

"Walt, in view of having two adjacent district deputies covering halves of your district, I thought I'd ride around it in kind of a circle and parade the badge a little."

"Sounds good, Sheriff. I figure the folks would be happy to see you patrolling."

"I will stop by and let Sarah know where I'm go-ing and head out," he said as he picked up the lighter carbine to substitute in Caesar's saddle scabbard. As soon as he put the big .45-70 in the rack in his office, he walked Caesar down the street.

Mattie Lane saw him tie Caesar to the hitching rail.

"Good morning, John! If you will be in here a few minutes, can I ride your stallion? I won't go far."

"Sure. Have at it. Caesar, be a good boy." Mattie flashed him a radiant grin and too much deliberate bare leg as she scrambled astride the almost sixteen hand horse.

He smiled at her and handed her the reins. He walked in and she rode down the street on his horse and with his hound leading the way.

"Hello, Sheriff," her sister said. "Where's Mattie?"

"She just stole my horse and is making her getaway, I'm afraid. I have to just let her go. No other horse in the county can catch Caesar, especially with a rider half my weight on his back."

His wife looked up from her desk and rolled her eyes. She was getting better about the Lane family flirt. She would rather have her riding his horse alone than making eyes at Pope unabashedly in her office, or worse yet, his.

The subject of these thoughts had been sitting asking intelligent questions about cases in the chair across from her until she made off with the black stallion.

"I just saw Miriam Isakson. I told her if she needed anything and I was not here, to come by and tell you," Pope said.

"You beat me to the draw. I was going to walk by later today and check on her."

"I figured you would. Still can. Or wait a day or two. Whatever you think is right."

Pope walked around town and spoke with his constituents for an hour. He was surprised when he arrived back at the Morse office. Neither his horse nor dog were there.

"Hmm. Longer ride than I figured it would be." He walked in.

"Have y'all seen Mattie? She's been gone with Caesar and Scout for over an hour now.

"No. I feared she was at the sheriff's office flirting with the sheriff," Sarah said.

"No. She hasn't been there."

He walked out the door to look down the street. He saw Scout running his way from several blocks off.

"This doesn't bode well," he thought.

"What is it boy?" he asked the powerful blue tick hound.

It was clear Scout wanted him to follow, as he yipped and turned back in the direction from which he came, then stopped and looked impatiently at Pope for not immediately following him.

"Stay Scout! I'll be right back." Pope went into the Morse office.

"Something's wrong. Scout is back by himself.

Get the buggy and let's follow him. I'll go ahead on your horse."

Before they could respond, Pope was already outside lengthening the stirrups for his lanky frame.

Millie stayed to watch the office as the two female detectives got in the buggy and followed Pope, now several blocks away.

Scout led them several miles and Pope continued to whistle for Caesar, fearing the worst. Perhaps the horse had stepped in a hole and broken his leg?

Into the third mile, he heard Caesar answer his whistle, but not make himself visible.

Around a bend in the road, he saw Caesar standing protectively by Mattie, who was sitting on her bottom leaning against a tree. She was not very happy.

Pope quickly dismounted and ran up to her.

"Are you alright?" he asked, seeing pain reflected on her face.

"Not really. A really big rattler crossed in front of us stopped and coiled. Caesar reared up to keep from being bitten. I fell off, but one foot got caught in the stirrup. It was just there long enough to twist my ankle. Then I pulled free. The snake is over there," she pointed. Pope knew exactly what happened.

Caesar hated snakes about as much as Pope did. To protect his rider on the ground, he stamped the snake to death.

Pope knew a poisonous snakebite on the horse was

life threatening. Whatever Mattie had could wait. He quickly examined him and did not find any snake bites. He petted the horse and told him what good stallion he was, then turned to Mattie.

"Better let me see your ankle, Mattie."

She pulled her skirt up above her bare hip on the right side and he felt her ankle.

They heard the buggy coming from the other side of the bend in the road. She hastily lowered her skirt to just above her ankle.

"I think it's just twisted. Nothing seems to be broken. We can have doc look at it. I fear his exposure to the grippe might be more harmful to you than limping around for a week," Pope said, almost more to himself than his admirer.

He stood and walked to the center of the road as Sarah and Martha rounded the bend and stopped the buggy.

"She's alright. Just a sore ankle from falling when a rattler spooked Caesar."

Martha unconsciously touched the butt of her gun. These two were city born and raised and snakes were nowhere in their experience. Martha had killed the only one she had ever seen.

Pope noted this and said, "The rattler is dead. Caesar killed it to protect Mattie and Scout came for help. See why these two are such good trail pards? Scout saved my life after I was recovering from being shot during the kidnapping rescue. A group of city thugs went to Grandpa's old ranch to kill me. One was drawing a bead when Scout appeared from nowhere like a cannon ball and knocked him off his horse," Pope said. Sarah had not heard this story and listened carefully. What other life threatening adventures had her husband not shared. She was surprised Israel, the great storyteller, had not shared this one. She did not know the reason he had not shared was because the former mountain man had shot the wounded survivors to death once he got back to the ranch.

"Let's get you loaded onto the buggy and back to town, young lady," Pope said.

He picked her up. She grimaced pain, but still managed to snuggle closely as he carried her and set her in the back of the buggy where she could lie down.

"Martha, can you drive a buggy?" he asked.

"Oh, yes. Have done it for years."

Pope raised the stirrups on Sarah's horse and held the reins as she mounted. "I'm disappointed you didn't lift me on," Sarah whispered, teasingly.

"I will. Later," he responded, closing the conversation with her smiling.

They rode back and the three women examined Mattie's ankle and concurred with Pope as to the lack of seriousness. All realized it was, and would be, painful for a while and somewhat debilitating. Millie urged the girls to come back with them and stay in

Pope's old bedroom until she was back to normal. She even noted there was a hand carved cane at the cabin. She had no idea where it came from.

After seeing Sarah's rapt attention to the story about Scout saving him, he decided to not immediately tell them about why his grandfather had carved the cane for him. Maybe later. Probably not.

The injury and having to be rescued like a child when her sister was a working detective seemed to settle Mattie some. At least outwardly, it cooled her ardor. But, her love for the lawman who saved her life would never die.

Bill Isakson proved to be a tough man as well as a nice one. Within days, his fever broke and he began to feel better. After a week, he went back home to recuperate. His wife plied him with enough meat and potatoes to build his strength and his weight back to its level before he became sick.

Pope found a telegram from the US Marshal in Nevada waiting on his desk five days later. It had been forwarded to him from Auburn.

"Sheriff Placer County Stop Stage robbery yesterday Carson City route Stop Red hair leader Stop US Marshal Nevada End."

"I have to get back to Lake Tahoe," Pope announced to Walter Wood, then his wife in her office. Sarah promised to send a telegram for him to the Placer office to advise of his return and an acknowledgement to the US Marshal.

"By the way, did you ever hear back from anyone at Pinkerton's about the mining robbery inquiry?" he asked Sarah.

"Nothing. I guess I don't mean anything to the sons. So much for the years of service, huh?" she said bitterly. He hugged her and headed out the door.

Pope switched the carbine for the heavy .45-70 rifle before leaving the office.

He rode back to his cabin and rolled some clean shirts and a pair of trail cotton trousers. Millie had stayed home today and he walked over to their cabin.

"Millie, I have to leave shortly to go back to Placer County. Do you want me to take the buggy and have you come with me? You are welcome to come and stay with Israel and me."

"No, my mood's been better with you and the girls here. You said this investigation is almost over. I'll stick around here and wait for my Israel to come home. Thanks for the option though!

What do you need for the camp on the way?" she asked.

"I have dry beans, jerky, and coffee left. I planned to pick up biscuits or cornbread and some tinned peaches in town on the way out."

"Don't waste your time, John. I have two tins of peaches, a quarter side of bacon and a whole pan of cornbread I'll slice for you. I have some store bought honey and have a little glazed clay pot with a cork for you to transport it in."

He accepted them and slipped some money on the table when she was not looking. He had not had a mother since he was ten and his step grandmother was a welcome addition to his life. His mother would have been forty-eight now. Millie was perhaps seven years older. He gave her a hug and kiss on the bun on top of her head and rode off. She watched for a long time. Millie Pope had a smile of pride on her lips as she did.

Pope stopped on the way out of town and bought a small shovel and tied it behind his bedroll on Caesar's saddle. The snow would be deeper by now. A real shovel would be needed to clear out a campsite instead of crawling around with his trowel. He abided by "always have enough gun." He added "shovel" to the mix. If he kept on, he would have a full felling axe and need a packhorse.

******

He rode into the night and camped at a familiar spot. Thanks to Millie, his dinner was better than usual, though the only hot thing he had was coffee. Pope was proud of his field coffee. He thought nobody made richer coffee than his grandfather or him.

Pope rode into Auburn the next day and greeted

his grandfather, Otha, and Tom Bond.

"Quick action in response to the telegram, Sheriff," Bond said.

"Tom, I want to get this man real badly. And, he's a murderer. I believe he killed the sheriff and others. We have to set an example about killing lawmen. Even ones who were wife-beating, child abusing pieces of crap."

"Do you want me to go up there with you to face the gang?" Bond asked.

"No, Tom. You are needed here. He is likely to come back alone or with very few men. I could be wrong, but I doubt he'd bring all four back here just to split the loot. According to village folks, his visitors don't stay long, if anyone comes at all. If he has a bunch staying there, I'll get word to you. I might meet up with Will Hastings along the way, too."

"Well, alright Boss. Just hate to see you take on a gang by yourself." Pope nodded at him in appreciation and stopped at a livery on the way out of town to buy a bag of hay for Caesar. He slung the lightweight sack over the saddle and tied it with a latigo.

He rode to the village without seeing Will Hastings. Neither the man at the store or Bertie had seen Willie Smith. He left the village and headed to his original campsite to pitch his camp.

The snow was two feet deeper. He was glad to have the short shovel to clear space for his shelter and for the fire pits. The ground for the latter was even harder than a week ago. He softened it with a tomahawk, his grandfather's third favorite weapon behind a gun and Bowie knife. Only in the direst of situations would either Pope use their precious Bowie to gouge out the earth. It was a slashing, stabbing weapon and its blade had to be kept sharp and clean of nicks along the cutting edge and the sharpened curve on the top quarter of the blade.

Pope piled the snow from his eight foot square space around its perimeter. It gave him a bit of a windbreak. He retrieved his cached poles and stakes from the woods and shook snow from the spruce boughs he used to hide them. He put the boughs down for his mattress as before. He put up the sapling frame and put the new, larger tarp over it and lashed and staked it down. It was tight, but he left enough flex to handle new snow.

His next trip into the woods before dark was to collect twigs for kindling and fallen wood for the fire. He reckoned he collected three days' worth of downed firewood. He needed to keep his fire going at night, so he did not bother to try to shorten it. He'd put one end into the fire and progressively push the unburnt part in as needed to maintain the fuel supply.

Pope melted snow for Caesar and put it in the canvas bucket with a small pile of hay in front. He melted more snow and put it in a small cast iron pot with the beans and a slice of raw bacon to simmer all night. Pope supped on cornbread and honey with his coffee. He checked on Caesar, intentionally unhobbled, and turned in. He almost wished he had brought Scout with him, but the dog was good protection for Sarah and Millie, as he had been for Pope and just a few days ago for Mattie Lane.

"Mattie Lane. The full length of leg she had deliberately uncovered was quite an alluring sight. She is no longer a teenager. She's a full grown, blossomed woman now," he thought. One he wished would go back to San Francisco and cease being a distraction in his life. An increasingly beautiful distraction to the man a scant decade older.

A light snow started and the woods became still. He heard a coyote call in the distance and an owl much closer. The twig breaking within his hearing had to be a deer. It was not a man, unless an Indian. While the Washoe tribe had been near the lake since early times, none were hostile now. It was live and let live. He seriously doubted a brave would be out stalking around in the woods now. He was positive Smith would not be either.

Pope drifted back to sleep.

The next morning, he restoked the fire for the beans to continue to simmer during the day. The rebuilt fire reheated last night's coffee. While it was reheating, he peered out of the edge of the woods at the rear of Smith's cabin. Nothing. No horses in the corral. No smoke spiraling from the fireplace.

He caught the slight smoke smell from Paulson's cabin. The smelly old fool had clearly reached the knife and cut himself loose from the bed where Pope had tied him with the strips of sheet. Which saved Pope from having to drag his rotten carcass around back to the pig pen.

Pope went back to camp and ate cornbread and drank coffee. He made sure he had enough wood on the fire to keep the beans and bacon simmering until lunch. The beans ought to be both soft and very warming by then.

He walked to the edge of the woods. Pope took his canteen, a couple of jerky strips, his small bedroll tarp, and the .45-70 rifle. He made a nest where he could watch the rear of Smith's cabin. He doubted Smith would show in the morning. If he had been within an hour away last night, he would have ridden in then.

He leaned against a tree and began his vigil.

Two hours later, nothing had happened. He ate a strip of bison jerky and had a swig of water from his canteen.

He continued to watch. The sun rose higher and the blue sky was bright at noon. There were no snow clouds anywhere in the sky. He closed his eyes, fighting sleep. It also allowed him to rest them from staring at the back of the cabin.

Something awakened Pope. A sound or a smell. He could not make it out, but knew it was something. He put all of his senses to work. There was the faint smell of horses, then the sound of men talking low.

He watched as five men rode in. Two went into the cabin and checked it. Three waited in the front. The first men came out and all walked their horses around back and unsaddled them. One, possibly Smith unrecognizable with hat and wool scarf around his face and head, brought out hay and threw it on the ground by the horses.

They went into the cabin. Soon a fire was built. A man came out and walked towards Paulson's cabin. It was a long walk. It signaled to Pope the horses were exhausted from a long ride. Like by a ride from the other side of Reno, Nevada.

The reprobate Paulson would tell him about Pope's visit for sure. Pope had known it from the start.

The man came back, walking fast. The autumn wind blew his hat off. Red hair!

"Who else would go see Paulson," Pope thought.

Pope chanced it from over two hundred yards. He aimed above the man's head and pressed the trigger of the .45-70, trying to account for the heavy rifle's rainbow trajectory. The man staggered and grabbed his shoulder. Pope imagined, more than heard, a profanity escape from his lips. Probably the same profanity Pope had uttered when he realized his shot had gone awry and not dead center.

The man ran as well as he could with a serious wound. He tried to zigzag back to the cabin. Two men came out with carbines. Pope dropped one and aimed at Smith again, but the corner of the cabin obstructed his view of the outlaw. The man he shot laid motionless on the ground. Pope had watched the massive chunk of lead hit him and how he reacted. He was pretty sure it was a kill shot. One wounded, one dead.

Pope yelled out "Placer County Sheriff! You are surrounded. Throw out your weapons or we'll smoke you out."

His stentorian yell caused a rifle barrel to break out a window. Pope sent a round through the window causing a loud scream and "thump" as body two hit the floor.

"Down to three alive. Smith is one of them and he's hurt," Pope thought to himself, always keeping count of ammunition expended and threats still breathing.

Pope changed position. A cloud of blue gray gunsmoke hung over his firing point, giving it away. He was unaware, but in a bit over a decade, smokeless powder would alleviate a shooter's position being given away by clouds of smoke. For now, he had to move every time he fired. Which was not bad tactics anyway. He rolled as more bullets cracked in the still air as they passed overhead.

Moving to the right, he had a better angle to see

the front door but lost his view of the rear. He could not shoot directly into the front door, but he could hit anyone who came out of it.

He heard a horse. At the same time, two men came out of the front, firing wildly in his general direction. He killed one with a single shot. The other disappeared back inside.

"Alright, my bet's on Smith with the horse and one man left in the cabin to cover his escape. What an idiot the second man is! Willing to die so Smith can get away, probably with the money," Pope mouthed to himself.

Smith, or so Pope thought, rode fast. He kept the cabin between himself and Pope, correctly assuming the man shooting at him could not show himself as a target to his confederate in the cabin. Pope could not see him. He could not shoot at him.

He had to let him go and deal with the remaining outlaw. He could and would track Smith down in due time.

He sent a bullet through the side window again and quickly moved further to the right. Pope had a pretty good angle on the front door now. He could call for the man to surrender. If he did, he would lose valuable time chasing Smith. A dead outlaw would be far more convenient.

Pope fired another round in through the front door. It was closed, but no barrier at this distance for the heavy Government round. The round could slice through it like a hot knife through butter.

Pope heard an unidentifiable noise. Then an identifiable one. A horse. The last man had slipped out the back and was riding in the direction Smith took.

He was not quite as bright as Smith. He did not keep the cabin between his route of escape and the lawman.

Pope knocked him off the horse. It was a solid hit and the bareback horse kept running.

Pope walked over to the cabin. All dead. He saw a canteen and picked it up. Reckoned he would need it for the man wounded about a hundred yard away.

He walked to the downed man. He was alive, but barely.

"Partner, you're shot bad. You were hit by a .45-70. They can bring down a buffalo. You have nothing to lose but a chance at heaven. Did Willie Smith's gang rob the stage over near Reno?"

"Water?" the man said painfully.

Pope gave him some.

"Did y'all rob the stage?" he repeated. The man nodded "yes."

"Where's the money?"

"Willie took it." This time it was Pope who nodded.

"What's your name?"

"John Easter."

"Where ya from John?" Pope asked.

"Reno, originally."

"Got family there I can notify?"

"My ma lives there. Her name is Hedda Easter."

"I'll contact her. One more question, then some more water, huh?"

Easter nodded.

"Did Willie Smith kill Sheriff Littleton, also known as Charles O'Brien?" Pope asked.

It was too late. Easter gave a death rattle and died.

"Sheriff!"

Pope looked up at Deputy Will Hastings riding towards him.

"Hi, Will. Glad you're here! Time for some on-the-job investigative training."

"A lot of dead bodies, Sheriff."

"No wrong ones, but not the right one."

Hastings looked at him quizzically.

"I got the gang, but Willie Smith rode away."

"Shouldn't we get after him?"

"No rush. I will track him tonight."

"Nobody can track at night!"

"I'll show you how later. Now, we have our work cut out for us. Let's take a quick
trip to my camp and get my kit and my horse."

They rode past Pope's spy nest and on to the camp.

"Nice camp, Boss."

"I have used it on and off for weeks. You can either stay here tonight if it gets dark on us or ride back five miles to your place. It you want to stay, I will leave you the beans and coffee and the stuff which goes with it. I will be riding light after Smith and won't need it all. Just my blanket and small tarp."

He saddled Caesar, put the bedroll on him, rifle scabbard, saddlebags, and the burlap sack with some hay. He left the rest in a pile in case Will Hastings stayed and needed it for his horse.

They rode the short distance back to the cabin.

Pope drew a diagram of the woods, road and cabin. They left the cabin as a rectangle, showing doors and windows. He put approximate distance lines on the perimeter of the site and of the cabin. He drew a stick figure where each body lay and had Hastings count the empty cartridge casings by each. Pope had both of them sign and date it.

They went into the cabin and searched it. Pope got a big smile on his face and walked out to the corral and open stable. He came in with the smile bigger.

"So, what's the good news, Sheriff?"

"There are three horses and five saddles. The man I was talking to as he died had a bareback horse for his ill-fated getaway. This means Willie Smith is riding bareback too, with no blanket, rifle or canteen. He may freeze to death before I can arrest him. At the very least, he will be hungry and thirsty. Have you ridden up the perimeter road?"

Hastings nodded.

"I put a number beside each body. Let's drag them in and put them against an inside wall. They will freeze, but not become food for coyotes or other creatures. I want them whole and recognizable for the pictures I want you to orchestrate," Pope said.

"How, Boss?"

"First thing in the morning, I want you to ride into the office in Auburn and tell the chief deputy, Otha, and Tom. I want you to lead the chief and Tom out here with a photographer and an undertaker wagon. I want the photographs along with our diagram for our records and those of the US Marshal over in Nevada. So, get several photographs of everybody and everything so we can have some and share the rest with the Nevada folks where their last robbery occurred. It was a stagecoach. Probably Wells Fargo from my memory of the stage lines over there." Pope pointed out to the perimeter road around the lake directing the conversation back to his question about the perimeter road.

"What's up there? Any towns or occupied cabins?"

"Not really. A few old cabins. I didn't see anybody around them. I guess he might find water from an old pump. Maybe steal a blanket. But, he will probably enter Nevada bareback, freezing his ass off, and thirsty."

"I will be chasing him on a fresh horse, with water, a coat and, sleeping gear. I'll have jerky to munch on.

And, a really big rifle. I will also be able to see at night. He won't."

"How can you see at night?"

Pope took out his Dietz police lantern and checked the fuel. It was full and he had a small metal bottle with more kerosene. He took out a Lucifer and struck it on his boot. He lit the lantern and showed Hastings how it could shoot a pencil beam or an all-around lantern light.

He doused it to preserve his vision for now. It was dusk but not dark.

"Sheriff, I have a blanket and small tarp. I think I may take you up on the beans and coffee and use your camp. Thanks for leaving hay for my horse. He'll appreciate it!"

"Oh! There's a smelly old reprobate next door. His name is Cletus Paulson. He has a shotgun so be careful. You may want to get the drop on him first in the morning before riding back. Tell him if we get back and find he's been to the cabin, he will be considered a member of the gang and you or I will shoot him to death. Remind him I want to feed him to his hogs out back. Say it with confidence and conviction. If you have to get a little rough to get his attention go ahead. Just watch him. He's a sneaky bastard, so don't let him get the jump on you."

Will Hastings grinned at Pope and allayed any doubts the sheriff may have had about the young deputy's commitment to convince Paulson to stay away.

Pope stuck out his hand and shook with his deputy.

"Will, you are a fine lawman. And, you are going to keep getting better and better. Stay safe my friend and Willie Smith and I will see you in a couple of days."

Pope turned and rode north on the perimeter road, his big rifle over the saddle ready for action. The young deputy watched him. He was perhaps seven years younger than the sheriff but thought he could never be as wise or deadly. Though a good man with a lot of potential, he was exactly right.

Pope rode until dark. The road had some traffic, but the snow was packed pretty hard and there were no discernable tracks to follow. He wished he had, once the shooting had stopped, tried to identify Smith's horse's hoof prints in the soft ground before the road. Then he decided it probably would not make any difference.

Pope walked Caesar along the edge of the road. Not where someone waiting in ambush would expect. By walking in the soft snow instead of the hard packed road, he was not sending sound messages to an untrained tracker either. Especially one who was probably shivering with cold by now. He rode through the night at a walk. Even in the cold, Caesar could continue this pace longer than the experienced horseman's butt could take it.

The night was clear but the wind was penetrating

and deadly. Pope turned up the collar on his heavy jacket and wrapped a woolen scarf Millie had knitted him around his neck and face. He wore heavy gloves, knowing while they might impede use of his Colt, the action of the big Winchester rifle would accommodate them handily.

Unless Smith was able to hide in the woods and keep his horse totally quiet, he was still up in front somewhere. The sun rose and Pope stopped and gave Caesar some water from his canteen and some of the hay sprinkled on the ground. He walked around and stretched, though always at the ready. He would kill for a cup of coffee. He chewed a couple of jerky strips and called it breakfast. Having walked a few kinks out, he asked Caesar if he was ready. The horse whinnied and shook his majestic black head.

Pope mounted and rode another half hour.

He saw a dead horse lying on its side in the road.

Pope dismounted. The horse had a bridle but no saddle. Was this Willie Smith's getaway horse, ridden to its death? He moved Caesar away from the horse and left him, reins down.

Pope began to search the woods on the side of the road. He found what he sought quickly.

Willie Smith was leaning against a tree. He was almost blue. He had died from exposure clutching a burlap sack full of the treasure taken from the Nevada stage robbery.

Gloves still on, Pope dragged the stiff, frozen carcass out to the road. He hoped for a southbound freight wagon.

In the meantime, he counted the cash and coins in the bag. It came to five thousand dollars even. He hoped Wells Fargo had posted a reward.

After an hour, a freighter pulled by four pairs of horses came by and Pope flagged it down.

"Sheriff of Placer County. Where you headed, Partner?" he asked.

"Oh, you are the new sheriff? The gunfighter?" the driver asked.

"There are some who call me such. I need your help. Other than southbound, where are you going?"

"To the village in at the south end of Lake Tahoe, then over to Auburn."

"I'll ride with you, but I need to transport this body of an outlaw either to halfway five miles above the village if the undertaker is there for other bodies, or to Auburn if not. Will you do it?"

"I charge two cents a pound, Sheriff. How heavy is that there fella?"

"I guess about one forty," Pope replied.

"So, that worth two eighty to you?" the man said, doing quick math in his head.

"You help me put him on and deliver to either place and I'll give you three bucks."

"You got yourself a deal, Sheriff."

They loaded Smith on the back of the freight wagon. It looked like a Conestoga pioneer wagon without a canvas top and with sides six feet tall.

They were unable to move the dead horse and just left it. Pope thought the stupid coward deserved to die for running the horse to his death but kept the thought to himself.

When they got to the part of the perimeter road where the shootout occurred, the deputies, photographer and undertaker were just arriving.

Israel Pope looked at Smith's body and the shoulder wound.

"You should have shot him harder, Sonny Boy."

"I know. I'll do better next time," Pope said.

"See that you do," Israel suggested. Pope nodded

The undertaker took possession of Smith's body after several photographs were taken of it. They would show him as someone who was virtually frozen and with a rifle shot to the deltoid muscle which had not killed him by bleeding to death. There were very limited bloodstains frozen to his body on either side of the through and through wound.

Unbeknownst to Pope, Israel had raised his eyebrows in appreciation his boy had killed four and badly wounded one in the gunfight at Tahoe. And, he had done it all alone. Israel knew he had taught him right.

They arrived in Auburn well after midnight. The

undertaker took his bodies away.

The lawmen met briefly at the office, then went to their homes for a brief rest before an early morning meeting.

By early the next day, Pope had his paperwork ready and let Otha announce the death of the gang which had not only robbed a stage coach in Nevada, but whose leader had murdered the former sheriff during the prior month.

The case was closed and Pope wanted to turn the office over to the new sheriff and new chief deputy so he and Israel could return to Marin County. He received due accolades in the Bay area newspapers, along with glowing quotes from the judge and his wartime friend, the governor. Israel received more than honorable mention in every article for keeping Placer County safe while the acting sheriff was solving the murder of the previous sheriff as well as a number of robberies.

Pope had one more stop to make. He wanted to provide the photographs and what he had learned about the Willie Smith gang to the sheriff and the US Marshal in Reno. He had his reasons to do it in person.

He arrived in Reno two days later, armed with his photographs and documentation.

Both lawmen met with him at the same time. Pope knew they were aware of the news coverage and would not really learn anything new.

Pope told him he had a source in California whose information led to most of the case solutions regarding O'Brien as a gang leader and his number two and murderer Willie Smith. He wondered if Wells Fargo had posted an award for the stage robbery, every penny of which he returned to the Wells Fargo office in Auburn. Money for which he received a receipt.

The US Marshal said "Yes, Sheriff. There was a seven hundred fifty dollar reward for information leading to the identification of the robbers. It's pretty clear your source deserves it."

"I was a Wells Fargo detective gentlemen. I know who to contact. I just wanted to check first during our debriefing here today. Thank you both for your support in these cases."

"I think we both owe you the debt of gratitude. You set out to solve a murder in California and also solved several here in Nevada along with the accompanying robberies. Based upon the evidence including photographs you have presented here today, we will be pleased to contact someone at Wells Fargo immediately and see if we can have your source compensated for the full award."

Pope wrote down the telegram address for James Hume, Wells Fargo Chief Detective, San Francisco in his notebook. He tore the page out and slid it across the desk.

"He's my old boss. Tell him I will provide the contact information for the source upon his request."

Pope took out the old wanted poster from Nevada. It was the one with no expiry date.

"Would you see to this for me? I will give it to the same confidential source. Just have them send the money in care of the Marin County Sheriff's Office." They agreed. The amount was four hundred dollars.

They all shook and Pope left for the south Tahoe village to see Bertie.

Again, he caught her without a customer.

"Well, it's the handsome sheriff again. I'm glad to see you," she greeted him, again with a hug.

"I need your full real name, Bertie. Something's in the works to let you leave this life and move to somewhere new. I cannot guarantee it one hundred percent, but I believe ninety percent would be safe to say."

"What on earth are you talking about, John Pope?" she asked with visible excitement.

"I have given evidentiary proof you gave me information about the Willie Smith gang—the red-haired fellow up on the lake's rim—which led to me identifying him as the robber of a stage in Nevada. I did not divulge your name or exact location yet. I also recovered the whole amount stolen and have returned it to Wells Fargo. I believe they will pay the seven hundred fifty dollar reward to you as a result. There's another reward for four hundred dollars from another source some years back. It's more iffy, but there's a good chance it will come through also."

She was stunned. It would be enough to cover her moving and a new residence. And, a new life.

"I am speechless, John. May I call you John?"

"Of course you may. Any idea where you might go?" he asked.

"We talked about San Rafael, or Saucelito the last time you were here. Either would be good. Tiburon, perhaps. I don't think I would bump into any former customers in any of them. I always made a point of trying to find out where people were from. As I said, most of mine were from Nevada and here making sales and deliveries. Almost none of the locals had any money to spend on my type services. I never gave credit. Except an offer to you once, which is good as long as I am alive and could be active, so to speak."

"I know. Thank you. I believe once it's approved you can show up at any Wells Fargo office and claim your reward. Or, the reward can be sent to a law enforcement office. Do you have anything in your name which can prove who you are?"

"Oh, yes. I have a family Bible showing my birth. I never really married so my birth name is still my legal name. I have letters from my family to me at a previous address when I had a café in Oakland. In fact, if I could afford the right place, opening another café is what I'd like to do."

"The owner of a café in Novato, north of San Rafael just had to close to move back east for family reasons. The café is small and might be in your price range. I believe she lived in rooms above it. An attorney in town is handling the sale for her. Let me write his name down for you."

He did and handed her the slip of paper.

"I own this place. It's probably worth five hundred or so, due to how close it is to the lake. I would put anything I got from the sale into a café deal," she said.

"Bertie, what is your real name so I can get used to calling you by it?" Pope asked.

"It's Helen Adams of Charlotte, North Carolina. I came west with my parents to escape the war. I am thirty-nine years old and have been a soiled dove here for five of those years. Before, I was a reputable woman."

"And, you will be again, Helen. The person who makes the payment decision at Wells Fargo for robbery rewards is my old boss. He is due to contact me on this matter. The other is being handled out of Nevada. I don't have any details, but my fingers are crossed it will come through to you at some point. What's the mail delivery like from San Rafael to here?"

"It's about a week from San Francisco. I am not sure from the towns north of the Bay," she said.

"I will get his response pretty fast by telegram and mail instructions to you."

"In the meantime, John, I will look into selling this property. One of my few local clients always said he liked it better than his own house, which is more valuable. Let's see if it's pillow talk or he will put his money where his mouth is.

I am ready to move and begin a new life with or without the reward, John."

"Good luck, Helen. I suspect you can get into the café in Novato for the sale price of this place. The owner has already moved and I understand she is pretty anxious. If you could sell here, the reward money would cover moving and some living expenses until you broke even.

I have to get going. Rest assured I will be in touch."

She hugged him again and he mounted Caesar and headed out. He had no idea where Deputy Will Hastings was. He hoped Will packed his gear and took or sent it back to Auburn. If not, Pope could afford replacing a tarp and some ironware.

He pointed Caesar west on an all-to-familiar trail and they trotted home at a comfortable, unhurried pace.

He had a telegram from Hume waiting on his desk. He replied back with the name of Helen Adams, formerly of Charlotte, North Carolina, currently in eastern Placer County, saying she has a family Bible and letters as proof of identity. And, that he would sign whatever necessary to indicate she was the one who gave him invaluable information about the location and names of the gang leader. Hume sent back the latter would be sufficient for monies to be picked up at any Wells Fargo Office, using this telegram as authority. Pope wrote Helen immediately.

CHAPTER 6

Placer County had a new sheriff and chief deputy, as organized by Pope before moving back to Marin. Pope settled back into his normal life and duties and Israel settled back into his interrupted retirement. Sarah was very busy handling cases for Harry Morse.

Pope learned Martha was coming along nicely in her transition to detective. Mattie was doing even better as an unpaid detective. Sarah had spoken to Morse. He told her Wells Fargo business diminished after the matter involving the capture of Black Bart. It was the incident where the company president had spun his version misreporting where the real credit belonged. Morse said this reduced his ability to hire detectives as easily as before. He suggested Mattie be used as an unpaid intern and be given job credit as an employee and a good reference when she left. Mattie, who was not worried about money, gladly accepted the assignment. She did not get a badge or a reason to carry a revolver, however. This grated on her, but she had grown up enough to learn how to not voice everything on her mind. Most of the time....

Two weeks after his return, Pope received a letter from Helen Adams.

Helen reported she had sold her house and small plot of land to the man she mentioned during his last visit. She had some furniture and cooking items and clothes to move, but little else. She had arranged transportation to meet with the attorney handling the sale of the café in Novato. If the meeting yielded a sale, she would stop by San Rafael and collect her reward, then return to the village on the lake to work out moving herself and her belongings to Novato.

Pope shared what he had done with his grandfather who told him "As usual, I'm right proud of you. You have done the right thing. You can never go wrong helping somebody who's in need. Bertie is a good woman fate stuck in a dishonorable job. But it doesn't mean she is dishonorable. In my one meeting with her she seemed a fine person.

Nobody needs to know her background. As I said, the first time you mentioned her name, a lotta women fell into her profession because it was their only option. Your grandmother was in her first night in a crib as a Hell Town whore. It was at the boat landing in Front Royal, Virginia. Luckily, I rescued her from her first customer. He was beating the hell out of her. I left him unconscious and ended up with something I wanted and something I didn't want."

"What were they, Grandpa?" Pope asked.

"A fine Bowie knife. I gave it to your step grandmother's father, Lone Bear. He was chief and like a father to me. I got it back at his death. I wear it every day and you are very familiar with it," Israel said. Pope smiled, until then unaware of the origin of the big Bowie.

"What was the other thing? The one you didn't want."

"A wife I hardly knew. I was young and stupid and she was pretty. White Feather ended up her best friend and helped her birth your pa. I was gone and returned to find she died in childbirth and your pa was being raised as an Indian. It was something I heartily agreed with, John. When he was nigh onto the age where I took over raising you, I brought him out to California to live with my sister Maude and her husband, Arthur. I had run a flatboat up the Shenandoah with him and we were like brothers. Sadly, the two of them died during the war. Cholera. You have some distant cousins, but I regret I have lost track of them. They only knew me from occasional visits and drifted off. They were grown by the time their folks died."

"Grandpa, we never talked about your folks. I figured there was some reason. Am I wrong?"

"No, Sonny Boy. You aren't wrong. Your grandma was a good woman and a survivor. She just got exhausted and weakened by the life my pa created.

My pa was a dreamer who dragged us from place to place with no plan nor gumption to make it worthwhile. Ma died too young, beaten down by following him and living a hardscrabble life. He died while I was trapping. He always looked for the easy way. His last easy way was found at the bottom of a bottle."

"Was he a mean person?" Pope asked.

"Not at all. Just a dreamer without the giddy-up to be successful at anything. Honest, but generally a no account. He took up space and air on this earth and left nothing but your great aunt and me to show he had even been here."

"Thank God, he left you." His grandfather patted him on the shoulder and smiled almost sadly. The talk had brought up his memories of White Feather, who like his first wife, died during his absence from an attack by an opposing war party. He would love her until the day he died.

"Well, enough of this lollygagging. Placer County sent me a month's check as chief deputy, thanks to you. I cashed it and figure on taking the whole family to dinner tonight. Are you up for it?"

"I would be, though because of Millie, I guess 'whole family' will include the Lane sisters? Can we include my acting chief deputy. He may have some interest in Mattie. I am going to encourage it. Right now, I have to go back to Lake Tahoe for a day or two."

"I'll put it off until you get back. Is Mattie still hot on your trail? Millie won't mention you and Mattie in the same conversation."

"The ardor comes and goes, Grandpa, but I'm afraid the answer is yes," Pope said.

"Sarah has not shot her yet. Good thing. You'd have to arrest her," Israel quipped.

"It's not so funny. She might and I really would have to arrest her. Sarah seems to be getting better about Mattie's shenanigans, but I don't trust either one. How do you figure out women?" Pope asked his grandfather.

"Beats me. I never could. You just take what comes and generally keep your mouth shut. Smile and nod your head a lot."

Pope grinned and nodded.

"Yep. Just like you just did. Practice it a lot and you might survive."

******

Pope rode out to Placer County and the lake the next day. It was colder yet. He bought another tarp and more cookware for camping. Deputy Will Hastings still had his and he would let him keep it. The kid was short on money and needed it for his job. Pope knew the county was not as rich as he suspected it would be one day and did not adequately equip the deputies.

He wanted to check on him anyway. He would also ride by and see what Helen had worked out for moving to Novato.

Pope camped the first night and ate well with the prepared food he brought from home. He managed to find Deputy Hastings the next day through sheer luck.

"Howdy, Will," he greeted the young deputy.

"Oh, Sheriff. I have your gear back at the house."

"No, Will. It's your gear now. You need to add a trowel all the time and a short shovel in the winter. Try to carry enough hay in the winter to feed your horse one night and the next morning. Carry Lucifer matches and a flint and steel kit. Get a good hatchet and keep it and the cook gear in your saddlebags, Will. Also, some dry beans, coffee and jerky. Keep a blanket and tarp bedroll on your saddle. What caliber is your rifle and your revolver?"

"Both are .38-40's," he responded.

"Good. The ammunition interchanges. Carry at least one full box of ammunition also. Two if you have room or know you are going after somebody and it may take a couple of days.

When you broke my camp, did you see how I dug the two fire pits? Try to always use those. Either dig a tunnel or a covered trench between the smaller air hole and the larger fire pit. The setup burns hotter and with less smoke. You never know what hostiles might be skulking around out there."

"I have most of those things with me right now. I'll pick up the rest in the village."

"Good man! Now, I have something sensitive to ask you to do. Miss Bertie in the village helped my grandfather with information about a fugitive he was running bounty on when she first got here five years ago. A couple years ago, she helped me find a man when I was a Wells Fargo detective. More recently, she gave me the information leading to the apprehension of the former sheriff's murderer and Willie Smith and his whole gang as you saw a couple days ago.

Up until five years ago, Miss Bertie was Helen Adams. She was a successful café operator elsewhere. Circumstances made her what she is now.

She will shortly receive the reward for the Smith gang's apprehension.

She will resume her real name and move to Novato, where she plans to open another café.

I ask you to never mention who the café owner used to be or where she went. She is a fine woman and I wish to keep her name unsullied. You promise me?"

"I promise, Sheriff. I always thought it was sad what seemed to be such a nice lady had to be a soiled dove. Now, she won't be. I wish her the best of luck in her new life."

"Good, Will. I knew I could trust you to do the right thing."

They rode around Hasting's district a while and then back down to the village. The deputy stopped by the store and picked up a few things from Pope's list. They dropped by to check on Bertie as she still was known for the next week. All three sat out on her front stoop and sipped coffee. It was cold out, but the air was fresh. The coffee was hot and flavorful and the visit pleasant.

"Miss Bertie, soon to be Helen once again, I have spoken with Deputy Hastings here. I will with the former deputy, too. We will all be on board with your new career and help bury your past identity," Pope said as Hastings nodded.

"I appreciate it a lot gentlemen. You two and Israel Pope are truly gentlemen for helping a damsel in distress."

"Ma'am, if your café food is as good as your coffee, you won't be in distress long," Hastings said, winning a smile.

"When will you be moving for good, Helen?" Pope asked.

"The day after tomorrow. The owner of the store has arranged to take my things in his buckboard out to where the perimeter road meets the road to Auburn. A freighter will meet us there and take it and me to Auburn. I will collect the reward and find another freighter to deliver my things up to Novato."

"There is a wholesale grocery wagon which goes from Auburn over to Saucelito and up through all the northern town including Novato weekly. I used to drive it before I became a deputy in Placer County. I am still friends with the owner. I am sure I could talk him into including your items on the trip for a few dollars," Hastings said.

It seemed like a logical approach to solving her problem. Pope asked him to write a letter to the man.

"Helen, even if you get your belongings as far as San Rafael, we will make sure they get up the road to Novato," Pope promised.

"I have a small surprise. The old reward came through and I have a draft for it right here." He handed her an envelope. She peeped in and smiled.

"I showed it to my wife who served as the Wells Fargo manager in San Rafael. She said it was good as gold and they would cash it for you."

He reminded her to take the family Bible and letters to Wells Fargo for identification and to tell them to call him if they needed any further identification.

He rode back to the San Rafael. By leaving early and riding into the night, he made it home without camping.

The next day, he rode in with Sarah. Happily, the two sisters had returned to Martha's room in town.

"I have asked a couple of deputies to come in this

week for some additional training. Would you mind giving them the short version of some of your Pinkerton curriculum?"

"I believe I have time. Perhaps the first half of the day Friday?" she said.

"Friday would be great. Thank you.

Did Millie mention Grandpa wants to celebrate our return what he calls a family dinner at a restaurant in town. He's including the Lane sisters as family."

"It makes sense since Millie raised them and is more of a mother than that poor mentally ill woman who bore them."

"I would like to sit at the opposite end of the table from Mattie, please. I don't want her bare toe sneaking up my pants cuff," he said.

Sarah broke out laughing.

"You are scared of a girl barely twenty!" she said.

"Not in the least. It is the one who is thirty two I am scared of."

"*Moi?*" she said.

"Hell yes. *Vous!*" he said.

"No, *tu* when you are speaking to your beloved wife!" she said.

"Whatever! The point is you don't really think this crush thing is funny and I think you could be provoked to violence."

"How little you think of my professionalism and judgement. How can you love me and trust me to train your deputies if I am such a loose cannon?" she asked.

Completely forgetting his grandfather's advice, he responded "See? Now you're getting petulant."

They finished the final three miles into town in silence. He doffed his hat at her at the Morse office and rode on to his own.

"Things were a lot better when we were on cases and not with differing careers and complications!" he told Caesar as he tied the stallion to the hitching rail and stomped into the office.

"Anything new, Walt?" he asked the acting chief deputy.

"I dropped by to check on Bill on the way in. He told me his wife is pushing him to retire. He says he can afford to but is not yet sure it's what he wants. I may be telling you this out of school, Sheriff."

"No problem, Walt. I want you to tell me anything on your mind and anything you hear which you think is important. I'll always hold your confidence and expect you to handle whatever I say to you the same way. Now, this isn't confidential, but I asked a couple of the deputies to come in and get some more training this week. I am going to ask Sarah, who was a Pinkerton instructor to talk with them a bit. If you want to sit in it's fine. Your call completely, Walt.

My grandfather seems to think I might need some more shooting training, too," he added.

Wood laughed.

"You? Shooting training? Ha!" he said.

"Well, he thinks merely poking a big hole in Willie Smith's shoulder from only two hundred yards is pretty unforgivable."

"Hell, Boss. Even hitting him from such a distance is pretty impressive to me."

"Not if you are Israel Pope, I guess. I should have hit him more accurately. He could have died on the grass instead of riding his poor horse to death and turning himself into a block of ice. He was a selfish idiot, riding bareback, no coat, and with just the darn money like he did.

I reckon Grandpa remembers a decade ago when buffalo hunter Billy Dixon used a borrowed Sharps Big Fifty like his to kill an Indian chief. It happened at the fight at Adobe Wall in Texas. He shot him from somewhere between one thousand and fifteen hundred yards. The longer range was measured by army surveyors and is probably more correct.

Dixon always claimed it was just a lucky shot. I doubt it very seriously. I think he must have been a helluva shot to shoot nine tenths of a mile and kill somebody.

Since the man he shot was on a horse next to the head chief, Quanah Parker, the battle pretty much ended. So me winging someone at only two hundred yards is poor shooting to my grandfather."

"Sheriff, the real point is you killed, or caused to die, some dangerous outlaws. You solved a couple of murders and even more robberies. The papers think you are a hero for what you did. What else matters?" Wood asked.

"I guess I might shoot up a box of .45-70's soon at longer distance and see if I can regain some missing accuracy anyway.

I have to leave a little early tonight. Grandpa wants to take the family out to dinner with his month's salary as chief deputy for Placer County."

"Bet it will be a nice quiet meal with the two of you and your wives," Wood said.

"Hardly. The Lane sisters will be there. It won't be quiet."

"Not to be too forward, but does Miss Mattie make Detective Pope, er, jealous?"

"Does a bear have big claws?"

"I was afraid so. Miss Mattie is really pretty and even more forward it seems."

"She's both. I may try to sic her on you. You'd like her. And, her father is rich as can be," Pope said.

"Go ahead. I could use a little excitement in my life."

"Excellent! I'd like for you to join us." Wood agreed.

At the moment seconds after Wood said he needed more excitement, the cleanup man from the nearby Wooden Nickel Saloon burst in the door and said there was a fight in the saloon. A big one.

The two lawmen ran to the saloon. They could hear the ruckus well before arriving. Pope had the Darne twelve gauge on half cock below his coat, almost out of sight.

"You want to practice your authoritative police voice?" Pope asked Wood.

"You men! Separate right now or you will go to jail!" he yelled convincingly.

Nothing happened.

Pope eased the right hammer back on the twelve gauge and let go a full load of buckshot into the ceiling. He stepped away, pushing Wood with him, as particles of ceiling plaster rained down.

The authoritative sound of a shotgun going off inside a room froze everyone in place. Except for one drunk who took the opportunity to sucker punch the man he was fighting.

Pope had already reached him and laid the short barrels of the shotgun across the back of his head none too gently. He collapsed in a heap.

Pope swung the barrels around the room, passing everybody with the impressively large twin muzzles. Out of the corner of his eye, he saw Wood covering everybody with his Colt.

"Alright, then! Who deserves to go to jail?" Pope asked loudly.

Men began pointing at the one who they had been fighting. The actions by the drunks were so ludicrous, the sheriff fought smiling. A glance at Wood showed his deputy had lost the battle and was grinning broadly.

A big drunk came staggering up to Pope threatening him. Pope handed the shotgun to Wood and faced the oaf. The man had tremendous fists up and swinging around slowly in every direction, boxing the air. He left so many openings for a fist to the chin, Pope was tempted.

Real gunfighters tried to never hit anything hard with the hands which kept them alive. A knockout punch to this idiot's chin would put him down. It would also put Pope's gun hand out of commission. Pope could not afford to lose the use of either hand for even a day.

He approached the man, whose reach was similar to his own. He knew how close he could and could not get from a danger standpoint.

Pope grinned at him and walked forward, both hands clasped behind his back. Unbeknownst to everyone except Pope, his hidden right hand held a lead and leather sap or blackjack from his San Francisco Police days.

"You want to put your hands behind your back? Kinda like mine are. Then I can handcuff you and take you to jail to sober up," Pope said, deeply but quietly.

The big man stepped forward and the right hand which had outdrawn many killers flashed. The sap hit the man in the jaw and fractured it. He went down like he was poleaxed.

The acting chief deputy, without instructions, handcuffed the man behind his back and recruited two big drunks who appeared to be somewhat steady on their feet to pick him up. As he did it, Pope stood watch with his hands near the big holstered Colt.

"Doc's or straight to jail, Sheriff?" he asked.

"I guess Doc's. I think I heard his jaw break. Good thing it wasn't higher. He'd be dead now," Pope said thoughtfully.

"Anybody else want to fight some more?" he asked the crowd as he took the Darne, slid the action back and replaced the shell in the right barrel slowly and with purpose.

Pope and the muzzle of the twelve gauge scanned around the saloon once again. The crowd seemed much more subdued. He and Wood backed out the door behind the two dragging the prisoner to the doctor's office, which was in his house.

"I think it's more of a jawline fracture, John. I don't believe he will have to have his maw wired shut. He won't have to stay here. I'd put a bucket in his cell though. He will be sick when he wakes up from all the bad whiskey he has sucked down.

On a happier note, I released Bill to go home today. He won't be strong enough for duty for a while, but he's no longer contagious. He is pretty weak though," the doctor said.

"Thanks, Doc. We will see what his wife influences him to do."

"Yes. She has been pretty vocal about what her preferences are." Pope nodded and reminded the doctor to bill Marin County for his services.

The sheriff and acting chief deputy, half walked and half dragged the drunk back to the office and put him in a cell with a large bucket. The night deputy, George Dunstan, arrived and was briefed about the happenings of the day.

Pope went to the pitcher and bowl near the stove and its important coffee pot. He splashed water on his face and dried off.

"Walt, you might want to do the same. There are some pretty young girls you will be having dinner with unless you have thought about it and decided you have other plans," He said to Wood.

"Uh, well, no. I don't have plans, Sheriff."

"Make it John and wash up. We have about five minutes to show up fashionably late.

Pope washed his hands at the pump and dried with a towel he brought in every day. At least, almost every day. Wood followed suit. Both men had suit jackets on and their heavy coats. They rode to the restaurant. They rode so they would have horses there for emergencies. The eatery was only two blocks from the sheriff's office.

They walked in and found Israel had secured a private dining room. Millie, acting as family hostess, directed everyone to seats she arranged in advance with Sarah's input.

"Grandpa, I asked the acting chief deputy to join us. I believe everybody knows Walt except the younger Lane sister. Walt, this is Miss Matilda Lane, generally called Mattie. Mattie, Walter Wood," he introduced the twenty-five year old lawman.

"Walt, glad you could join us. Consider yourself family. There's a chair over across from Miss Mattie. Why don't you take it? John, you sit up here with me to tell me all about what happened. There seemed to have been a ruckus over at the Wooden Nickel. Somebody shot off a shotgun and scared the pudding out of the drunks. I wonder who could have done such a thing?" Israel asked.

Pope looked over at his chief deputy and nodded.

"Well, Mr. Pope, it was the sheriff who got almost everybody's attention with the sawed off. He took out a good piece of the ceiling and pushed me away before we both were covered like on a winter night by the lake. Plaster was falling like snow."

"Go on, Walt. What happened next?" Israel prompted.

"I said 'almost everybody,' because one big drunk did not get the full significance of the sheriff's words. He staggered forward swinging his fists in the air.

The sheriff handed me the alley cleaner and walked towards the man with his hands behind his back."

"What happened then, Chief Deputy?" Mattie asked.

"He told the man to put his hands behind his back to be handcuffed. The man did not comply and I never saw anybody move so fast. John's right hand held a sap and he fractured the man's jaw before anybody knew what was happening! It was amazing!"

Sarah turned to Mattie who was sitting next to her and a table away from her husband. By her request.

"Mattie, someone who has to draw and fire quickly has to keep his hands pliable. He doesn't chop wood without gloves on. He tries to avoid hitting something hard enough to break or even stiffen his hand. John always taught me to punch something soft and chop, elbow, or head butt something hard," she said.

Israel nodded in agreement and asked, "Walt, what was next?"

"Let me jump in here," Pope said.

"Walt immediately cuffed the unconscious drunk and recruited the two biggest and most sober drunks there to pick him up and assist him to the doctor's office to get checked out."

"He was completely unconscious, then?" Martha asked.

"He was. The doctor somewhat revived him with an ammonia ampule, then checked his jaw. He pronounced it fractured, but not bad enough for further action. John and I picked him up and half dragged him to a cell."

"John, what will you and Walt charge him with?" Mattie asked, careful to include and look at the handsome deputy.

Again, Pope looked to the deputy for an answer.

"The only thing I can think of is felony stupid. So, unless the Sheriff disagrees, we will probably kick him out with a stern warning when he sobers up."

"Y'all are much nicer than my first action as a deputy sheriff," Israel began, signaling the start of one of his famous stories about the old days.

"I was a young pup, younger than you Miss Mattie. I came into rendezvous. Had a load of beaver pelts to sell from a whole season's cold and wet work at the eastern portion of the Wind River Range.

Some fellas robbed the top fur buyer of his cash purchase money and rode off. We saw them in the distance and the sheriff was there for the rendezvous. Things could get a little out of hand at rendezvous, you know.

He jumped on his horse and I ran along to where my mule, Amos, was to see if we could catch up with the thieves," Israel said.

"What happened then, Grandpa?" Pope said, knowing the answer.

"I shot one of them, dead, from a hundred yards. I loaded while we were riding after the other one. I shot and knocked his hat of and scared him so bad he fell off his horse. Fool broke his arm and we took him into custody. They did not have a jail near, so the sheriff let him go to suffer with his bad arm on his lonesome. We recovered all the money. The trader we returned it to paid me a real fair price for my pelts and I rode back to Kentucky and brought John's grandmother back to the mountains. She was with me a year or so when she died giving birth to John's pa. Both my boys are named John Hunt Pope. John Hunt was the name of my mountain man teacher who taught me all I know about tracking, trapping and living in the wilderness. I buried him on the prettiest mountain top you ever saw. He overlooks the blue mountains just like he wanted."

"Israel, how did he die? A bear like attack like you experienced twice?" Sarah asked.

"No, old age. He knew he was dying and where he wanted it happen."

The stories were interrupted by the waiter who took their orders. San Rafael was close enough to San Francisco to draw good chefs and offer excellent cuisine.

After pie and coffee the stories continued into the evening, mainly told by Israel and Sarah. She talked about being a female detective at Pinkerton's, then when she was at Wells Fargo and had partnered with Pope.

Pope, though he was the center of some of his grandfather's stories, did not tell any himself. He was a private man, almost to a fault. He did not consider any of his gunfights or investigative prowess much more than luck. He did not want to mess up the luck by boasting about his deeds.

Walt talked about growing up and his first jobs. Pope and Sarah watched Mattie's rapt attention at the young man's stories. In his own way, he was almost as eloquent a storyteller as the old mountain man. The more the evening progressed, the happier Pope was he had brought him to dinner. And, the more convinced he was, when the time came, he would make Wood's chief deputy job permanent.

They broke up around nine and Walt Wood escorted the two sisters back to the hotel where they rented.

Pope and his grandfather rode beside the buggy with Sarah driving and Millie happily content with how this dinner had come off. Israel rode with him.

"Grandpa, thanks for welcoming Walt. He's a good man. I want to give you a little something to cover his meal since you didn't plan on it."

"Not necessary. You know, Walt is a good story-teller. He fits in this family darn well."

"Mattie seemed taken with him," Sarah said more hopefully than confidently.

"I thought so, too," Millie added.

"Good seating choices, Millie. Thanks!" Pope said.

"It just happened," Millie said as the rest looked at her incredulously.

She smiled. "I am not used to lying. It's kind of fun," she giggled.

"Grandpa, so you just shot the hat off the robber's head? How far was he?"

"A couple hundred yards, riding away hard."

"Like Willie Smith was when I shot him?"

"Not at all. I was at full gallop on Amos. You were stationary and had the opportunity for a good aim," Israel said with two of the fingers holding his reins crossed. Crossed out of sight.

"I see," Pope said, unconvinced. His grandfather turned away so Pope could not see the fun he was having. He decided he won this one and would not bring it up again.

They arrived back at the cabins. Both men saw to the horses and both women retired to their cabins to restoke the fires for the cold night and roll down the comforters.

"You didn't add much to the stories, husband," Sarah said as she snuggled up to Pope.

"You, Grandpa and Walt are such good storytellers. Y'all were on a roll. Besides, Mattie was captivated with everything Walt said."

"I told Millie and Israel what we were planning. Both were in cahoots with us. I did not have the opportunity to tell you ahead of time," she said.

"My luck would be he'll marry Martha instead."

"Oh, no. You have good luck. Quite good luck," she said and she took both ends of his mustache between her fingers and drew his lips down to hers.

"She's right, damn good luck," Pope thought, unable to speak at the time.

******

The next morning the Pope's joined for breakfast. Still not knowing how long Mattie's visit would last, Millie decided to go to the office again with Sarah.

Israel decided to go squirrel hunting for stew meat. He had treated himself to a new .22 rimfire Ballard single shot and wanted to try it out on some small game for the pot.

Pope rode into town beside the buggy, then veered off at the Isakson home to check on Bill.

He detected bacon and coffee smells, so he knew it was probably not too early to call.

Pope tapped on the door and his chief deputy answered. He was already dressed for chores but not the office.

"Bill you look better, my friend," Pope greeted him.

"Thank God, I am, John."

"You take whatever time you need to fully recover, Bill. Your job is secure."

"I have been wanting to talk with you about the job, John. Come on in for a cup of coffee, if you have the time," the chief deputy said.

Pope came in and greeted Bill's wife, Miriam, who handed him a steaming mug.

"I'll let you men talk," she said.

"No, honey. What we are going to talk about involves you. Please sit with us."

After she was seated, he began. Pope knew where this was going to go.

"Miriam and I have talked a lot. I came close to buying the big one with the grippe. Life is short, John. I want to spend it with my gun shooting squirrels and rabbits, not a big gun befitting a big badge.

I want to give you notice of my retirement right now. I will get you a letter later on today."

"Bill, I really hate to see you go. I understand completely, but wish you'd stay on a while and break Walt in. He was your pick and a real good one," Pope said.

"How about this? I will come in next week for two more weeks. I will spend those ten days training Walt everything he needs to know to be a chief deputy. He already is a top man. I just have to train him some of the paperwork and particulars like taxes, license enforcement and foreclosures. He already knows the rest.

A friend of mine drinks a bit too hard. He was at the Wooden Nickel when you broke up the fight last night. Sounded like Walt backed you up very well, John."

"He did a fine job. We communicated like you and I do. Instinctively and without words. I have no qualms about him being chief. I just want him to be trained by the best. You."

The chief looked at his wife and she nodded affirmatively.

"You have a deal. Let's only share the retirement date with Walt. He's trustworthy."

"Not meaning to be too personal, Bill, but are you all ready to live without a salary?"

"John, we have been planning for this for years. We don't owe anybody a penny. We have enough saved to take care of us. Miriam grows half our food. We sell eggs to lots of folks and it brings in a good income. I think we can offer some of the stores fresh and canned vegetables, too. Don't worry about us. We'll be fine."

Pope nodded. He wondered if he would be in the same financial shape thirty-five years from now. He knew he would have one hundred thirty acres of valuable Marin County land. But he reckoned he might be cash poor. Maybe this was a wakeup call for him. He would discuss it at family dinner tonight.

He shook with his chief and Miriam gave him a motherly hug. He rode back to the office and tied Caesar to the hitching rail.

Acting chief deputy Wood was already there

being briefed how quiet a night it had been by the night deputy.

"Anything I need to know?" he asked the night deputy who was wrapping up with Wood.

"Not really, Sheriff. Like I told the chief, it was pretty quiet. I walked the beat and no problems at the saloons. The retail stores' doors were all locked."

"Sounds like a good quiet night. Go home and get some sleep."

Later, Pope said to Wood "Glad you came last night. You're a good storyteller. And, you were paired with the best one I ever heard."

"Your grandfather is some man, I'll tell you. Somebody ought to write a book about him," Wood said.

"He killed two bears with just a knife and you heard about him and me knocking off a whole war party. Well, another whole war party which killed his Indian wife 'way before I was born. He killed them all by himself. He's a quiet, kind man until you attack his kin. Then, the devil comes out and there is hell to pay. Everything good I may be is due to him and his example raising me from age ten. The bad? Hell, I don't know where it comes from. My folks were not bad people. From what I heard, my real grandma was a bit of a character. The Indian wife who raised my pa during his early days sounds like an angel. I am sorry I never met her."

"So, he has raised you since you were ten years old?

Must have been something. The things a man like him could teach. I cannot imagine, John."

"I have been blessed alright. Him. Sarah, first as a great partner at Wells Fargo, now as a wife. No complaints.

On another subject, Bill advised me of his retirement today. I worked out a deal with him. He spends the next week recovering some more, then the next two finishing training you the administrative aspects of being a chief deputy. I'll swear you in at the end of the training. Alright with you?" Pope asked.

"It is, if you don't think I am too young for such a responsible position?" he said.

"Only if you think at only five years older, I am too young for my responsible position."

"I don't. So I guess we have a deal!" He extended his hand to the sheriff to make his acceptance official.

Deputy Will Hastings came in later from Placer County.

"Hello, Will. I am surprised to see you here. Did a mutual friend come with you?"

"She rode with the freighter, but I escorted them. I took a couple days off. It seemed like the right thing to do. A handsome woman riding with freighters seemed a bit chancy. After today, she will be carrying a lot of cash money. I will escort her up to Novato, then head back to Placer County. She is over at the Wells Fargo office getting ready to claim a reward and cash her other draft," Hastings said without going into details.

"I was just going over to see my wife at the Morse Detective Agency office next door. Why don't you walk with me?"

"Walt, I'll be back in a little while then I may ride north a bit today or tomorrow."

"Okay, Sheriff. See you whenever."

Pope and his former Placer County deputy walked to the Wells Fargo office first.

He walked in. He had already met the new manager through Sarah. The manager was well aware the husband and wife team were two of the greatest detectives in company history.

"I just wanted to say hello, to Mrs. Adams and verify to you she is who she claims to be," Pope said.

"Yes, Sheriff. Mr. Hume wired me to say you may corroborate her identity. She seems to have sufficient documentation, but I appreciate you adding to it."

He counted out two separate sums of cash to Helen Adams, never Bertie again. Pope noted the two amounts. The older reward had come through the same time as the newer Wells Fargo one.

She walked out with the deputy and the sheriff.

"Did Will's former employer agree to move your belongings all the way up to Novato, Helen?" Pope asked.

"He did. In fact, they are on the way now. I will pick up a ride on the stage in about an hour," she said.

"Why don't you two get some lunch before the stage arrives? It's a long, cold ride this time of year," Pope said slipping a five dollar gold piece into Hasting's palm unseen by the woman.

"Won't you join us?" she asked.

"I have a conflict, but I will surely see you in Novato before too much time has passed. Have you had further communications with the lawyer who is acting as agent for the café?" he asked.

"Yes. He said the relatives are eager to sell. He's so confident the sale will happen he said it would be fine to store my things in the upstairs apartment of the building and even live there before the sale closes."

"Perfect! I wish you the very best in your new life and will check on you later on, alright?"

"Sheriff John Pope, you will be welcome anytime. And, your money is no good at my café once it opens."

"Very kind of you. However, it goes against a rule I put into effect. Nothing free because of the badge."

"If it was not for you, I would be stuck back in my old life by the lake forever, John," she said so nobody but the three of them could hear.

He smiled at her and said "See you soon."

They walked off to eat and he went into the office of the Harry Morse Detective Agency.

Four women looked up and gave him differing but genuine smiles.

"Any big cases today?" he asked.

"One new one. A thousand dollars missing from a bank in Bolinas," Martha answered.

"Interesting. Any suspects? Inside job?" he asked.

"Our former company's stage delivered a strong box. A new teller put it in the safe without verifying it. When the bank settled for the day, using the amount from the delivery on the cash side, the tally came up an even thousand short. Knowing the care Wells Fargo exercises in computing deliveries, I have to believe it was at the bank," Sarah said.

"What do you know about the teller?" he asked.

"Nothing yet. Martha and I are riding up in an hour and interview everyone, including him."

"And, I am going to spend time with Millie. Our home misses her so much," Mattie said.

"I am sure. But you can't have her back. She's finally happy and the official queen bee in her own home," Pope said.

"John, if we come up with compelling evidence, how do you want to work it? Martha and I can arrest him and bring him to you to charge. However, Harry does not push the lack of true arrest powers as hard as Jim Hume does. Hume had us arrest people and deliver them, pretending we had the authority to do it. Pinkerton did the same thing. Harry is more careful," Sarah asked.

"Send me a telegram. I will figure out who and how."

"Thanks, darling!" He smiled at his beautiful raven-haired wife, put his Stetson back on and walked back to the office, where he had a cup of coffee for lunch and reviewed new wanted posters.

Deputy Hastings came by the office to say goodbye before returning to his county.

"Chief Deputy Walt Wood, meet Will Hastings. He's a good deputy from Lake Tahoe. We worked together when I was helping out in Placer County."

"The lady get off alright?" Pope asked.

"She did."

"Do I know her?" Wood asked.

"No, just a person from Placer County who I met over there. She is relocating to our county to open a café up in Novato. She is a fine person and Will was kind enough to take some time off and help her move," Pope said.

"They could use another café or restaurant up there. I believe the one I used to go to when I was passing through is closed now," Wood said.

******

Sarah and Martha left in a hired buggy to ride to Bolinas to conduct interviews. The trip took three hours.

They went to the First Miner's Bank of Bolinas and met with the president and the cashier. Since they were two women meeting with two executives privately, the teller incorrectly assumed they were there about a loan or something other than investigating him.

"Mr. Galloway," Sarah began speaking to the bank's president, "How did you hire the new teller?"

"He told us he had worked with a bank in San Francisco as a teller," he responded, giving her the name of the bank.

"Did you speak with anyone at the bank, in person or by letter or telegram?" she asked.

He reddened and said "No, we usually take a man's word on his personal history."

"How stupid," she thought without any facial change. She was conscious about "tells" after a recent conversation with her husband.

"I will telegraph the Morse head office in San Francisco before speaking to the teller, Mr. Gadsden. They can send a detective by to check on his history with them. Do you think Gadsden has any idea he might be a suspect?" she asked.

"If he's guilty, he is probably paranoid. Otherwise, neither the cashier nor I have given him any hint we suspect him. He believes we think it was a Wells Fargo mistake."

"How about this: Detective Lane and I will publicly shake hands with you two gentlemen and leave smiling like we just got a big loan approved. We will go straight to the telegraph office and have a San Francisco Morse detective check at the other bank and see what they say about Gadsden before any other action is taken?" Sarah asked.

"Sounds good to me. I will expect to see you when you have learned something from his prior employer," Galloway said.

They parted as planned and the two detectives sent their telegram. Morse replied back he would sent Detective Lee to make bank inquiries. Lee was a Chinese detective both Sarah and Pope had worked with on several cases and held in high esteem. Morse said it might be late in the day before he would be able to tell her anything.

Sarah suggested they find a room for the night. By the time they found out anything and questioned Gadsden, it would be too late to make the three hour trip back to the county seat. Additionally, they preferred not to transport a prisoner back in the small buggy during darkness.

They checked back at four and nothing had arrived. They waited at the office another thirty minutes and Morse's response came in.

He said Lee had found Gadsden had worked for the San Francisco bank less than a year when he was fired. Gadsden had been suspected over a mysterious loss. The amount was small, so the bank terminated his employment and did not pursue anything further.

The First Miner's Bank closed for business at two o'clock each day. The tellers settled and were ready to leave by three. The two executives, the president and the cashier, were usually there until six.

Sarah knew Gadsden had left for the day, so she and Martha went to the bank and apprised the president and cashier of their findings.

"We will want to question him in the morning when he gets in. We will be inside first so we can move him to one of your private rooms immediately. I suspect we will take him into custody and transport him to San Rafael to be further interrogated by the sheriff and arrested. We will make every effort to recover your thousand dollars, including searching his room before leaving."

"I sure would like to get the money back, Detective Pope. As for Gadsden, I should have done my due diligence and checked him out before putting him in the teller's cage. I will never make the same mistake again, I assure you.

He gets in around seven thirty in the morning. Why don't the two of you come to the rear door at around seven and knock. One of us will let you in," the president said.

"We will see you around back at seven," Sarah said.

They left for dinner after sending a telegram apprising the sheriff of the impending arrival of a prisoner around midday tomorrow.

******

They arrived on time and were ushered in by the cashier. Per plan, Sarah went into the room where they would question Gadsden. Martha sat in a chair next to the front door. She had a newspaper to hold up as if reading, but in reality, to hide her identity.

Half an hour later, Gadsden walked in the rear door to the lobby.

He was medium height, about thirty and had thin blonde hair. He was dressed in a white shirt and bow tie and had sleeve protectors to keep the ink from his rubber stamp off his shirt.

Sarah stepped out.

Martha dropped her paper and stood.

Time seemed to stand still for everyone present.

Gadsden did the unexpected. He punched Sarah, knocking her down. He then focused on Martha and drew a revolver from the waist, hidden by his vest.

There were two loud "pops!" and he crumpled to the floor.

Martha had beaten him to the draw and fired twice before he could use his gun. Martha approached, gun still at the ready.

The bank president bent over Gadsden and saw his eyes staring blindly. He put his hand on the teller's heart, avoiding the two bullet holes.

Sarah stood there dizzily.

"Is he dead?" she asked.

"I believe so. We'd better have the doctor look at

him though," Galloway said. He sent the cashier to bring the town's doctor back.

Sarah picked up the revolver Gadsden had drawn but died before he could fire. She slipped it in her jacket pocket.

"You alright?" she asked her trainee detective, who had lowered her gun and was holding it pointed downwards, finger off the trigger just as Sarah had taught her.

"Do not reload. John will want to inspect it as it is. Put it back in its holster and leave it there, Martha. You did real well. You probably saved my life and maybe the bankers' lives.

Mr. Galloway, could you not open the bank on time? Put some sort of sign in the window please. This is now a crime scene. Martha and I will go to the telegrapher and send telegrams to the sheriff to respond and to our boss in San Francisco. He will probably come too. I believe your case is solved. I further believe we will find your money in his room," Sarah said as she began to guide the shaken young detective out the rear door.

The telegrams were sent. Pope made it there in a bit more than two hours on Caesar. Harry Morse had jumped on the ferry and arrived right behind Pope.

Pope and Morse jointly interviewed each witness separately. Their stories matched. The large bruise on Sarah's jaw added reinforcement to the reports.

The two sat Martha down and asked her to recount from the beginning.

"Sarah and I arrived yesterday. We found out the suspect was a relatively new teller. He was Mr. Gadsden, the deceased. The bank president admitted he had not checked any references on him. Sarah telegraphed you, Mr. Morse. You sent Detective Lee to his prior bank.

Detective Lee found Gadsden had been fired over the suspicious loss of a small amount of money.

By the time we got his message, Gadsden had left for the day. We spoke with President Galloway and decided to catch Gadsden for questioning when he first arrived today.

Sarah was in a side room, the president at his desk and the cashier was in the teller cage at his desk by the vault door.

I was sitting by the locked front entrance, holding up a newspaper as a disguise when he entered.

Sarah stepped out and he slugged her. She went down and he saw me. He started to draw, but I got my gun into action first and shot him twice in the chest. He fell. Mr. Galloway checked him for a heartbeat and could not find any. He sent for the doctor. The doctor pronounced Gadsden dead at the scene.

Sarah told me to not reload. She said you, John, would want to inspect my revolver as is. It has been in my holster untouched since the shooting," Martha said.

"Martha, please stand up so I can remove your gun and look at it," Pope said.

She did and he removed the revolver and broke it open and viewed two cartridges with their primers dented by the firing pin and three untouched rounds. He sniffed he muzzle. It smelled like a black powder cartridge gun which had recently been fired.

"I have to keep this to compare the bullets taken from the suspect. Get Sarah to loan you a replacement in the meantime. If she does not have one, I do.

Harry, do you have any questions or ideas?" he asked the famous detective.

"Martha, you gave a comprehensive rendition of what happened. As you saw, both John and I took extensive notes. I suspect he will write his up and get you to look it over and sign it as a statement." Pope nodded.

"How are you after all of this, young lady?"

"Shaken. I killed somebody Mr. Morse. I shot him dead. I need to deal with what I did."

"You do, Martha. Just remember he made the decision, not you. You did what you were taught and expected to do," Harry Morse said.

"Harry is right, Martha. Gadsden was the bad person. You were the good one. Those facts will never change. You did what you had to do. There's no other way to look at it," Pope said. "I sent Walt Wood over to tell Mattie and Millie you are okay. I would send a telegram to your dad to let him know the same before he reads it in the San Francisco paper. Get Sarah to help you write it," Pope added.

While Sarah was helping Martha with the telegram, Pope, Morse and the bank president went to Gadsden's room and searched it.

They found and counted the money. All was there. They did not find anything else of value in the case, which was now closed. As to Gadsden, they found some letters to a sister and Pope would contact her once he got back to his office to advise of her brother's death and allow her to work out the burial and the return of his possessions.

They returned to the bank and Galloway gave Pope a requested receipt for return of the embezzled funds. Morse sent a telegram to Hume at Wells Fargo stating the missing First Miner's Bank money had been located and there was no wrongdoing on the part of the delivery driver or guard.

As expected, one of the few female detectives in the country killing a bank criminal was big news in the Bay area newspapers. The Harry Morse Detective Agency got good press. The young detective received more infamy than fame. Morse warned her such might be the case and to just roll with it.

CHAPTER 7

Bill Isakson made good on his promise and fully trained Walter Wood as chief deputy before moving out of his desk in the sheriff's office and retiring.

Pope insisted he keep deputy authority and his badge. He presented him with a nickel plated stag gripped Smith & Wesson .38 in a presentation box as his retirement gift.

Wood was sworn in as chief deputy. After several romantic weeks, Mattie Lane was there to pin on the new badge. This change did not go unnoticed by Detective Sarah Pope who was there at the ceremony smiling.

Her father had immediately demanded his older daughter leave the detective business and threatened the Morse Agency might not get any more work from Wells Fargo.

Morse reminded him he seldom did anything for

the company as it was and his daughter had largely solved a Wells Fargo case. Morse stopped short of telling Lane where to go, but the senior executive got the idea. He was a smart man and realized it was not Morse who was the problem, but his daughter's insistence on her career choice. He realized he had enough on his plate with a wife with serious mental problems and a somewhat wild younger daughter. One who would worry him even more if she told him about the job title of her newest love interest.

Mattie got a job with a local merchant and her own room on the same hotel as her sister.

Somewhat to Sarah's chagrin, the young woman who seemed to get lovelier by the week appeared to be a permanent fixture in San Rafael.

Pope made his notification to Gadsden's sister and did the ballistic test on Martha's gun. It proved what everyone already knew. Pope thought it was a procedure he should always follow after a shooting where the gun and the autopsy removed bullet were available.

"Every time I think no part of California is the Wild West anymore, somebody robs a bank or a stage or shoots somebody," Pope mentioned over dinner one night some months later.

"Have any of those happened?" his grandfather asked.

"Not in the last six months, Grandpa, except for Martha shooting the banker a few months ago," he responded.

"Sounds like you are just aching for some action, Sonny Boy!" his grandfather observed.

The two women at the table nodded with resignation. Sarah had always worried a California sheriff's job would be too tame for her wild cowboy gunslinger husband. She always thought he might be happier as sheriff in Laramie County, Wyoming or Yavapai County, Arizona where they met. This was just more indication she was right.

The next morning, Pope saw the back of a young woman sitting in his office when he arrived.

"John, it's Sophie O'Brien. She's Littleton's daughter," the chief deputy said.

"Oh, I sure know who she is, Walt. Did she say what she wants?"

"Just to talk with you. Alone."

"Oh, boy. This will be interesting."

He walked in and closed the door. The office was partially glassed in. They were visible but nobody could hear conversations.

"Good morning, Miss Sophie. How have you been?"

"I'm worried and scared, Sheriff."

"Want to tell me why?" he prompted.

"I know the case of my horrid father's death has been solved. The record shows his friend Willie Smith did it."

"Yes, you are correct," Pope said.

"Well, you got it all wrong. Willie did not do it. He was a terrible man. But the one thing he did not do is kill my father."

"How do you know this, Miss Sophie?"

"Because I killed him."

Pope sat there for a moment looking at her and trying not to evidence the stark shock he felt.

"Why are you coming forth now. You were totally in the clear, Sophie."

"I have been guilty. I could not confess it as a Catholic. Nobody else could know, even a priest. I don't think what I did was wrong. But, it was illegal. I was always waiting for you to knock on the door again. I knew it would be you, if anybody came after me."

"Please tell me about what happened," he asked.

"Charles O'Brien was a poor excuse for a human being. He was a bully and a rapist. He beat my mother senseless and sexually molested me as a little girl all the way up to when we left him. I dreamed of killing him from eight years old on."

"How did you go about doing this? He might have been an awful father, but from what I know about him, he was a hard man to kill."

"I went by the sheriff's office in Auburn and asked for Sheriff Littleton. I had figured out who and what he was by accident. I saw him in Oakland a few months before with Willie Smith. He had a sheriff's badge on. They were arguing and he did not see me pass by closely. I read the county name on the badge.

The old chief deputy in Auburn told me he had gone over to Lake Tahoe patrolling.

I said, 'oh, it's not real important. I may check back later. There's just a question I have to ask him.'

I turned my rental buggy towards the lake and drove it to the little village.

A man at the store said he was just there and had ridden north along the perimeter road. I whipped the poor horse into a lather catching him but catch him I did. He was by the lake smoking a cigarette like he was waiting for somebody."

"What happened then?" Pope asked.

"He recognized me after four years though I looked a lot different grown up.

He asked 'what the hell are you doing here girl? I've a mind to whip you until you are black and blue,' he told me.

"He had gotten down from the horse and I climbed down from the buggy. I had the shotgun covered by a shawl on the seat.

My father came walking towards me. I knew what was going to happen next. When he got close, I pulled the shotgun out and let him have it! I stood there looking at him lying there and I was laughing and crying at the same time. Damn him to hell!"

"Where did you get the shotgun? It was an odd one and probably cost a pretty penny," Pope asked.

"I stole it from a rich man whose house we cleaned. Ma didn't know because I hid it in the bushes out back and came back and got it later. The owner was old and since he has died. He had no idea the gun was missing.

Remember how I told you I held my father's gun while he sawed the front sight off with a hacksaw?" Pope nodded.

"Well, I still had the hacksaw. I used it to saw off the barrel and the butt stock. I even put varnish on the sawed wood to blend it in."

"Then you threw it in the lake, about twenty feet out from where you killed O'Brien," Pope said.

"I threw it as hard as I could. I had no idea anybody would ever find it."

"Miss Sophie, it was set to spend eternity there. Something was calling me from the lake though. I had to look. When I found it, I knew it was the murder weapon. There was not a speck of rust on it. Anywhere! I almost froze to death, even with a fire and blanket and tarp because of the swim to find the murder weapon."

"Sheriff, will I hang for what I did?" she asked matter of factly with no sign of a tear of remorse.

Pope looked at her a long time. He turned wildly divergent thoughts over in his head before he answered.

"No. You won't hang."

"Why, Sheriff?"

"Because the case is closed. Whether Willie Smith

did it or you did it, justice has been done. I take it your mother does not know? She seemed pretty shocked at news of his death."

"She does not have a clue. Only you and I know, Sheriff," Sophie said.

"I want you to get up, then thank me for telling you about your father once we walk out of the office door.

Go live your life and never mention this to another soul. Walk out the door and breathe in the cold clear air. Go back to Oakland and know you will never ever have to look over your shoulder for a man with a badge behind you for what you did.

Do you understand?"

"Yessir. I understand. Thank you, Sheriff. You are a good man."

"No, not all of the time. I am just being fair. Take advantage of it and leave."

Both got up and walked to the door.

He opened it and as told, she said in front of the chief deputy "Thank you, Sheriff for everything. What you told me about my father fills in a lot of blanks. Now I know. I will never think of him ever again." She proffered her hand and he shook it.

Sophie O'Brien walked out of the sheriff's office and never looked back.

Pope walked back into his office. Walt Wood was busy going through the morning's mail. He thought what Pope wanted him to think. The young woman came in for closure and received it. Nothing more.

Pope sat at his desk and took his gold badge off. He turned it over in his hand for a long time thinking. What did his authority really mean? Enforcing the law only? Or, maybe dispensing justice. Perhaps justice was his real calling and the law just was a way justice was served.

John Hunt Pope, the Sheriff of Marin County, pinned the badge back on and sighed.

This case was closed once and for all, though with a very different ending than he expected. He would never second guess his decision regarding Sophie O'Brien.

Nor would he ever mention the case again. Even to Israel Pope. It was a serious resolution. He had never held anything back from his grandfather. However, he would keep this to himself and only himself.

Pope got up and poured another cup of coffee and sat for a long time savoring it.

After a while, he stood up and put his heavy coat on.

"I'm going to go out to walk around and clear my mind a bit, Walt. I'll be back in a while."

Pope did not think about Sophie, or her father, or Placer County. None of those things worried him in the least.

He really did not think about much of anything as he walked around the county seat.

He just enjoyed the crisp air and the badge on his vest. It seemed like it hung a little lighter today.

Pope saw Sarah come out of her office door a block down. He waved and smiled at her.

Maybe another cup of coffee at the café with his beautiful wife was in order. He picked up his pace.

A LOOK AT: ARIZONA GUNMAN

A WESTERN STORY OF GOOD OVER EVIL, LAW OVER CRIMINALITY.

County Sheriff James Duncan is fast and honorable. An Arizona lawman who rides rough country, often going up against dangerous men and gangs alone. Dealing with bank robbers, kidnappers and rustlers with his fast gun. Much of his tracking ability comes from his Scottish father, who served as an Indian scout. Valuable experience as a Rough Rider with Teddy Roosevelt, then as an Arizona Ranger.

Outlaws and corrupt government tend to stand in Duncan's way, but he manages to overcome all obstacles with integrity and really fast guns.

AVAILABLE NOW

ABOUT THE AUTHOR

G. Wayne Tilman is a full-time author. He retired from the Federal Bureau of Investigation several years ago. Prior to the FBI, he was a Marine, bank security director, deputy sheriff, investigator, and security contractor. He holds baccalaureate and master's degrees from the University of Richmond and has been an adjunct faculty member there, as well as the University of Phoenix, St. Petersburg College and Florida Metropolitan University.

He wrote his first novel over thirty years ago and has now written thirteen novels. Genres include espionage thrillers, mysteries, and Westerns.